"Come on, open your eyes again, honey."

Holly did her best to obey.

There, silhouetted with sunlight, was a familiar face. Dark eyes, a baseball cap shielding them. Nose slightly too long, cheekbones slightly too high, the charcoal shading on his cheeks from stubble answering one question—he did get a shadow well before five o'clock.

Reese examined her critically, staring into her eyes for what seemed like forever. He nodded, slightly, as if he'd found what he expected. "How did they get you? Where were you when you were taken?"

Taken? Her arms were heavy, but she managed to rub at her eyes. He pulled her up, wiry strength evident in his grip on her arm. Despite that, he was gentle, and she was glad, because she ached all over. "I... There was a van. I was...I was going for coffee. With you." The fog in her head was breaking up, but not nearly quickly enough. "Why are you in my house?"

"I'm rescuing you."

Dear Reader,

This book started as a gift to my writing partner, who really needed a story to get her through some stressful days. Now it's a gift to you. I had so much fun writing about a waitress and a superspy, and in the end, Holly's strength and Reese's tenderness worked their way into my heart. I hope you enjoy their story as much as I enjoyed writing it.

Sincerely,

Lili

AGENT ZERO

Lilith Saintcrow

HARLEQUIN® ROMANTIC SUSPENSE

Recycling programs for this product may not exist in your area.

ISBN-13: 978-0-373-27935-7

Agent Zero

HARLEQUIN®
www.Harlequin.com

Lilith Saintcrow has been writing stories since the second grade and lives in Vancouver, Washington, with two children, two cats, two dogs and assorted other strays. Please check out her website at lilithsaintcrow.com.

Books by Lilith Saintcrow

Harlequin Romantic Suspense

Agent Zero

Harlequin Nocturne

Taken

To Mel, from the beginning.

Part One

Fourteen hours after the hit, he was out of the stink and the heat of Mosul, stitched up and stinging from the antiseptic, and the debrief was going…well. Or as well as could be expected, in this airless white-painted concrete-floored room with the one-way mirror on the east wall. There wasn't anyone behind the mirror—Reese would have outright smelled an onlooker—but that didn't mean there wasn't a camera. Recording him and combing frame by frame might give them an edge, and they weren't idiots.

Idiots couldn't build agents—it took civilian egg-heads to do the drafting and drill instructors to do the training—but they could certainly *run* them.

Which explained Bronson, sort of.

"And that's it," Reese heard himself say, dully. Now that he was coming down out of redline, he felt the lit-tle vicious nips and bites all over him. Scrambling over the scorching clay rooftops to avoid mujahideen and other surprises, not to mention getting almost blown out of the safe house because his contact was compromised…it could have been much worse. The deepest of the cuts had already closed, with the almost painful itch of wounds sealing themselves faster than they should. "Target, secondary target, collateral."

"Collateral." Bronson was a hatchet-faced, bespectacled wall, but that's what they wanted in wrap-up. He'd debriefed Reese several times now, and it was always the same. No surprise, no affect at all. Bad skin, probably from the fried food coming off him in invisible waves, but a great poker face. Even his ties were all the same, a maroon that looked dirty under fluorescents.

If Reese hadn't been able to smell the fear on the man, he might even have believed him unaffected. "Nobody told me there'd be guests." *Armed, nasty guests. As well as not-so-armed, innocent ones.*

"Ah." A single syllable, that was all.

Reese decided to prod a little more. "In other words, I took out the entire installation."

"And?" Bronson's tone plainly said he considered that the whole point of the job, which was reasonable enough. From an operations point of view, that was.

Not from an agent's, but who ever asked one?

And if I needed a psych eval, now would be the time for you to suggest it. The physical evals had been daily during training, the psych ones every other day. Looking for a weak spot, checking for breakdown, degradation, a sign that the virus wasn't going to play nice forever.

There was a brassier note in the fearsmell now, and Bronson's eyelids flickered once. His blood pressure was probably spiking, if his pulse was any indication. Reese's was normal, nice and low. They wouldn't get anything from his vitals, not even if they had him strapped in—as long as he had enough spare concentration to keep everything flatline. Just another benefit from the happy little invaders.

Most of all, he suspected, they were looking for agents having trouble with the idea of infection. It did funny things to your head, after a while, even if the Gibraltar virus was what gave you an edge.

Bronson glanced down at the file in front of him. "We didn't have intel on the guests."

The hot wet scent of a lie smacked Reese in the face. What the hell, it wasn't like it mattered. "Sure." He took the water bottle, considered it. A whole lot of things were possible, if you got them going fast enough. He could ghost this idiot and get out the door. Go to ground. Become the Invisible Man.

They had to know he would be thinking about it, right? When you train a dog to dig, he goes and digs. Simple logic.

An obvious corollary to that was that the people who built him were the enemy, too. Or so close to enemy it didn't matter.

Bronson nodded, tapped a paper clip on the table-top. One of his little tells, meaning he was almost done. Probably unconscious, like most patterns, but if he was doing debriefs for program agents, or even just for any shadow-side operative, he obeyed the rules and had a classified box inside his head. "You're scheduled for eval in two days, but we can move it up for tomorrow—"

"Two days is fine," Reese answered with just the

right note of rawness, giving them what they expected. How many other agents were there? It was a question he sometimes considered during long transit times, waiting to touch down in a whole new place and start causing havoc. "I'd have to come back for blood draws anyway. Might as well have it then. I'd like some rest."

"Any, ah, headaches? Physical degradation? Unwelcome thoughts?"

"No." A long swallow of water. He could tear the bottle open, get some sort of flimsy edge. There was the table, too. No great task to go straight over it, or even apply enough force to send the man against the bare concrete wall hard enough to rupture or break something internal. There was that paper clip, too, and Bronson no doubt had a pen. Reese's guns were checked, but he had the ceramknife and his hands. As well as strength, and speed, and apparently the ability to not let little things bother him. "No more than usual."

That got a response. "What?"

Weren't you listening? "No physical degradation. No unwelcome thoughts other than the usual. You know, the ones that spring from killing people for my country. If I didn't have those thoughts, I'd be a program failure, now wouldn't I."

"Emotional noise is also a variable, agent."

"Then consider me at the lowest level of static." He eyed the brown paper of the file cover. How many of those had he seen so far? Each one full of dates and death. The question of when one of them would have his own dates and death was pretty much academic. He'd never expected to survive any of this. "Are we done?"

"You know this is just wrap-up. We had confirmation of the kills before you left the country. They'll be too busy fighting each other to give us trouble for a little while."

Probably not as long as you think. "Good." He pushed himself up, and Bronson actually flinched. The movement, small but definite, almost managed to get through the deadly exhaustion weighing down Reese's every nerve. As it was, he just set it aside for future thought. Like so much else. "Two days, blood drop."

"Try not to get into any trouble." The light winked off Bronson's steel-rimmed glasses, a sharp headache-making dart.

"Yessir." A sketched salute, and the door opened for him. Whoever was taping behind the one-way mirror must have thought he was all right to go, too.

A glare-white corridor lurked right outside, anonymous doors opening off either side, full of disinfectant and the colorless reek of pain. Another agent had been this way recently. Reese inhaled, filing the markers away—male, healthy, with the bright buttery note that generally meant blond.

The desk was manned by a petite civilian brunette with a pert smile, part of the subcontractor apparatus calcifying over every defense-spending teat nowadays. She switched her hips while bringing his clearance packet back, and if he hadn't been so tired he might have felt a faint flicker below the belt.

Don't think about that.

No use at all. He'd tried again in Paris, a good town for getting off if there ever was one, and paid half again as much when the inevitable happened. Failure to engage, failure to load, failure to take off.

There was a fix, and he knew right where to find it, though. Didn't he?

I said don't think about it. Christ. Focus.

The watch was set; he checked it against the clock behind the brunette's smile. Red silk shell, cute tartan skirt and the pulse in her throat fluttering a little. She smelled of recent exertion, probably a workout, and in the time it took him to check the wallet and slide it into his pocket, get the watch on and pick up the sunglass case while making small talk he knew her name was Donna, she was ovulating, she'd had one too many gin and tonics last night, and the patent-leather pumps she wore had been cheek-rubbed by a very affectionate cat. Probably Siamese.

He checked the watch again, ran a hand back over his dark hair. It wasn't perfect, but it was adequate. There was an hour and a half to kill, and the apartment to check. He'd only been gone two weeks, but it was good practice to force himself to make sure nobody else had gone in and looked around.

Reese gave Donna the lonely a smile, and got the hell out of there.

"He's cleared the base, sir." An anonymous male voice, a brief burst of static through the handheld receiver.

Bronson pressed the button, wincing at the thought of the next budget request forms to be filled out. "Ten-four. Eyes on the prize all the way."

"Affirmative. Red Rooster out." The man on the other end didn't sound happy about the overtime, but that wasn't Richard Bronson's problem, no, sir. He turned the talkie off and set it in its lead-lined drawer, then leaned back in the creaking black ergonomic chair, settling with a sigh and regarding the screen on the other

side of the room. The stack of paperwork wasn't enticing, but at least he had a good report.

Buried down here in this windowless black-walled office, it was hard to believe there was a world outside sliding toward chaos and terrorism, a world that needed people like him to fight the good fight and prop up democracy. There wasn't a lot of satisfaction to be had sitting behind a desk and pushing paper around, or in debriefing arrogant superhuman jarheads. He wondered, not for the first time, if he should bring a poster down here, something motivational. A kitten—*Just Hang On*.

And, like he did each time, he dismissed the thought as a little less than manly.

There was no sound from behind him, where she would be standing. There never was. He cleared his throat, made a mental note to have lunch delivered. He couldn't stop thinking about it. Sitting across the table from the Frankensteins gave him the willies. Their matter-of-fact recitations of the things they did, even with all the code words and jargon, wore on him. "Three?"

"Sir." Flat and neutral, her voice, just like a computer's. Despite that, it was pleasant; she had a light alto purr. Before she'd been…modified…it had probably been a phone-sex siren's song.

"Anything to add?"

"No, sir."

There rarely was, but he still asked. Sometimes it was good to have a ritual. Really, he liked hearing her, even if it might as well have been a recording. If there was such a thing as full success when dealing with modifying a human being, she represented it. The only trouble was the hands-off bit of the contract. If they could just make a more…physically amenable…version, the applications—and profit—of the induction process could be intriguing indeed.

The viral process, though, couldn't be sold. There was probably profit in it, but selling *that* to Commies or terrorists wasn't a good, red-blooded American thing to do. That was why Division had government oversight.

"Okay." He spent a few moments tapping at the pad, keying in passwords, the thumblock scan giving him a brief shiver, as always. The secure uplink began loading, and on the other end, a light would be flashing.

He was precisely on time. Control disliked tardiness.

The bluescreen came up, a smear showing as the scrambler ticked along a stripe at the bottom of the picture. The blurred figure sharpened, but only so far, enough to give you a headache if you stared for too long. Control settled into a chair as well, and the familiar click. Cigarette lighter, perhaps? Or recording equipment? Why would Control bother with analog when digital was so easy and secure?

Scrambled and modulated, Control's deep voice burbled from the sleek speakers. "How's our boy, Bronson?"

"Which one, sir?" Always best to be precise. He'd learned that early on in this job.

A weirdly modulated laugh. "The one who just came back. The news is full of running and screaming. Goddamn chickens, all of them."

Well, that was a good sign. It was the intended effect of sending Six out—that, and eliminating a troublesome rallying point for the opposition to some very important policies. "I've sent my notes, the feed of his debrief and analysis—"

"I know, Dick. I'm asking you for a verbal rundown. How's Number Six?"

"Just the same, sir. Low emotional noise, performs beautifully. Can't find a damn thing wrong with him or his work. The only problem is—"

"—his habit of going off by himself, yes." Control paused. "I interrupted. My apologies. You were about to tell me something else?"

How did the man do it? It was goddamn unreal.

Bronson's stomach rumbled a little. Maybe a salad would be better; his last doctor had clucked something stupid about cholesterol at him. "I have an analysis that says he's got more noise than he's showing."

"Yes, your pet actuary. I'm sure it's dressed up with percentages."

"Never been wrong before, sir." Really, once emotion was taken out of it, the human brain was a fine instrument.

The thought of a bacon cheeseburger cropped up. Maybe with onion rings. He could treat himself. Maybe he'd even send Three to carry it up from the front desk when it arrived.

A short silence. Whatever was going through Control's head was probably unpleasant, but at the moment Bronson didn't care as much he might. Finally, the voice came through the speakers again, a little sharper this time. "You want resources to keep following him around?"

"Yes, sir."

"Not as sure about your wonder boy as you used to be?"

As if this wasn't Control's project all the way, and the profits from the civilian side going into deep, deep crony pockets. The economic benefit to democracy was ancillary, but that was enough for Mrs. Bronson's boy Ritchie. "I believe in being safe, sir."

"Humph." Another slight click, a tapping noise. A pen against a desktop, maybe. "Granted. He's due back in two days?"

"Yes, sir."

"I want a full psych workup on him then. Let's see if your little insurance adjustor is right."

"Yes, sir."

"How's Eight?"

Bronson almost winced. "Still unfortunate."

"Still hiding that girl, huh? A shame. Well, as long as his performance doesn't suffer, he can keep going. They can't all be as bright as our boy Six."

"No, sir."

"Carry on, then." A sudden movement, and the screen blanked. Bronson held his breath until it powered down all the way. Then he exhaled. His armpits were damp.

After a short while, his chair squeaked a little as he turned. Across the office's dim interior, he could barely see the slim womanshape near the door, hair sleeked back, a gleam of her eyes, just the barest suggestion of the tailored blazer. Even if she wasn't as voluptuous as he might have preferred, she still had good legs, and he liked seeing them. "Lights, Three."

"Yes, sir." A brisk, efficient movement, and the sudden flood of light stung. He blinked, surveyed her legs again and once more noticed her depressing dearth of chest. She was getting skinny.

"Analysis, Three."

"Confusion, sir."

Well, that was unexpected. He blinked, examining her blank, serene expression. Like a doll. No makeup, but flawless skin. Maybe he should order her to wear lipstick. Something slut-red. Now that would be exciting.

"Yes? I mean, ah, please explain." *Goddamn it.* They should have succeeded in complete emotional noise suppression with a man; it grated on you to have to ask something with breasts for an *explanation*.

She didn't move, her hands empty and loose, her stillness eerie. Her shoes were functional black nurse's brogans instead of a nice pair of heels. Of course, she was supposed to be a bodyguard, too. "Control is exhibiting less attention to detail, and is also allowing emotional noise to become more of a variable in program processes. This is a marked change. It indicates the program itself is drifting."

Bodyguard in a skirt. What was the world coming to? "Damn." Now that he thought about it, she was right. That was the shortest call he'd had with Control in a while, and there had been other program agents brought in and canceled for less deviance than Eight was currently displaying. Were they loosening protocols, or...

Bronson tapped a paper clip on the desk's glass surface. Eyed the stack of paperwork. "The question is, changing to what?"

"I would require more data, sir." She was even pretty, in an unremarkable way. Maybe he should tell her to wear her hair down.

He heaved a sigh. Program protocols weren't his problem. Command and control was his problem, and paperwork. "Go on down and send someone for a bacon cheeseburger, Three. And onion rings. Use the petty cash. Then come on back. There's forms to fill out."

"Yes, sir." The door closed behind her. Even the ass wasn't sufficient.

Well, a man worked with what he had. Would it have killed the gene jockeys to put a little more meat on her while they were taking all the emotion out? "*Damn it,*" Bronson muttered, and dragged the first file folder across the desk.

It was a good thing Holly was habitually early. *Ten minutes before is right on time,* Dad used to say, squinting through the truck windshield every morning as he dropped her off at high school. It was one of the many things he'd learned in the army, like how to fill out forms, how to heft a rifle and just how wrong your country could do you when you believed in her. Or in the men claiming to speak for her.

Which added up to Mike Candless's daughter getting to work just as Doug was threatening to quit again. Ginny had just poured a glass of ice water on a grabby-hands patron, and the espresso machine was making that wheezing noise again.

Just another day at Crossroads Diner. In other words, *welcome to hell.*

"Thank God someone sane is here." Barbara cracked her gum, the sound lost in the ancient time clock punching Holly's card. "Can you talk to Doug? I've got a guy threatening to sue—"

"I saw that." Holly struggled out of her coat, clipped her name tag on, and was in the process of twisting her black hair up. "Ginny strikes again."

"You'd think her ass would come with a warning

label." Barbara fishhooked a wad of pink gum out, flicked it accurately into the scrap bin and sallied through the swinging doors to pour oil on the troubled waters of a businessman with wandering fingers.

Steady cursing came from the other end of the short hall. Holly finished twisting her hair into a bun, slapped a band around it and called it good. She stepped into the kitchen's heat and vapor. "Doug?"

"Holly!" Doug Endicott waved a knife while skinny Bart, his understudy, rolled his eyes. Bart was hunched over the grill, tending what looked like the mother of all breakfast rushes. "I can't work like this!"

"You say that every week. What's wrong now?"

"The fan!" Broad-shouldered, buzzcut, and loud, he was more of a sonic assault than a visual experience.

Holly took a deep breath, reaching for patience. "What about it?"

"It quit working." The cook was the very definition of *built like a brick outhouse*, and the tattoos on his neck were pure jailhouse art. However, right at the moment, he looked like a balding, petulant three-year-old.

Holly put her hands on her hips. "Did you check the fuse box?"

Silence, broken only by the sizzling from the grill. Holly sighed, marched past him into the utility closet, and a few seconds' worth of fiddling had everything set to rights. "Honestly," she continued, stepping out and kicking the door shut with her heel, "it's *two steps away*, Doug."

"He just wants you to talk to him." Bart grinned, his gold-capped tooth flashing. He was a little slow sometimes, but those knob-knuckled hands of his could coax the balky old grill into behaving and clean it to spotless, and he was pretty laid-back even when Doug went on his rampages.

"Shut up." The senior cook's ears had turned bright pink. Looked like the special today was something to do with asparagus. At least it wasn't like the time he'd brought in buckets of oysters. *Got such a deal on them*, he'd crowed, and nobody had the heart to disagree.

Who's going to pay for oyster anything? Antony had moaned, but he didn't get rid of Doug. Or the poor oysters.

Antony was a softie. Also, nobody had gotten any food poisoning, which was damn near miraculous.

Holly clucked her tongue and escaped before Doug could find something else that needed attention. It was going to be a long day.

As soon as she hit the swinging doors, Ginny descended. The tall girl, whorls of color marching up her arms and her bottom lip pierced, was afire with righteous indignation. "Can you *believe* it?" She swiped at her Bettie Page bangs with the back of one hand, and her kohl-smeared eyes blinked rapidly.

"Second time this week? Or third?" Holly tucked a fresh order pad into her apron. "What's it look like?" She could very well glance over Ginny's shoulder and see the usual brunch rush, but getting the girl distracted would make the rest of her shift easier.

"Hell." Ginny swayed a little. She was in the combat boots again. At least she wasn't trying to work in heels like she did at first. "And your weirdo's here."

"Which one?" But she saw him, and her heart sank a little bit.

It was the usual table, tucked against the corner. He always moved the chair, though, resting it against the mirrored wall. Dark hair, dark eyes, wide shoulders, in jeans and a T-shirt most of the time but with a nice watch. Always ordered coffee, sat for at least an hour…

…and left a humongous tip, which would have been great, except he asked for Holly every damn time. He never even drank the coffee.

All of which added up to potential trouble, and attention Holly didn't want. She was trying to slide by unnoticed, but people just kept latching on wherever she landed.

She put her smile on, hipchecked the closest undercounter fridge door to make sure it was closed and headed for the espresso machine. Antony had picked it up somewhere and kept putting off the servicing. *Can't afford it. I got a sinking ship here, folks*, he'd say, rubbing at his salt-and-pepper stubble.

Didn't they all.

She put it off as long as she could, but the tables filled up fast and she had to make a coffee round eventually. She saved him for last, glancing out the window at traffic heaving slowly by on Merton. Crowded pavements, too, even in the rain. The Crossroads had a great location, near both downtown and the naval base butting up against the river, and that was probably its only saving grace.

Well, that and the fact that staff turnover was low. Antony was irritating sometimes, but he did right by his workers. All in all, she was lucky to have ended up here. Sometimes, though, it didn't feel like it. Mostly when she got tired, and the thought of something malignant crouching somewhere inside her body, quietly growing in the darkness and listening to her heartbeat, filled her throat with a rock and her eyes with hot water.

Don't brood on it. Just keep working. The doctor's office had stopped calling, finally. Holly had changed her number, too, just to be sure. Twenty bucks she couldn't afford, but it was worth it to have the damn thing stop ringing.

Holly halted near the table near the window, summoning a smile that felt like a mask. Ginny called him "your weirdo," and Barb kept bugging Holly to use those customer-service skills to find out more about him. Dark hair, dark eyes, aquiline nose, wide shoulders; dark blue T-shirt, jeans, the same canvas jacket with a high collar as always. His capable-looking hands were scraped up pretty badly, and there was a shadow of a bruise on his cheek.

"Morning." She couldn't help herself, even though she knew showing any interest was probably a bad idea. The quiet, borderline-handsome ones were never a good idea—they wormed their way in and before you knew it, you were eating your own heart out missing them. "Looks like you went through the wringer."

He waited until she got close enough to pour to cover his coffee cup with one banged-up hand. The bandages were fresh, and his hair was damp. Of course, there was the rain. "Hi, Holly."

One of these days she'd get a job without a name tag, or she'd finally keel over and the whole thing would be academic. Still, she couldn't help smiling, more naturally now. He looked pretty pleased to see her, even if he was a little…weird. "Ah. Hey, you were in a couple weeks ago. I think you left the wrong tip." *Because a twenty for a cup of burned coffee isn't strange at all, no sir.* "I put the change in an envelope up at the register. I'll go get it."

"No." He leaned forward a little, as if he was going to reach out and stop her, and Holly noticed his watch again. Nice, heavy, expensive but restrained. What was someone who could afford that doing sitting in the Crossroads as regularly as he did? "Don't do that. I left it for you."

"That's really nice." She reached for diplomacy, the coffee slopping inside its glass carafe as she stepped back. "I think you meant to leave a single, though."

"I didn't." He wasn't quite staring at her, but it was close. His gaze flicked away, came back, and there was the ghost of a smile around his mouth. "It was for you."

Oh, man, this is not going to end well. Still, she could use the money. "Well, thank you. You look a little tired."

"Jet lag. Got in a couple hours ago." He was freshly shaven, though, and something about the way he sat bothered her. Too tense. His back was straight, too. Good posture, but something about it warned her that he was ready to move at a moment's notice.

"You should get some rest." She had four other tables needing some attention, though, one of them with kids. If he wanted to drop twenties just for sitting there, it wasn't her business. This was the big bad city, and she carried Mace in her purse.

"I will, but not for a while." The smile was real now, and for such a nondescript guy he had a pretty good one. She couldn't figure out what about him made her so nervous. Was nervous the word? "Thanks."

"You're welcome. It's pretty busy, so flag me if you need a refill, okay?" *Coming over and making awkward conversation with you is not on my priority list.*

"I will."

Did he watch her walk away? She had no way of knowing, though she could have sworn she felt him looking.

Probably harmless, she decided. Maybe lonely. Although why he'd pick a washed-out divorcée in a sinking diner to fixate on, she had no idea. The world was full of strangeness—she'd seen more than enough of it working retail and food service.

She racked the coffee carafe just as Bart hammered the order-up bell and yelled her name. Holly winced internally, put on her best smile and got back down to business.

He hadn't slept on the plane. That made about ninety-two hours since his last kip, and he felt a bit draggy even with the little invaders working overtime to keep him tip-top. He should have stayed in the apartment and caught some lights out, given the little guys a break. Even if you could function without sleep, it wasn't a good idea to keep doing it. The apartment was as close to a haven as he had now, and it could be blown at any time. Because of course they would know where he laid his head; it would be stupid of him to try to hide *that*.

Still, Reese stayed through the end of the rush, watching. Right here wasn't the safest spot to sit—no self-respecting agent would put himself willingly so close to that window—but it caught the air currents just fine, and each time she passed across any of three different lines he could get a whiff.

It wasn't her soap. Or her shampoo. She didn't wear perfume, and the fabric softener on her was harsh and cheap. But under it, like heatshimmer off pavement on a fry-an-egg day, was something…

He couldn't quite figure it out. He kept taking lungfuls trying to, and getting distracted.

Badly distracted.

The trouble had really started after Tangiers. They kept agents supplied, of course—you used protection, stayed away from the fertile or diseased ones, paid the girls and forgot them as soon as possible. Just like brushing your teeth or washing your hands, another routine to keep the head clear. After Tangiers, the blood and the smoke and the screaming and those huge, accusing eyes, well…

They asked during psych evals and physicals, of course, so he gave them dates and places. He didn't mention that he just sat motionless until enough time had passed for a good old fashioned hygienic clearing of the vas deferens, paid whatever girl sat uncomfortably on the bed to keep him company, and left.

Sometimes he wondered if the docs tested for VD, and wondered if the invaders would eat any of those illnesses the way they ate every other sickness or infirmity. He also wondered if anyone would work his back trail and figure out he didn't touch the girls. It could be a bad sign, and his continued existence probably depended on giving the program whatever it wanted to hear.

The rush slowly cleared. The tattooed girl worked her tables aggressively, bending over and leaning in; the brunette with the bubblegum habit bounced along with a maximum of efficiency and a minimum of fuss or emotion.

Then there was… Holly. It wasn't just that she smelled

so delicious. The more he watched her, the more he liked her. She was just so…kind? Was that it?

He inhaled, deeply, and it wasn't just a twitch. It was definitely his body taking notice.

Twenty blocks from the apartment was this run-down squatting tin cube of a diner. He'd come in on a whim, scouting the lay of the land near the base, part of an agent's habitual recon. At first he'd thought it was a bakery; his mouth started watering as soon as he hit the door. He'd figured out it wasn't fresh bread. The smell shifted—he could never quite pin it down—but it was definitely her. Whenever she brought the coffeepot, the hormone rush almost blinded him.

Black hair, sweat-raveled on the back of her neck under the sloppy but effective bun. Dancer's calves— she walked to work, too. Smoky blue eyes, fringed with charcoal lashes. No makeup, except maybe a bit of ChapStick. Cheap and sensible shoes, and the green of the polyester uniform did nothing for her—she really deserved red, a nice clingy number with spaghetti straps. Fingernails bitten down, no pantyhose. Sometimes, when she was coming through the swinging doors, she had a small smile, just a curve of pale lips.

It never lasted. She set her shoulders, put her chin up and got her job done. She gave the kids an extra peppermint at the end of their meal, even the brats. Unfailingly polite, even with the trouble tables—the bubblegum and the tattooed girl both handed the problem ones over to her. She tipped in the kid doing the bussing and probably the cook, too.

The regulars asked for her, and she always had a soft word for them, remembering names and asking about kids, coworkers, hospital stays, if the vitamins worked, if they wanted their usual. The kind of employee nobody thought much about until they left and things went to hell.

Thousands of women in dead-end service jobs all over the country, just like her. Used up and put-upon their entire lives. Maybe in a while she'd turn bitter instead of polite, and those eyes would go dark. Before then, maybe he'd get a chance to...what?

Stupid. If he got close he'd foul her, smear all the blackness he carried over an innocent person's life, and that was the last thing he wanted to do. She deserved better than this goddamn job, and he wanted to figure out how to give it to her.

It was no use. He had to get some sleep.

Still, he wrapped his hands around the stone-cold coffee cup. Nine months ago a man at the counter had dropped like a felled ox. Heart attack. Reese could close his eyes and *see* the light on Holly's hair, how a few strands had come loose and fallen down, the high flush in her cheeks, the way she'd cradled the man's hand and bent over him, whispering. *It's going to be okay, Ernie. Just hold on. Help's coming, just be okay.*

She'd kept on talking to the man, even when he'd been strapped to a gurney, harried EMTs wheeling him for the door. She'd only let go when they lifted him into the ambulance, and after it had peeled away, siren shrieking, she'd come back in, pushing her hair back, and restored order with a few smiles and free coffees.

At least they'd kept the siren on until they were decently away. He'd heard the sound cut off abruptly, and watched to see if she had...but nobody else in the diner was jacked into the red with happy little invaders. As far as they were concerned, the battle had been won.

They were so busy congratulating each other nobody had noticed how pale Holly was, or how she shook. She covered it well.

That was the first night he'd followed her home, and she'd walked with her head down all the way from the subway, wiping at her cheeks and sniffing quietly. He'd kept repeating to himself that he was just doing it as an exercise. Just practicing.

He surfaced from memory and scanned the diner again. The rush was over; bubblegum brunette had a couple at a table all the way across the diner. Tattoo Girl had vanished. Holly finished filling a napkin container, grabbed the coffeepot and darted a glance in his direction.

The closer she got, the more that maddening smell teased at him. It wasn't fertility, it wasn't danger, and it wasn't interest. It was something else. Something good, and he inhaled as deeply as he could, stealing while it lasted.

"Hey." A tired smile. There were shadows under her eyes. Sleeplessness, or something else? "Need a refill?"

He shook his head. The world swam for a moment, came back. He'd start cannibalizing reserves in a little while. Sleep was definitely best. This close, he was almost dizzy. Was he sniffing like a coke fiend? No, she'd probably be looking at him strangely if he was.

"Okay." She paused, examining him. "You look…a little tired. Maybe you should catch some rest, mister."

"Reese." It surprised him. "It's Reese. I think I should." Very carefully, he pushed the chair back. She was only average height, just up to his shoulder. "Thank you. For letting me sit. It must seem pretty strange."

"We see strange in here all the time." She took two

steps back, not precisely nervous. Just like a doe on delicate legs, moving restlessly. Coffee sploshed inside the glass pot, and that fragrance spilled over him in a wave. "Want me to call you a cab? You really do not... I mean, you look a little pale."

The way she said it probably meant *sick*. "I'll be fine." He dug for the wallet, not breaking eye contact. *Stay here. Just for a couple more seconds.* Nothing good ever lasted, but if he could get just a few more seconds, it would help, right? "Just, you know. Jet lag."

He didn't even look at the bill he laid on the table. Neither did she. Instead, she studied him, a faint line between her eyebrows. A tinge of lemon-yellow worry to that marvelous scent now, and he couldn't *think*. She looked worried. About him, and he was a virtual stranger.

Christ. What would it be like, to care that much about random passersby? It sounded exhausting. Maybe that was why she looked so haggard.

She nodded, the worry a little sharper now. "Maybe you should drink some of that coffee. You know, keep you awake until you can go to bed. Jet lag'll keep you turned around if it can."

"Thanks." He forced himself to take a step to the side, another. She was still watching him, and the concern was full-blown, now.

He wasn't blending in. This was dangerous, it was flat-out unprofessional, and he could not for the life of him figure out why the hell he was doing it.

"Thank you," he said again, and turned about-face, as if he was on the parade ground. He could hear her heartbeat, murmuring along under the traffic, and even when he got outside in the stinging-cold rain his head didn't clear.

He made it back to the apartment, forcing himself to check and double-check everything, and fell onto the bed, into velvet blackness.

That maddening smell followed him down.

"I don't like it." Holly frowned at the table, crossing her arms. Her back ached, a deep drilling pain.

"It's forty-eight bucks for nothing. Take it." Barbara cracked her gum again. Doug hummed something in the kitchen, obviously over his morning snit.

"Who leaves a fifty for a cup of coffee? He looked hungover, Barb. Or sick." *Probably a junkie, one who hasn't gone down the drain yet. Bad news.* He seemed too...with-it, though, to be on drugs.

"So? He left it, it's yours now. Pay your light bill. Donate it to charity—I've been looking at a pair of nice shoes lately." Barbara's nicotine-yellowed grin lit up her whole face. "I think he probably likes you."

Now she knew what a slug felt like when salt was poured on it. Everything in her curled up at the thought of someone else who might miss her when she finally disappeared. "Oh, God. You see them everywhere."

"Not my fault you're terminally single. I keep trying, you know. When the fleet's in there's good pickings. Can't be gun-shy forever, Holls."

Terminally single. If you only knew. "If I wanted to date, I would." How ironic was it that she didn't even want to right now? She was just too tired, and whatever time she had left was better spent elsewhere. Holly didn't talk about the divorce, either, especially with inveterate gossipers. If Barbara wanted to draw conclusions, well, let her. The fifty lay there, bearded President Grant looking vaguely worried and disapproving. Just like her father. The temptation to take it was well-nigh irresistible, even though she had her arms firmly folded.

She finally swept it up, and Barbara blew a vile pink bubble in triumph.

Holly restrained the urge to roll her eyes. "I'll put it in the envelope. I'll talk to him about it if he comes back."

Barb's grin probably wasn't meant as predatory, just the glee of a congenital meddler. "Which he will. Seriously, Holl, I think he likes you. He's always watching."

I noticed, thanks. "Creeptastic." She sighed. "You want fills or spills?"

"I'll do both if you clean the board. When Ginny gets off break she can do the restrooms."

"Fine." It wasn't a fair division of labor, but it got them off the subject of Mr. Watch Her and Leave a Huge Tip. For now, because Barb would no doubt circle back to it. She was like a terrier: just couldn't leave anything alone, and since she had no shortage of boyfriends, she apparently wanted to share the wealth. A woman wasn't complete without *something*, apparently, and Barb felt it her sworn duty to help Holly realize her potential.

Getting so tired she never even registered the lack of sex was an unexpected side benefit to being…sick. *Always look on the bright side, Holly. Daddy would be proud.*

Now *there* was an unwelcome thought.

The ancient cash register glittered under fluorescents as Holly wiped everything down, bleach water stinging her raw, much-washed hands. The next time she passed that slice of counter, she dug in the shelves underneath, pushing aside the mittens someone had left last week and stacks of fresh and leftover order pads. Register tape, fire extinguisher, a pair of rain boots that fit nobody employed here now—a real wonderland of the lost and just-in-case, most of it so familiar she didn't even see it anymore.

The envelope was right where she'd left it. She pulled it out, frowned at the numbers scribbled on the front, and tucked the fifty in. The twenty went into her tip pocket, a reassuring weight, and she rang the coffee through, sighing a little as another twinge went through her lumbar region. Even cushioned shoes didn't help. *It's a symptom, Holly. Deal with it.*

She was about to put the envelope back when she stopped, grabbed a pen, and wrote *Reese* on the back flap. It went back into the dark, and she told herself it wasn't anything. Just a name.

Still, it was more than she'd known before. Maybe Barb wasn't the only waitress at Crossroads who liked a mystery. And with so little time left on her clock, why couldn't a girl think about what she pleased?

"Goddamn it," Ginny yelled from the other side of the diner, "why do I have to do restrooms *again*?"

A single file folder was all it took to finish destroying Jacob Heming's career. He was the first to find out, and his reaction—to pour a nice stiff drink with shaking hands—was perhaps too cliché for his taste, but it went unwitnessed. No, here he was in a crappy little apartment instead of his house on the bay, because Connie had gotten the house *and* alimony, most of every paycheck from even this cushy position, and even the dog, for God's sake. The windows here didn't look out on anything but Sixteenth Street and headlights, the rumble of traffic a constant reminder that he'd married that bitch and was now taking his lumps.

He poured himself another two fingers of Glenfiddich. Might as well, what the hell. He turned around, a balding man with glasses in a pair of baggy boxers and his undershirt, the garters holding his socks up rubbing at his calves, a familiar, ignored irritation.

You weren't supposed to take charts home. Data breach, security issues, the whole nine. But you couldn't keep up with the damn paperwork unless you spent hours in those cube offices, with Bronson breathing his halitosis over your shoulder and that ghostlike secretary of his moving silently in his wake, and the damn nurses skipping out on work to go do whatever it was they did—probably chase all the brawny military types.

Just like Connie and that tennis coach. *He actually listens to me, Jacob.*

Why anyone would listen to her cheese grater of a voice was beyond Hemings, despite the fact that he'd graduated summa cum laude. He'd left the university even though he was possibly about to get tenure, because the offer from the defense contractor had been too good to ignore…and now here he was.

And there, on the bed, was a pile of innocent-looking file folders, all the tasteful mauve that said *patient*. It also said *anonymized* and *safe*, and while he might be reprimanded for taking those off the base to work on, he was sure some of the others had also taken one or two home to finish. They weren't the problem. The problem was that thin thread of crimson in the middle.

A red file, in the middle of the patient files. How the *hell* had it gotten in there? Red files were scan-counted at the end of the day. They would know one was missing. Good luck slipping it back in, too—they'd be on high alert. Donna at the front desk would begin checking IDs and passes again, like the officious little cocker spaniel she was. *No, Dr. Heming, I'm afraid I can't go with you Saturday. Thanks for the invite, though!*

He scratched under his belly, sipped at the scotch. God's perfect drink, full of wonder. It never let you down, like a basketball scholarship gone because of one little hazing incident, or a tenure position because someone else had slept with a board member or two, or a blonde, bubbly trophy wife who forgot her proper place.

There were all sorts of things that…bothered him. Something military—the men were all young, strapping and added *sir* to every sentence. The tolerance tests were thought provoking. Allergy tests, the higher-ups said. As if allergies were a threat big enough to warrant these kinds of resources thrown at them. Really, Heming was a glorified PA in this job; the research facility was in White Oaks. Or at least, that's where the samples were sent for processing. All Heming did was take the vitals and ask the checkup questions and write the prissy little reports to Bronson's exacting specifications.

They were his patients, right? Six, Four, Seven, Eight, Twelve and Fourteen—where were all the other numbers? And those scratches and scrapes on them, healing up so nicely.

So *quickly*.

They were his patients, and he had a right to educate himself, didn't he? It would make his treatment more effective.

He turned back to the dresser, poured himself an-

other scotch. The silver-framed picture next to the bottle
was the wedding photo—oh, the cash he'd shelled out
for Connie to have that white wedding she wanted—
and their wide, fake smiles glared at him from under a
few months' worth of dust.

"I'm a *doctor*, dammit."

Nobody spoke up to disagree.

Jacob sighed, strode across the room and settled on
the creaking bed. The folders slid around sloppily on
the crocheted bedspread his own mother had given him.
Brown and yellow and blue, and tacky as hell. But a
man's arthritic mother had made it — he couldn't very
well throw it out like Connie had wanted, could he?

He pulled the red file out, lingeringly, from the middle of the pile. *Classified* stamped across its cover, the
black ink faintly smeared. Maybe that weed-smoking,
perpetually lazy bitch nurse Fleming had just grabbed
a stack in a hurry. Who knew?

What mattered was, it was here now. Why couldn't a
doctor take a look? There wasn't any harm in it. Maybe
tomorrow he could slip it somewhere, or even throw
it away.

You're an idiot, Jacob. It was Connie's voice, loud
and nasal. She was so pretty, and had been so sweet in
the beginning. *A little two-bit horse doctor.*

Well, he'd graduated top of his class. He could find
a way to get rid of some paper.

He flipped the folder open and began scanning.

A few minutes later, the glass of scotch tipped out
of his hand and splashed onto the cheap carpet. His
heart beat, a harsh thin tattoo in his ears and throat
and wrists.

Virology control, one sheet was titled. *Tolerances*, another. *Infection vector*, a third.

He kept reading, mouth dry and heart pounding, while the stink of spilled alcohol simmered in his lonely apartment.

Same medical suite as last time, bare concrete walls and supplies locked down in neatly organized, color-coded bins. They took blood, swabbed his cheek, poked and prodded. Looked at the scrapes on his hands, already closed up. Crackle of the paper onesie they gave him, the disinfectant smell overpowering. The nurse was a lean-faced young tomboy, Dr. Heming the same sour-faced civilian douche bag he'd always been, his hair combed over his bald spot in strings and his lab coat indifferently laundered.

Heming's steel-rimmed glasses almost matched Bronson's. He asked all the usual questions. *Any headaches? Any ringing in the ears? Change in sleeping patterns? Change in digestion?*

No, no, no. Other than the fact that he'd been drinking water that would give a tourist dysentery, no.

"You're a little lighter than we like." Heming peered over his glasses. "Been living rough?"

"Yessir." They said that with the little bastards swimming around in your blood you could even digest grass, but he hadn't had to prove it yet. Not even on the BS scavenger hunt meant to test his survival capabilities in the wilderness.

No, he'd eaten meat all through that. Catching it yourself was supposed to make it taste better.

Heming nodded thoughtfully, paging through the mauve-jacketed file. He never slipped up and left the paperwork where Reese could get his hands on it. Maybe one day—hope sprang eternal and all that. "Well. You're scheduled for psych after we're done here. We have a couple tolerance tests this time, and an extra blood draw. Did you sign the consent form?"

"Yessir." *Like I could refuse.* It was just going to be uncomfortable, whatever they injected him with fighting with the…

The virus. The happy little buggers who made him stronger, faster…and smarter. That was the main thing, right?

"Good, good. Well, we'll get those done, then you can go talk to the headshrinkers." Heming grinned as though the thought pleased him. Maybe it did. But under that pleasure was a sour whiff of fear. The man was sweating, and Reese filed that away. It wasn't usual, but what medical man wouldn't get a little shaky around an agent? Especially if they were poking one with needles. Even an idiot might wonder why he was in such great shape. The disclosure agreements, the high pay, the security arrangements—

An internal shrug. There were better things to think about. If he got out of here before 1600 he could get off-base and get in position for the walk home. It would be good practice.

Sure. Just keep telling yourself it's practice.

"Yessir." Reese caught the tomboy nurse's frown. She didn't think much of Heming either, and deliberately moved away from him every time he stepped close. Smart girl.

He'd slipped up. Told Holly his name. Not a cover, not even a fiction. His *name*. What was he going to do about that? Make a confession? As if they'd put him in the stockade.

Maybe they would. Maybe they had one especially for agents.

Your head's not a comfortable place these days, Reese. Besides, he shouldn't be thinking about Holly. He should be paying attention to the here and now and giving them what they wanted so he could get offbase and see her again.

Heming coughed a little. The sweatsmell intensified, a sourness of bad laundry and nervousness, the very antithesis of Holly's clean, beautiful scent. Maybe the doc knew more about the program's other side than was comfortable, too. Either way, not Reese's problem. "All right. Marty here will be back with the doses in a few minutes. Pleasure seeing you again."

"Yessir," Reese murmured. He watched Heming try to pinch the girl's bottom as he crowded her out the door, and his jaw tightened. *Officious little prick.*

He made it offbase just in time, and when quitting hour rolled around he was in position. The employee door gave out onto an alley; his vantage point provided him a good clear field of vision. When she stepped out, laughing over her shoulder at something said inside, his throat went dry. He had to wait for the breeze to shift before he could get a whiff of her, and the jolt went through him high and hard. His arms itched from whatever they'd injected. He was due back for another blood draw in forty-eight, to see if the invaders had eaten whatever it was. Heming had ordered more than the usual vampire bites.

Holly hitched her bag up higher on her shoulder,

walked quickly with her head down against the fine
misting rain. The crowd swallowed her; she headed
upstreet for the Mierkele Street station.

The subway was glare and noise; he got the car behind hers and watched through the glass, hanging on to
a pole as she settled into a seat and opened a battered
paperback with a red cover. It took a little while before
he could figure out what it was. Raymond Chandler, a
collection.

Interesting. The cars weren't packed, and every once
in a while a man would glance her way. Those glances
bounced off her obliviousness. She didn't make eye
contact, didn't look up and the *don't come near me* vibrated off her in waves.

It was a good thing, too.

Almost a half hour later, he watched her step into
a small bodega on Perelman. This was a rough neighborhood, but she moved with easy familiarity, ignoring everything because it was the usual, the expected.

She came out just as the street lamps were flickering
on, with a small net bag. Oranges, and something green,
and a bottle of cheap red wine. A small bit of cheese.
No wonder she was so thin, if she ate rabbit food all the
time. Looked like a night alone for her.

At least, he was pretty sure she was alone. He didn't
smell anyone else on her, not even a cat.

Four years ago he wouldn't have known, just a regular soldier with dim connectors in his brain, a happy-
go-lucky idiot. How the hell had he ever managed to
get through basic training without the invaders? How
had he survived the state home, and the tours of duty,
or anything else?

At least the virus gave him a *chance*. You got used

to the perks pretty damn quickly. You went through a phase of thinking you were invincible. Then came something like Tangiers.

He shook his head, dropping back as she sped up. She nipped aside into a run-down four-story building; he gave her a good head start. Most of the time he just made sure she got to the door all right, just like a gentleman should. Tonight, however...he'd been a good boy. He could use a little reward, right?

Inside the foyer, there was a wall of brass-door mailboxes. The place had seen much better days before being chopped up into studios and one bedrooms. She'd definitely passed this way, heading for the stairs. Cheap food, desperation, the close fug of people living all piled together. Four big black trash bags jammed against the opposite side of the foyer, someone's bicycle chained to the newel post of a Gilded Age staircase. Wood flooring peeked out from under scarred linoleum.

It was child's play to find her mailbox. It all but reeked of her, and he put a fingertip against its chilly metal door. CANDLESS, the tag said. Could be a previous tenant. Top floor, 4D.

Not even a buzzer on the front. Security nightmare. Did she have real locks? He glanced around to make sure he had exit routes, then climbed the stairs and peered down the hall. She was down at the end. There was an emergency exit, but it was chained shut. A fire would trap everyone in here like rats in a cage.

The building breathed around him, roaches in the cracked walls, someone on the bottom floor cooking enchiladas, and that door at the end of the hall, reeling him in like a fishing line—4D. What would the space behind it look like? Pink and frilly? She was girly, but maybe not in that way. A woman, living alone—he'd bet she didn't even have a goldfish. She didn't go anywhere after work, except occasionally the bodega. No parties, unless she sneaked out past midnight.

He'd stayed a long while, once or twice, just to see.

Reese had his hand raised to knock on her door before he realized what the hell he was doing and backed away.

She was a civilian, for God's sake. He was just making sure she was safe.

It took him the entire way home to make his hands stop shaking. Now he knew precisely where she lived, not just the building. So what if he'd been tempted to knock? What the hell would he have said? *Hi, I followed you home, but don't call the police*? Christ.

He got the hell out of there.

It didn't help that when he got back to the residence, he had his first respectable hard-on since Tangiers. He took an icy shower—his bathroom was probably as big as her entire apartment—and told himself to calm and never, ever go near that diner again. The needle pricks in his arms ached deeply, relentlessly.

He already knew he wasn't going to listen.

Working the Friday middle shift always gave her a headache. Antony was not making it any better, because he was getting desperate and kept following her around. "You can close up. Help me out here."

"You're not paying me overtime, Tony." Her feet ached, too. That fifty under the register could buy another decent pair of shoes. Either that or a hammer to fix her headache. She hadn't been able to eat this morning, either. A beautiful salad, gone to waste. Not even oranges tasted good anymore. "No dice."

"Like you've got something to do after work? Come on, Holly! I've got courtside seats!"

She shook her head, four plates in her arms and a fresh ketchup for table eight tucked in her apron. He'd been after her ever since she arrived. It wasn't his fault Angie had come down with the flu and they were already one short. Nobody else was due in until eight, and it was going to be a long time until then. Maybe she should be flattered that he trusted her to close up, but he probably would sign the diner over to the devil himself for a stand-in at this point.

"Anything else I can get you?" she asked every table, and of course there always was. Some days were like that—none of your tables were outright awful, but they all changed their minds a million times or they thought of some extra thing they just *had* to have.

At least when she was running through the dinner rush Tony couldn't really put the screws to her. Even the counter was full, each stool taken, and she didn't notice the guy on the far end in the familiar canvas jacket, a blue baseball cap pulled low over his dark eyes. Working the counter was Tony's job, with Brenda doing backup, and Brenda had enough trouble taking half Angie's tables as well.

The crowning event of the night was a piss-soaked drunk passing out in the men's room, but Juan the night cook took care of that, heading right back into the kitchen to crank out special after special. Bart was in there, too, furiously chopping and prepping, and the busser tonight was dreamy Eduardo, who was *excruciatingly* slow but at least never stopped shuffling while he stared into each tub of dishes like it held the Holy Grail.

Her calves and lower back were solid bars of nauseating pain by the time she looked up and noticed it was seven thirty and the rush was clearing. Two minutes in the ladies'—her first break since she'd walked in—got her face splashed with cold water and her hair pulled back again, this time just in a ponytail. She barely managed to haul herself upright after sitting on the toilet, scrubbed up and headed back out to get her last tables sent off with a smile even though she'd dry-heaved over the sink a bit. The nausea just wouldn't quit.

At least the tips were good.

Tony started in again as she was bent over a table, scrubbing up the last of a toddler's birthday ice cream. Cute kid, chubby cheeked and flaxen haired, but he'd spread the damn dessert everywhere and probably eaten the cheap stick candle, too.

Tony's tie was a little askew and his cheeks were flushed, his proud beak of a nose dotted with sweat. "Come on, Holly. I'm dying here. I can make the second half if you close up for me."

"No, Tony. I can't."

"What you got that's so important?" He waved his hands, his gold pinkie ring flashing. There was a diamond in it, a microscopic one he was inordinately proud of.

Her temper almost snapped. *None of your business.* The rag went into the tub; she hefted it and stepped back, almost colliding with him. Even with the weight she'd lost recently she could knock him over, having a head's worth of height on him. "Laura and Benny are due in at eight. Maybe one of them can help you out."

"You're killing me!" Tony moaned, and she was startled into a laugh. She set off for the counter, hissing an out breath as her back cramped a little.

"You're the boss, Tony. With great power, you know. Great responsibility." She cut the corner too close and almost bumped into a customer. "Whoops, sorry."

"No worries." The voice was familiar, and she stopped dead.

It was the mystery man, and he'd actually eaten, for once. Looked like a short stack and over-easy, four stripes on the side. And orange juice. Breakfast for dinner. Well, some people liked that. The thought of over-easy eggs made her even more queasy, though.

They had been Phillip's favorite. *I want a divorce, Holl.* She'd sat at the kitchen table for a long time that day, then gotten up and hadn't stopped moving since, it felt like.

"Oh." All the breath ran out of her. "Hi. Reese, right?"

"Yeah. Hi." That nice smile, and he looked just fine. Not pale or anything, and she could have sworn he was bruised the other day, but he didn't seem to be now. Maybe he'd just been jet-lagged. Nobody ever looked good coming off an airplane. He looked at her face as if she had something growing on it, dark eyes narrowing just a little. "No coffee this time."

"Did you want some?" She was suddenly, acutely aware of the sweat soaking through her uniform, her sloppy ponytail, and that she probably looked like hell. Certainly not worth the once-over he was giving her.

Why do I care? It wasn't like it mattered. Sooner or later her body was going to just give out. Until then, she was simply marking time, getting along with the least amount of mess possible. If she vanished tomorrow someone would grouse about how she didn't show up for her shift, but nobody would feel any wrenching pain. Tony would hire a new waitress, maybe one even younger and more brassy than Ginny, and that would be that.

At least, that was the plan, and Holly intended to stick to it.

A ghost of a smile showed up on Reese's face. "Only if you're pouring."

Did it taste better when she poured, or was it just this guy being weird all over again? It didn't matter, she decided. Even if he did look a lot better now. He probably cleaned up very well. Imagining him in a suit didn't hurt anything, and it even made her feel a tickle of amusement. "I can, sure. Just give me a minute."

Tony muttered as he punched at the cash register down at the other end of the counter, running off the after-rush numbers. He really did love his basketball. She almost felt charitable enough to agree to close up for him.

Almost.

Brenda, her spray-lacquered hair in place and her drawn-on eyebrows giving her a perpetually surprised expression, shook her chunky blue plastic earrings as she put together a fresh pot of coffee. "If he asks me one more time I'm going to dump him in the fryer."

"I'll help," Holly muttered. "Hey, what's with the guy at the counter?"

Brenda peered around the coffee cubby's edge. "Him? Polite, no trouble." It was the highest praise a waitress could give. "Why?"

No reason. But she had one, thankfully. "He's a regular. Tips well."

"Good. I could use it." Brenda sighed. "God, I need a smoke."

A long time ago Holly might have told her to quit anyway, it was a bad habit. With things as they were, though, she didn't waste the breath. "Go on, I'll handle it. Just don't let Tony talk you into anything."

When she came back, Reese was looking down the long polished stripe of the counter. "Busy night."

"Fridays." She set the cup down and poured. At least it was fresh. Eduardo had cleared the mystery man's plate and moved on to Brenda's half of the diner. "You did it again last time."

Did he look startled? His eyes really were very dark, barely any difference between iris and pupil. "Did what?"

"The tip." She felt her eyebrows go all the way up, a comical feeling. Tony had headed to the office—he was probably going to call his bookie and complain about missing the game.

Reese shrugged. That was it. No explanation, nothing. Was he embarrassed?

"I can get you your change right now, if you want," she persisted. "Because, you know, I thought it was a mistake."

"Again?" He leaned forward on the counter, bracing his elbows. "No. No mistake."

How could a place go from being so full one minute to practically empty the next? Eduardo had another tubful and was heading back to deposit them for Jackie the dishwasher. Who was no doubt listening to ranchero hip-hop while he scrubbed and kept up a steady stream of half-whispered invective. Brenda was in the alley smoking, and the office door closed behind Tony with a thud. Every table was bare.

"Okay. Well, thank you." She took a step back.

"You're welcome." He kept watching her. "Can I ask you something?"

"I guess." She braced herself. *Aha. Here it comes.* She was already rehearsing how to let him down easy. *I'm married*, she could say. She'd said it before. Or even *I'm a lesbian*. Now there was a new one. Would it work?

His shoulders relaxed a little. Maybe he was just nervous. "Do you ever wonder where people go when they leave here? You know, try to guess who they are, what they do?"

It wasn't what she'd expected, so it took her a couple seconds to shift mental gears. "Doesn't everyone who works this kind of job? I mean, it's natural to wonder about people." She rested the coffeepot on the counter. Juan, back in the kitchen, yelled something at Bart, who replied in the same tone. Something about scrubbing down the grill. "Like you, for example."

"You wonder about me?" He even looked a little pleased, that faint ghost of a smile intensifying.

Well, now she'd gone and done it. "We wonder about all our regulars."

"I'm a regular?" Surprised, and maybe a little horrified.

His expression was pretty priceless, so she actually laughed, cupping her free hand over her mouth as if to catch it. "Sort of. Barb—she's here in the mornings— well, we call you the mystery man."

His smile in return was…really nice. The image of

him in a charcoal-gray suit, the tie loosened just a little, wouldn't go away. "Oh. I'm really kind of boring."

Well, that's a relief. Me, too, and I want it kept that way. "Oh?" Everyone wanted to talk about themselves. As long as you let them, you could get away with not saying much about your own life.

Mostly.

"Yeah. I work…security."

Huh. And you have such nice big shoulders. I'll bet you loom really well. She examined him, critically. "You don't look like a rent-a-cop."

"Not that kind. I'm sort of a consultant." He lifted the coffee cup, blew across the top. No bandages, just some pretty livid scratches.

"Your hands are a lot better."

"It looked worse than it was."

"Oh." She searched for a polite escape. "Well, I'm glad. Listen…"

"I'm listening."

She reached over and scooped up his ticket. "This one's on me. Okay?"

Now *that* got a reaction. "There's no need for that." His hand shot out, but she was too quick for him; she already had it tucked in her apron.

She stepped back, hurriedly. "Call it relief. Last time you were in, you looked pretty thrashed. Jet lag can really wallop you." *Why am I doing this?*

Even if you were looking to leave a room quietly, there was no reason to leave a mess, right? No reason not to be kind while she was waiting to go.

"Holly…"

The grin on her face felt strange, because it was genuine. "You can say *thank you*," she informed him. He wasn't so bad after all. Just strange, but that was okay. She headed for the register, her back not cramping so much now that she'd had a bit of a breather. "Leave a good tip for Brenda. She's got kids."

"Thank you. I really wish you'd—"

The swinging doors burst open, and Benny—six foot plus of good-natured pacifist Samoan, with gentle eyes and light feet—threw his hands in the air. "I have arrived, good peoples!"

"Benny in the house!" she called back, and didn't notice Reese the mystery man's hand slipping away from his waistband. "Be careful, Tony's going to try to con you into closing."

"On a Friday? Oh yeah, the Toppers are playing." The front doorbell chimed, and Benny dropped his arms, a little sheepishly. Sometimes people thought his size meant he was scary. "Was that a dine and ditch?"

"Hmm? No, I've got it right here." Holly glanced up and stopped. "Huh."

The Crossroads was empty. Reese was gone. He'd left a twenty, though.

Brenda was happy about that; she didn't even notice Holly was a little…disappointed? Was that the word?

Let it go, Holl, she told herself yet again. Getting involved, even just overly friendly, wasn't a luxury she was allowed.

Even if she—useless to deny it—wouldn't mind just a tiny taste of it, one more time.

His arms itched, and he'd almost put the drop on the guy. Just a waiter. That would be great, to walk into his next eval and lay that on the table. *I killed a waiter. Because he startled me.*

It had been going pretty damn great up until then. She'd dropped her guard, visibly deciding he wasn't a stalker. Laid the groundwork, nice and careful, then almost ruined it.

He could still call off the strike. All it would take was staying away. He wasn't real enough to get close to her, even. He was an agent, a ghost in the machine, an invisible man. It was pretty likely that he'd try to help her and get misinterpreted, or worse, mess everything up just like the idiot he was. He should stay well away—it was best for her.

So why was he here in the rain without his hat, watching the alley? Why hadn't he gone back to residence, dried off, poured himself a shot of something alcoholic and useless? You had to drink a lot to outpace the invaders.

His fingers drifted across his hip. He couldn't feel the little telltale bump under the skin, but he knew it was there, a small silver cylinder inserted under the skin. He hadn't been able to determine if it was live or just a passive beacon, though he'd gotten offgrid with it a couple times now. Technology was great, but transmitters still had a hard time with foil.

That little bump was a very good reason for leaving a kind, pretty little waitress alone. No matter *how* good she smelled.

It was dark when she came out. No laughter this time, just the head down, don't-look-at-me walk. Her hair was loose, spilling against the shoulders of her plastic-gleaming raincoat. He probably could have followed her a lot more closely, but why? Hanging back was good practice.

No need to make her skittish. Sometimes your mark

caught on for no reason—instinct, or their subconscious working overtime.

She pulled out another book on the subway. Chinese history. But she didn't turn a page, just stared at it and swayed, obviously exhausted. She was too thin. Someone needed to hold her down and feed her cheeseburgers. Was she a ketchup person? Mustard?

I want to know. The itching got worse, and so did a nameless tension. His own instincts twitched. Most people didn't pay any damn attention to what their senses were telling them, even without little invaders jacking them up into the red. Lots of the agent training was just common sense, tuning in, paying attention.

Look harder. Look again.

There. He found the source of the nagging. Brown and brown, black baseball cap, hooded sweatshirt, eleven o'clock. Sweating a little, through the rain-dew and condensation hanging on everyone. The man's gaze kept sliding over Holly from top to toe, flicking away and returning far too many times.

It was like watching a hungry cat eye a distracted mouse. He added the man up, didn't like the answer he got. If she looked up, stared him down or made the effort to appear a little less tired and oblivious, he might move on to another target. As it was, she was broadcasting weakness, and predators were at the water hole.

She telegraphed her stop, tucking away the book and stretching, wincing as if it hurt. When she got off the train Mr. Black Cap did, too. Reese swore internally, drifting behind them. Footsore and exhausted, she might as well have had a neon *Rob Me* sign over her head.

Why was Reese speeding up a little? Why were his

hands tensing and his pulse picking up? How would he explain it if—

She turned sharply into the same tiny store she had last time, maybe on impulse. It gave him the opening he needed, and Black Cap never knew what hit him. A silent, ghosting dash, a low "Hey…" to grab Black Cap's attention, quick shot to the knee, another to the throat to keep him quiet. Crunch of bone breaking—it was just the man's arm, and he was lucky Reese didn't want to kill him.

What the hell am I doing?

A handy alley loomed nearby; it couldn't have been more perfect if he'd planned it. Propping the jackass next to an overflowing Dumpster didn't take long. The pain would wake him up soon, but by then Holly would be home safe and sound. Anything else wasn't Reese's concern.

Bad part of town. Should get her out of here, somewhere safer. How exactly to do it was tricky, but he'd already achieved primary contact, so…

He halted at the alley's mouth, flattening himself against the right-hand side. Tried to get his pulse back down. He could almost hear Bronson's dry, uninterested tone.

Emotional noise is also a variable, agent.

Well, fine. There was noise. Now he had to decide what to do about it. How likely was it that he could keep her hidden? Just like kiping a blank passport from stock or hoarding cash, the medkit he kept taped inside a heating duct and the little hidey-holes, potential or actual, in different cities.

You trained a dog to dig, and he went and dug. Simple, really. They had to have expected it.

So what was he going to do? She might not even be interested. What would she believe? He wasn't much of a honeypot agent, preferring the more direct methods. There might have been Romeos in the program, but he wasn't one of them.

Familiar footsteps. He went completely still, gapping his mouth and slowing his pulse. The wind had picked up a little; he caught a breath of that elusive, mouth-watering smell. A shadow against the streetlight shine outside, her wet hair dripping on her coat, stuffing a bottle of ibuprofen into her purse.

Of course. She'd been on her feet for hours, running around taking orders from idiots.

She sniffed, wiping at her nose with the back of her hand, an impatient movement. She should really have an umbrella. A better raincoat. Something.

And you're going to get right on that, huh, soldier?

Even the rain wasn't keeping him down. At all. The one time he needed to be thinking with his big head, and he couldn't manage it.

He kept back, just waiting until she got inside her building. He couldn't follow her home every day. They'd send him out as soon as he cleared his next blood draw; the itching was already going down, which meant the little buggers in his bloodstream had eaten whatever he'd been dosed with.

That was another worry. *Hi, I've been mutated. They injected me with a virus that changed some of my chromosomes, I'm starving, and you smell like cupcakes.* Yeah, that would go over really well.

He checked the street and stepped into her building. Just the same, her smell on her mailbox, stealthy sounds in the walls. A baby crying somewhere, and a tang of smoke. Someone had burned dinner.

He touched the mailbox's closed, secretive door again, quelled the urge to go up the stairs and decided that was enough for one night.

Her face was a mask, and Three took care to keep it that way.

The windowless office surrounded her, familiar from its short vinyl carpet to the sleek black electronics and Bronson's chair off center, pushed up against his desk. Beside Three, gazing at the screen bolted to the wall, was the stolid, middle-aged, rancid man himself. It had something to do with the garbage he poured into his body on a regular basis, congealed grease masquerading as food. Halitosis, his sweat full of cortisol and the poisons his body couldn't metabolize, all contributing to a cloud-haze of nastiness.

Three leaned back slightly, away from his reek. How many inches would give her a little relief from the smell and still keep him within striking distance? If, of course, she had a reason to disobey her orders.

It was a puzzle she was no closer to solving, for all her careful thinking. Why did she even have the capacity to contemplate disobedience? They hadn't answered *that* in training.

On the screen, the video feed showed a blond man, at ease in a hard metal chair from the debrief room. Lean and fit, a half smile as he stared offscreen, his blue eyes direct and sunny. His hair was mussed, his jacket unzipped, and everything about him screamed *sloppy*.

Except for that gleam in the back of his eyes and the

careful placement of his hands. Loose on the table, but ready. This, then, was Eight.

She had never seen his face before.

From offscreen, Bronson's voice. This interrogation masquerading as a debrief was two weeks old, judging by the date at the bottom. *"You went offgrid for four days."*

The man shrugged. *"Suppose I can't say I had business."*

"Smart-ass," Bronson breathed next to her. She considered telling him to be quiet. Analysis was rendered more difficult with his bloviating commentary.

She didn't, though. Three concentrated, a faint line appearing between her eyebrows. Something about that face seemed...familiar.

It was probably a neurological ghost. They'd warned her about that when she woke up from the induction, that she would think she remembered...things. Such memories were only phantoms, having no bearing on the present. Her file was classified, they told her, at her own request. She had signed the papers and agreed. It was for science, and for her country—two things Three was told she had believed in enough to sign herself over to the program lock, stock and amnesia.

The interrogation continued on-screen. Three watched, ignoring Bronson's commentary. Why did the blond man look so familiar?

"You're in deep over this, Eight. If you didn't have a reason—"

"Look, you train us to do this. Even on home ground. What kind of reason can I give you? Seriously? Look at my file. You know I'm considered impulsive. Maybe I just started walking and a direction looked good."

Three's head began to pound. The headaches were growing more frequent, 20 percent more this week. She was supposed to report any chronic pain, any digestive disturbance, any amenorrhea. The last wasn't strictly their business, but she obeyed.

"I'm going to have to put you on standby if you keep this up."

"I was just practicing, sir. Come on." That winning, wide smile. Eight probably thought himself very charming.

That was, however, conjecture, and insupportable. The pain intensified, the inside of her skull shivering, and Three's heartrate rose slightly. Not that the man beside her would notice.

Her analysis was...troubling. Eight was showing emotional noise. He had dropped offgrid for some purpose, and didn't particularly care what punishment would be meted out. He could very easily disappear again, that slight smirk said; it was indeed what the male agents were trained for.

Not Three. Her talents were...otherwise. Although a certain facility with the standard regimen was necessary for her to analyze, correlate, and predict what the male agents would do.

"Wanted to put him on standby." Bronson coughed, a deep, phlegmy sound. His chances of surviving more than ten years, with his current weight and habits, were comfortingly low. "But there was a situation in Eastern Europe, so—"

"Ukraine," she corrected, quietly. "Eighty-nine percent chance of success, given mission parameters."

"And with this?"

"The same." She calculated again, frowning. The

machine in her head returned the same answer. "That particular operation is low risk for impairment, given his profile."

"Well, at least *that's* good news."

The pain in her head eased a little. On-screen, Eight tensed slightly, and leaned forward, as if he was thinking what Trinity thought every time Bronson invaded the space normally judged personal in their society.

"Sir? Did you change your cologne?"

Bronson, sounding irritated. *"What?"*

"Never mind." A flicker of unguarded expression, and Three's breath caught in her throat. What was that? He looked almost…interested? Intrigued? It was there and gone so quickly a regular wouldn't notice, but *she* had.

She was still trying to decipher the expression when her head gave another flare of pain. A small dinging noise interrupted her—Bronson's cell phone, an alarm.

"Damn." He coughed again, hit the pause button, checked the phone. "It's checkup time for Six. Put the tapes away and finish the paperwork."

"Yes, sir," she murmured. The sharp twisting in her brain eased as Bronson moved away.

"Good girl, Three." He slammed the door on his way out, and she wondered what the crawling all over her skin was. An allergic reaction, perhaps? It eased as well. She stood for a few moments, staring at the screen, where Eight had been caught blinking. With his eyes closed he looked almost serene, and her hand rose, surprising her.

A fingertip touched the screen, right at the bridge of his nose. A shadow of crookedness—perhaps an old break. No doubt he received sympathy from the woman he had hidden away. What was her name?

Tracy Moritz. There were already contingencies in place. Civilian entanglements were frowned upon.

Her throat was oddly constricted. Three's hand dropped back to her side. The screen blanked into power-saving mode.

How long had she been standing here? She shook her head, and a thought occurred to her.

Three. That's not a name.

Curiosity, then. Perhaps, since she was a mystery even to herself, she could *choose* a name?

"Trinity." There. That would do. Her lips shaped the word, and her headache eased all at once.

The strangeness in her throat did not, but she set it aside to concentrate on work.

"I'm getting too old for this crap." Holly leaned back a little, stretching. At least she'd been able to get some dry toast down this morning. Her weight was holding steady. Maybe she wasn't going to be called to the big rodeo in the sky just yet.

"I hear that." Barb cracked her gum, grabbed another saltshaker. Thin fall sunlight streamed through the window, liquid gold showing every crack and chip in the tables underneath. The street steamed, and everyone was either irritated by the sudden glare or doped up on yellow light. Sunshine drove everyone crazy. "Any word on Angie?"

"Ginny's going by today to check on her."

Barb snorted. "Well, that's no help."

"She's just young." *And stupid. We were all stupid once.* Growing out of the stupidity was painful.

Sometimes it took a hard jolt to kick-start the process. Sometimes it took a double punch, one-two, like coming home from a doctor's office and hearing your husband say *I want a divorce* as though he was telling you what was for dinner.

"So are you." Barb filled the shaker, screwed the cap back on with a savage twist and cracked it down like a shot glass.

"Ha. I feel pretty damn creaky." Holly's hands moved on their own, wrapping silverware. Fork, knife, spoon, crease the napkin, the gummed band nice and tight.

"You're just a baby. What about Mystery Man?" With a bright avid smile, Barb picked up another saltshaker. Her fingers lingered.

"Haven't seen him." *Not since Friday, at least. Stop asking.*

"Shame. I could use one of those tips."

"We all could." Fork, knife, spoon. A roll, a tap, the gummed band.

"What did you say his name was?"

Reese. "Can't remember."

"You think he'll be back?"

"Probably not." *Hope not.* Did she?

That was the trouble. Life was uncertainty. She should have gone back to the doctor once or twice, to get some sort of idea *exactly* how long she had, but what was the point? Better just to vanish.

"Shame."

"If he does, *you* can pour him coffee and make awkward conversation." Another band, smoothed down. Just like a pillowcase. Right after the divorce she'd done housekeeping in the Five Seasons downtown; it was a relief not to think. To move so steadily you didn't have to brood about anything. All during her father's final illness she'd perfected that skill to a fine art.

By now she was probably at Olympic level in that sport. One day at a time. She'd read a "Surviving Cancer" book from the library once, and it was full of little gems like that. Dad had refused to read any of the literature they gave him. He'd retreated into himself like a snail into a shell, and the military hadn't done a damn thing to help. All those years he gave to his country, and they threw him out like trash.

Don't think about that. He did what he had to do.

"Deal." Barb grinned, arranging the shakers on a tray, and hefted the whole thing with a single, oddly graceful movement. The bell at the front door tinkled, and Holly suppressed a sigh. Someone *would* show up right in the middle of prep time.

Barb laughed, swinging away. "Speak of the devil."

Holly's head snapped up, the glare of the sun on wet pavement and crawling-past cars turning to shutter-clicks as she blinked.

Reese stood in the flood of light, droplets of water caught in his dark hair. His broad shoulders were tight, his face shadowed, and his jeans were wet to the knee, as if he'd run through puddles or had a losing battle with a street corner–surfing cab. Another sigh worked its way up, got caught in her chest, and she looked down at the silverware tub again.

"Well, hello again, stranger." Barb took over, familiar patter tripping off her tongue. The saltshakers were perilously close to tipping off the tray, she was in such a hurry. "Your usual?"

"That's okay." Nice, polite. "I'll sit up there. Hi, Holly."

She glanced up, and it was no use. He was heading right for her.

Suddenly clumsy, it took her twice as long to get the next set of silverware wrapped up. She stared down into the tub as if it held gold dust. She had to dredge up a smile and be pleasant, and somehow palm him off onto Barb.

The very thought made her tired all over again. "Hi, Reese. Coffee?"

"Sure." Did he have to sound so pleased? He moved almost as if he was military, but the hair was wrong. Civilian hair, Dad had called it. "I always wondered how that happened."

She finished another set. She was thinking about her father more and more these days. "What?"

"The little paper things. I wondered how they got around the silverware."

So did I, until I found out. Now I've done a million of them. "Me, too." Why did she want to smile? When she stole a glance at him, he'd settled on the stool to her left, not too close. Not too far away, either. "You left in a hurry the other night."

"You didn't put the tip behind the register, did you?"

A laugh surprised her, and she dropped the last set into the box of finished settings. "No. Brenda was really happy with it. Thank you."

"Good." He turned the coffee cup at his place over, set it precisely on its paper coaster. "Sorry for leaving so fast. I realized what time it was, had to catch the train."

Well, that made sense. She waved the apology away and picked up the box, bracing it on her hip. "It was pretty late. Hey, Barb will take care of you—"

"I'm just here for coffee. And I wanted to ask you something."

"Again?"

He paused for the barest second, studying her expression. An answering smile tilted up the corners of his mouth, and she caught a breath of cologne. Had he dressed up? No, it was just the same as usual—navy-blue T-shirt and jeans, that dark nondescript canvas jacket with a high collar. The same watch, and his bare, ringless fingers. Not even a betraying divot on the left third finger that would shout *on the prowl*.

I'm not looking, she told herself. *I don't care.*

"Yeah, again. Unless you're busy."

"You can see they're beating down the doors." She let her gaze swing critically over the empty tables. Traffic outside whispered and rumbled. In the kitchen, there was a hiss of steam and Doug turned the radio up, some country song about a woman in need wailing its reedy guitar over the static. Was there anything she could say that was polite yet brisk, or even just neutral?

Barb swung by and set the coffeepot down with a splash. "I'm going on my break," she announced and, of all things, *winked* at Reese. "Be good, kiddos."

Oh, for God's sake. There was absolutely no way around it, so she set the box back down and poured him a cup of coffee. Barb's giggle as she popped through the swinging door was a masterpiece of mischief, broken only by a crack of her gum.

He curled his hands around the thick ceramic mug, shifted a little on the stool, shot a glance over his shoulder. The light brought out shadows on his cheeks—he would rough up well before five o'clock—and bright threads in his irises, matching the highlights in his hair. Little bits of gold. He'd probably tan well.

Holly took a deep breath. *Be kind. It costs you nothing, Dad always said.* "So what's your question?"

"I've got a million of them, actually. I wonder about a lot of things. Occupational hazard." He blew across the top of his cup, steam gilded for a brief second before the air dispersed it. "I could keep you here until doomsday asking things."

What did that mean? She waited, holding the coffeepot, wondering what the hell she was supposed to say.

"But really," he continued, "it would just add up to me wanting to talk to you. So I'll settle for a cliché, I guess. Would you... I mean, do you think you could have a cup of coffee with me?"

Oh, Lord. "Um."

"I kept trying to figure out how to ask you." Was he nervous? He shifted a little, shot another glance at the front window. "Then I thought, well, just come right out and say it, and...because, well, hanging out here and just staring is sort of...creepy."

It is. "Um." *I've gone preverbal. Great.* She licked her lips, wished she hadn't, because he kept looking at her mouth. "It's not exactly..." *Professional? I'm a waitress, not a therapist.* "I guess. I mean, sure. Okay."

Wait. What did I just say?

For a second she was sure he would laugh, that it was a joke. Instead, he rocked back on the stool a little. He even looked surprised.

Well, that made two of them. The thudding in her ears and throat was her heart. Outside, a semi shifted and nosed past, rattling the windowglass.

"Really?" As if he didn't believe her.

Last chance to back out, Holly. Don't do this. You don't have time for it. "Really. But not here."

"Where, then? And when?"

"I work. You do, too. So—"

"I'll make time."

Well, maybe I can't just duck out whenever I feel like it. "It's just coffee."

"I know." He ducked his head, just like a teenager. "Look, I'm rusty. I haven't asked a girl out in years."

"I'm not a girl."

A quick lift of one eyebrow, and his expression plainly shouted he was very aware she wasn't a *girl*. "So tell me when and where."

Am I blushing? Either that or her cheeks had just acquired a sunburn from nowhere. "Give me a minute to think, all right?" How long had it been since someone had looked at her like this? It was awkward as hell, sure, and maybe he could still turn out to be a creeper...

Or maybe he wouldn't. And having coffee wasn't a proposal or anything. She could just do it once, to see what it felt like again. One last time around the block, so to speak, before she took matters into her own hands.

Is that what I've decided to do? Some things you couldn't think about straight-on—they just crept up on you until you knew, all at once, that you'd decided.

A cup of coffee with a guy who found her mildly attractive would relieve some of the crushing loneliness, and it didn't have to go anywhere, right?

"Are you going to change your mind?" Quick downward tilt to his mouth, rueful and oddly vulnerable.

I guess a nice tip or two gets you the benefit of the doubt. "No." Was that a big stupid grin on her face?

It was. It was probably all right, though, because he

was wearing one, too. It did great things for his velvet-dark eyes, wrinkles fanning at the corners telling her he was maybe too old for this crap too. Maybe old enough to have a little sense.

Not that it mattered. She tried to shove that thought away. Even though something in her cringed at knowing another person here in this city, she still...well, she *wanted*. There was no harm in it, was there? It wasn't like it mattered. One coffee date, then she'd make her arrangements. He'd never see her again afterward.

"Good." He set the mug back down, and she remembered she had a job to do. The entire place was deserted, though. Barbara was due back any minute from her break, unable to keep her nose out of whatever was going on.

Still, just this once, maybe Holly could steal a minute or two. One of the benefits of finally making a big decision, maybe. Funny how knowing made it feel as if she had all the time in the world.

So Holly pushed the coffeepot aside and leaned against the counter. "So. Reese. We'll do coffee. You got a last name?"

It was still sunny, but you wouldn't know it down here. No guns, just the ceramknife, because he was coming in from street level, getting onbase with the ID kept just for these visits. Signing the consent form, giving the same answers over and over again.

No headaches. No digestive problems. No dizziness. No bad dreams. No hives, trouble breathing. No, no, no. No degradation.

Different exam suite than last time. The tomboy nurse was nervous. Her pulse was up, and the serrated tang of fear rasped against his nose. What did they tell the medical personnel here? As far as Reese could figure, they thought it was allergy research. Which, he supposed, was incredibly ironic.

Heming probably knew something. He had to, looking at their bloodwork. The big brains, the architects of this operation, were most likely far away in nice offices, looking down from their heights at the little chess pieces below.

Wait.

What was bothering him? That tickle of instinct again, one wrong note throwing everything out of tune.

"Go ahead and disrobe." She had a cute snub nose and freckles, but the slight sheen of perspiration on her forehead was too much. Something wrong in her personal life, maybe.

Then why was he so damn uneasy? Maybe it was the fact that he had a coffee date after he finished here. He'd planned for this to take a while, but if they decided they wanted another MRI or something, he'd be late. Or miss it, and Holly would think…

Now *there* was a distraction. Just thinking about that delicious, indefinable smell would make things really interesting once he got into the paper onesie on the exam table.

The nurse left, closing the door with a soft snick, and he almost unbuckled his belt.

Stop.

He stepped close to the door, tested the handle.

Locked.

That's interesting. Never done that before. He cocked his head. Sealed door. No windows. Huh. A quick glance up showed him the ceiling wasn't standard, either. A slight hiss as something exhaled from a grill-work vent, and his skin roughened all over.

Time to think fast.

The ceramknife in his boot was great for avoiding metal detectors, but it didn't have a thin enough blade to jimmy the door open. Fortunately, nobody really looked at a keyring, so you could have all sorts of interesting things jangling on it.

Paper clip. Always keep a jumbo one on the ring for emergencies. A hot second to bend it, slide the wire into the small hole on one side of the doorhandle, and he paused only to yank the knife free of his boot before slipping through the door. Behind him, the hissing intensified, and whatever it was, it irritated the hell out of his eyes. *Lock it on the way out, Reese.* Quick exhale—he waited until he was down the featureless concrete hallway to inhale again, and the flimsy lock on the broomcloset door was no match for enhanced musculature.

The T-junction at the end of this hall was alive with the sound of movement. Someone was on their way, and he stepped inside the closet's darkness, blinking his streaming eyes furiously. *Damn. Am I blind?*

The burning crested, and he almost knocked something over. Froze, the terror of a hunted animal bursting low in his belly, filling his mouth with chemical sourness. If the soldiers had been outside the door when the nurse exited, he might be bleeding out on the hall floor right now.

They came past the door pretty quietly, moving in standard bottle-it-up. They weren't agents, which might have made him feel a little better if his eyes didn't feel like they were being scooped out of his head.

Just regular soldiers. Creak of gear, the brassy note of male adrenaline, the smell of discipline, canvas and disinfectant. He weighed his options just as the tearing pain in his eyes receded. His fingers tingled as well as his toes. Some kind of nerve agent, maybe? It hurt, goddammit, and he couldn't wait to kill that freckle-cheeked nurse.

A slight sound—they'd tested the door to the exam room. Found it locked. What were their orders?

Analyze. Fast-acting gas—was it antiviral? The nurse's nervousness. The reception desk, where Donna the friendly was pale and nervous, checking ID the way she hardly ever did—had the bored NCO on duty at the "secured" door hesitated for a moment before passing him through? The itching from the tolerance jabs last time, lasting a little longer than it usually did. The extra blood draw.

The burning and tingling receded all at once. His own sweat, sour with something inimical, metabolized, itched. He had the knife, keyring, wallet, and if he'd just been erased they were probably already at the apartment now, tossing it over and wrapping things up.

Whoever they sent to hit the apartment would know more than these stupid soldiers. If he got out of here in time, he might be able to catch them at their work.

Bring the heartbeat down. Listen.

Five pulses outside the door. One of them was talking, muffled by something—probably a gas mask. A gossamer-fine tremor in the middle of his bones. Whatever they'd pumped into the room might have effects beyond the immediate.

Carefully, ready for the burning again, he opened his eyes.

Sliver of light under the door, enough to give him something to work with. Mop bucket, a forgotten raincoat that smelled of fried food and dung, shelves of cleaning supplies. A hazmat cleaning station, with a bottle of eyewash he longed for, but the burning had gone away. The trembling receded as his brain clicked through alternatives.

The physical changes were useful, yeah, but not the most useful. Everything before he woke up in the hospital bed with his head bandaged and the fever sweat on him thick as grease was gray and dull, seen through a fog. Challenged, they'd called it. Developmentally disabled.

Stupe. Retard. Moron. All those nasty little words.

After the mystery flu, so sick he'd thought he was going to die, he heard different things. *Neuroplasticity. Cortical restructuring. Off the charts.* Waking weak and shaky, the entire world crystal clear in a way it never had been before, suddenly grasping connections in a way he never had. Agent training, where it was drilled into you: *it's the virus, stupid.* Lose the microscopic invaders and you lose your edge.

Was it an antiviral? Probably not in aerosol, but still. Had they decided he couldn't keep the little bastards?

First step was getting out of this hole, then getting offbase. He was already moving. One against five, and they were armed—but there was the jacket, a whole array of chemicals, his knife and the mop.

"Merry Christmas," he whispered, very softly, and set to work.

It wasn't a bad apartment. A nice view, even if that meant a chance of being trapped with nothing but glass between him and a six-story fall. There was chrome, and stainless steel, and glass, and leather. It was a stage set more than anything else, but it was *his* stage set, and no matter how much they cautioned against getting attached to your hidey-hole, it was still where he slept and kept a few things that mattered.

So it was the first place they would send a cleanup team, and if they had found the bodies he'd left behind, more would be on the way to net him and back the cleaners up, too.

Why? Why are they after me now?

No time to worry. This was what he was trained for.

Now, he bolted down the hall. Everything depended on speed. They'd sent a three-man team to clear the apartment, but again, none of them were agents. The one watching the hall he'd taken silently from behind; now there were just two.

They'd been busy. Garbage bags, latex gloves, window open because something was smoldering in an ashtray. Probably a passport, but if they could find it, he could afford to lose it.

There goes the security deposit. On his knees, sliding, taking out the first linebacker in a suit. Real gorillas, these boys, but if they were doing this they were smart muscle. Both of them had extra weight on him, and he'd almost dislocated his shoulder during the little brawl in the hallway. His eyes still smarted, his cheeks slicked with salt water, and he could still smell the janitor's jacket and the battlefield bowel reek as the last soldier died hard.

A patriot ought to feel bad about killing his own.

Even the biggest man went down when a knee was taken out. Splintering crack like greenwood, and the reason Reese had hit the ground too was for the gun under the glass-and-steel coffee table. Gorilla One dropped like a head-tapped ox, and Reese's aim was off. The gun roared—middle of the day, and the complex was usually deserted, but someone might call the cops.

The way his day had been going, it was pretty damn likely.

It was a gutshot instead of a good clean kill, which meant he anticipated even more noise as he hauled himself up and took care of Gorilla One on the floor. Gorilla Two was writhing in shock, sucking in air and trying to scream. Still, Two had presence of mind enough to strike out wildly as Reese was on him. He did not go gently, but the crack of a neck breaking and the foulness of loosened sphincters followed each other almost immediately.

Only three of them—it was a good thing.

A glance at the watch told him he had less than ten minutes before he had to jump. Probably more like seven. He already had a mental list of what to grab.

Keeping one of them for questioning had been an option, but he didn't have time. Getting the hell out of Dodge was his best bet.

I'm not going to make my coffee date. Dammit.

Or so he thought, until five minutes later, when he circled the parking garage below the building, pressing the unlock button on the key fob the lookout had been holding. A nice black SUV lit up like a beacon, and as soon as he got it open and started searching, he saw the files tucked under the driver's seat. He slid inside, closed and locked the doors, and decided he had thirty seconds to do some reading.

Two folders. There were no cameras down here; still,

he glanced nervously over his shoulder before flipping through the first one.

There he was, his name and vitals, a good black-and-white of him clean shaven and walking. Another of him scruffy and slouching, looked like it was on the Krakow job. Now that had been a balls-up, and he hadn't thought anyone could catch him even with a telephoto. Time to rethink his movement strategy between hides.

The second file…

He sat for a moment, staring, his pulse leaping and thudding in his ears. His eyes welled with more hot water, but it was probably just left over from whatever they'd pumped inside the sealed room.

Holly Rachel Candless.

Reese flipped through it, once, hoping he wasn't losing cognitive function. Name. Vitals. Marriage and divorce dates. CV and medical précis—looked like she'd lost a lot of weight since her last checkup. Huh. Bloodwork a little odd, but that was two years ago. Maybe they hadn't been able to pull her recents?

Goddamn them. He'd spent too much time talking to her, and someone with a telephoto lens had noticed. Or there had been a wrong note in his psych eval, or something else. It could just be as simple as a random check on agents, easier to do inside the borders of the good old US of A with a camera on every damn corner.

The point was, he'd gotten too close, and she was going to pay for it unless he got to her in time.

Unacceptable, Reese.

He came back to himself with his head resting against the steering wheel, an ache building in the very center of his skull. How long did he have, if whatever they'd dosed him with was killing the happy little buggers in his bloodstream?

Doesn't matter. He tucked the files into the backpack. Black, heavy-duty and modified ever so slightly, it was now his lifeline. If he carried it, he could be sure of not losing one of the few edges he had left.

Getting out of town was his safest bet. Going deep and far, keeping his head low, and finding a corner of the globe they didn't care about was the smart thing to do. Vanishing as soon as he left the SUV and the parking lot. He had wheels elsewhere, and there was probably a transponder in this piece of government-issued metal.

Reese jammed the key into the ignition. He needed a few minutes to get the bump out of his hip—passive beacon or not, they would soon begin to scramble to find him. The faster he could find some place to ditch it, disinfect the incision he'd have to make and move on, the better.

Damn. What am I going to do?

As if he didn't know.

Looked like he was going to make his coffee date after all. The only problem was, someone else might have met the lady first.

A cloud drifted over the sun, and Holly hunched her shoulders, hurrying along the building side of the pavement. The bus had been limping along twenty minutes late, for God's sake, and maybe he'd think she'd changed her mind.

Maybe she *should* change her mind. It was her day off, and she had better things to do. There were the dishes, for one thing, and laundry to haul up the block, and figuring out next month's food budget. Although working at the Crossroads meant she'd never go hungry, there was only so much greasy spoon you could take, and if it was one of the days she couldn't eat, she preferred to dry-heave at home.

Of course, she had her plans to step neatly out of her life like a woman sliding out of her slippers as she got into bed, but all the planning in the world didn't mean everything would go smoothly. Life had taught her that much, at least.

Why was she so nervous? It was just coffee. It made sense that he was just shy…but still, there were things that bothered her. She couldn't think of them just now, but she was sure there were things that bothered her.

Maybe it was just that she couldn't let anything good through the door after Phillip.

God, are you even thinking about him now? You're divorced. Let it go.

What was the word for feeling sad even when someone who was nothing but a user was out of your life? Was there even a word for it? Maybe she was nervous because Reese might be…well, decent, and she wasn't going to be around long enough to—

A horn blared to her left, out in traffic, but she didn't even glance back, shaking her head to get all the second-guessing out. *I shouldn't have agreed to this. I should turn around and go home.*

If she had, she would have seen the black van in the right-hand lane, slowing down as it reached the end of a line of parked cars. In half a block Montrose Street narrowed, the parking lane whittled away to nothing. It was the same black van that had been circling her route to the Starbucks on Montrose and Fifteenth, but then again, vans were as common as colds, in the city.

Even black ones.

Should have picked a place closer to home. Should actually go *home. This is crazy.* She sighed, jamming her hands deeper in the pockets of her gray hoodie. Picking a place closer to home wasn't a good idea, though, if you were a woman alone in the big city. She could turn around right now; it was only a bus ride to—

Someone bumped into her, hard, from behind. Holly glanced up, the curse on her lips dying as she realized the crowd wasn't bad enough to warrant that sort of thing, and that it wasn't a bump. More like someone was pushing her, and—

"What the fu—" she began, but he'd already shoved her across the sidewalk. It was a black van, the paint job neither glossy nor dusty, and she was bundled in like a bag of laundry.

She couldn't even scream. A gloved hand popped over her mouth, her hands yanked back and a slight zipping sound—something bit her wrists, cruelly—and by the time Holly realized she was being kidnapped she had already been jabbed with a needle the size of the DeriCorp skyscraper downtown. Right through her jeans, too, and it stung. Her right buttcheek promptly went numb, but she found her wits and began to kick.

She was still trying to scream when the chemical took effect, and everything went black.

She surfaced, groggy, blinking, the world smears of wet color on a glass plate. It felt like only a few seconds, but she was now sitting up, at least relatively. That was, if "sitting up" meant "slumped in something hard and uncomfortable," and her mouth was cotton dry, too.

What just... I was walking down the street, and then...

Her head was stuffed with something dry and crackling, and all she could do was listen.

She heard her own voice, slurred and slow as a sleepwalker's. Questions being asked. It was important that she concentrate, if she didn't concentrate bad things would happen.

Sudden light searing her eyes. She whimpered, and remembered her name.

Holly. I'm Holly.

With that came other things. She'd been just walking down Montrose, about to go to a coffee date. With... who?

A sharp, frustrated sound. "How much did they dose her with? She's useless." Male, a light tenor, each syllable precise and crisp. Very businesslike, and somehow...cruel.

"Just let her metabolize." Another male, this voice deeper, and somehow...anxious? Worried?

What the hell? *She was in a chair. The light was too bright, but her eyes wouldn't close properly.*

"We may not have time. Whose bright idea was it to scoop her up?" Flipping paper. The precise tenor voice sounded distinctly underimpressed.

"We're thinking Six—"

"Oh, yes. Tell me again how that happened?"

"The civilian doctor went A-45. Pumped a nerve agent on the—"

"That was rhetorical, Caldwell. Three, do we have anything?"

"Nothing yet." This was a new voice—contralto, female and weirdly uninflected. Sounded like a teacher Holly had once hated. *"We had a ping on him near the site where we picked her up. A meet, maybe."*

She concentrated on sitting up and blinking. It sounded almost doable.

"There's nothing here. No gray-side contact, nothing." The tenor sounded disgusted. *"It wasn't necessary to pick her up, for God's sake."*

"Protocol, sir." The woman sounded like a robot.

More shuffling paper. *"What a mess. Caldwell, can't we give her something to wake her up?"*

"If we want a dead body on our hands, sure. They overdosed her, medics say, anything else and her heart might shut down. She's lighter than she looks."

"Fine. Three?"

A slight noise of shifting cloth, and the woman spoke again. *"We either keep subject until she metabolizes, or we return her. We watch, and see if Six bites... I calculate ten percent odds he may."*

"He's probably not even in the city anymore. Give him another twenty-four and he'll be out of the country." It would be hard for the tenor to sound any more disgusted.

"Then this subject is collateral damage. A forty percent chance of breach, given Six's apparent interest in her and subsequent events." The woman was very calm. Her voice...it just wasn't right. Too flat, weirdly uninflected.

The tenor sighed. *"Fine, fine. But put her back, for God's sake. I don't want to sign the paperwork for a cremation."*

This, *Holly decided, is a dream. One she would wake*

up from in a little bit. Then she'd hop in the shower,
check the clock and hurry to make her coffee date.

That's what I was doing, right?

The light faded, receding down a long tunnel. That
was nice, because it was giving her a pounding head-
ache through the cotton filling her skull. Everything
turned warm and gooey, and she slid down a long
greased tunnel into velvet blackness.

Four calls logged on the desk, three on his phone,
but he'd been busy, dammit. Bronson toggled the trans-
mitter and was only halfway gratified when it immediately went through.

Control must have been waiting.

Yep. He had been. "What the *hell* is happening out
there?" Control did not sound happy, even through the
identity-protecting modifications.

Bronson sighed, pinching the bridge of his nose. He
finished settling in the chair, and was glad his hand
would cover his expression. "Civilian doctor went A-45.
Thought the operatives were contagious. Had himself
convinced they were going to infect the whole popula-
tion, that he was going to be a big damn American hero
and stop it. He's in interrogation now with Caldwell."

"Well." Control paused. "This is…unfortunate."

He was used to the man's habit of understatement,
but this was a little much. Bronson pinched a little
harder. Next Control was going to ask how the hell the
doctor had cottoned on, and—

"I'd hoped we had a little more time." Control's sigh
was audible even through the filtering. "We're looking
at a mess, Dick."

The world rocked underneath him. Bronson's hand

fell away from his face. Sweat began at the small of his back, his underarms prickling, and he was suddenly glad this office didn't have any damn windows. As it was, he already felt horribly, nastily exposed. "You mean…oh, *damn*."

"There was always a chance," Control said, pedantically.

"Fifteen percent," Three murmured. "Mutation, that is. Communicability chance is even lower, unless—"

"Shut up." Bronson didn't need to hear that. He leaned back in the chair. "Jesus Christ."

"The Gibraltar virus mutated. The eggheads are calling the new virus version Gemini. Some of the operatives were finding nice, cozy little socks for their wieners and thinking they were in love. Apparently the girls they were boning started showing…signs, and turned up infected. Three so far, one liquidated with the operative responsible for infection, the other two… it's a mess."

"Four percent," Three said, softly. "Unless…" She stopped when Bronson glanced at her, but he wasn't sure if it was obeying the unspoken order, or that something else had occurred in that computer she called a brain.

Control kept going. "They're going off the rez all over. I was hoping you had some good news."

"Huh. Well, we're containing here. We have one off the rez, and are taking steps to regain contact. Eight's back from Eastern Europe—"

"Ukraine," Three corrected, quietly.

Bronson's temper almost snapped. He couldn't yell with Control on the line, but good *God*, he was about to demote the computer-brained bitch to a secretary and be done with it. "Will you *shut up*? As it is, the only one who isn't causing problems is Three, here." *And she's beginning to get on my nerves.*

"Well, that's a silver lining. I'm sending resource allowances as we speak. Get yours in, by whatever means necessary. Prep them for transport. Mama's calling the chickens home. They'll be reeducated, or liquidated."

"What about the civvie doctor?"

"Disappear any civilian noise you can, fox the rest."

Really? "They're pulling the plug?" That loose, squirrely feeling in his guts couldn't be fear. It had to be the mozzarella sticks. At least he'd given the right order when it came to Six's little waitress.

"Not quite. We want to salvage what we can, but we need time and a little bit of quiet."

Well, now, wasn't that a relief. "Who's on firewall?"

"You don't need to know. Suffice to say our investors are chagrined, but not angry."

"That's...good. What about Three here?" Although he couldn't care less. It was probably time to move the nest egg offshore, and start making plans. Serving one's country was a fine and honorable thing, but getting cut loose and flushed wasn't.

Control paused. Three didn't move. Ice-cold, a woman reduced to a terminal.

"She's the program's greatest success so far. Keep her secured."

"Yes, sir." That would be easy. Unlike the boys, she was never any trouble, except for when she started *correcting* him, for God's sake.

"You're a good man, Dick. Clean your part of this up, and certain people will be very grateful."

"Ten-four." *My part of this? Already spreading the blame, you bastard.*

Control apparently thought that was that, because he disconnected. The screen went blank, Bronson sagged in his chair, and he suddenly wished for a bottle of vodka. A nip of something hard would go down *really* well right about now.

"Lying." Three's soft, uninflected verdict. "He's lying."

"Three?" He had to work not to shout. "Unless I ask you a question, you keep your damn mouth *shut*."

No response. He didn't look at her, but if he had, he might have seen a very small, very satisfied smile on her doll-like face. It was there and gone in a moment, a flicker of emotion shocking on such a blank canvas.

"Okay," Bronson said. "Okay." All he had to do was get Six back. Four and Twelve were already onbase; it would be easy to scoop them up. Eight could be called in and that civilian bitch he was seeing tied up, and all would be well. All Rich Bronson really had to worry about was Six—*Reese*, that was his name. The civilian girl he'd been stalking was already dead, no worries there.

Another silver lining. They were few and far between in this messed-up situation.

Bronson sighed again and reached for the desk phone. He'd already forgotten Three was in the room.

No sign of her. He waited as long as he dared, throttling the rabbit-run of panic under his skin, then hit the streets. The back of his neck itched, telling him he'd just avoided something—instinct or his perceptions picking up on something too small to be consciously noted. Maybe they were the same thing. Or maybe the itch was just the little helpers in his bloodstream dying off.

Quit thinking like that.

Maybe he was supposed to think she'd changed her mind, but he had both files tucked in his backpack. It was far likelier that she was screaming in a padded cell somewhere, doped on something meant to get her to babble about him. It wouldn't do any good—she didn't know anything, and he'd contaminated her just by going back to the diner once too often. Who knew they were watching so goddamn closely?

He should get the hell out of town. That was the safest option, and the most unacceptable one.

Because it left her behind, just like a discarded shirt, and *that* wasn't…what?

It just plain wasn't acceptable. So he visited a drugstore, and an hour and a half later found him in a familiar, run-down neighborhood. He ducked into the little bodega she often stopped in and bought a black baseball cap, put it on. Just in case. There was also an emergency exit at the back of the store that might prove useful.

The proprietor, a graying Sikh, barely glanced away from his flickering television to take Reese's money. The street outside looked normal, no breath of surveillance, and that was bad. If they weren't watching, did it mean they already had her? Or did it mean he was slipping, since he hadn't thought they were watching him trail Holly?

Don't rabbit. Walking down the street as if he belonged, stepping through the sudden glare as the sun came out from behind scudding clouds. The wind freshened, holding a promise of rain later, and he could smell faint traces of her as soon as he stepped inside the apartment building. The front door wasn't the greatest way in, but at least he'd scoped this place thoroughly.

He spent a few moments at the emergency exit at the end of her hall, breathing in the stale fug of a dejected apartment building in the dead time of afternoon, when even babies were napping.

With that done, he went back to her door—4D. Was now the time to admit he'd wondered just how easy the locks would be to coax? She had a dead bolt, thank God, but it wasn't enough.

Less than sixty seconds passed before he turned the knob and stepped over the threshold. The smell was there, wrapping all around him like a warm blanket. A rush of images—black hair, her smoky eyes, that little smile she sometimes wore. What would it be like to see her really happy? Baking bread, fresh strawberries, the tang of an adult woman...

He shook his head, almost staggering. A small kitchen opened up immediately to his right, ruthlessly scrubbed and gleaming. She wasn't looking for her security deposit back, it looked like, because she'd painted the cabinets a soft yellow, like sunshine.

The bathroom was the size of a postage stamp, but also scrubbed, the fixtures all redone. Probably salvage, because they didn't all match, but they were all brushed nickel, and he wondered how she was strong enough to turn a wrench, thin and tired-looking as she was.

The more he saw, the more he liked her.

She'd probably chosen this place for the light. The rest of the apartment was a single room, a futon with a cherrywood frame folded neatly into a red-cushioned couch and a small bookcase painted crimson. A skylight overhead filled it to the brim with mellow afternoon sun, and even when the clouds came again it glowed like the inside of a pearl. Bare wood floors, polished until they shone—had she taken out carpeting to expose the original hardwood? Or had it been a reason to rent this place?

Her smell was everywhere, drenching him. There was a battered leather recliner set near the large window, which looked down on Fifty-Eighth Street. He could see her curled up in it, watching the traffic go by. Probably with a book—and there was a small notebook with a pen clipped to its cover. Diary, probably—girls loved diaries.

Her dresser was in the closet, painted a glowing pale white. She'd taken the closet doors off and hung a rippling curtain of red and gold there instead, a sunburst of color. It was a restrained, beautiful nest. The small table next to the futon was ruthlessly bare except for a lamp and an empty glass.

The urge to lie down on the couch and work that wonderful smell all over him was incredible. He made another circuit of the room, checked the bathroom. The mirrored cabinet over the sink held toiletries and pill bottles, all over-the-counter remedies. Looked like she had trouble with her digestion, and also trouble sleeping.

I could help with that.

He stopped, staring at the antique cast-iron tub. What kind of thought was that? Why was he even here, instead of getting out of town?

Because someone will come to clear this place, and they might know where she is.

It was crazy. It was impossible. It was the riskiest possible maneuver.

I don't care. He let out a long, soft breath, and his ears perked. At least he wasn't degrading just yet; his hearing was as acute as ever.

Footsteps. Two men, moving with alien purpose. Coming down the hall, a wrong note in the regular symphony of a sleepy city afternoon.

Great. He eased the knife free—time to be silent and quick. Kill one, and see if the other knew anything. There were ways to wring all sorts of information out of people, and he was aching to try a few.

He was out of the bathroom and at the end of the short entry hall, tucked out of sight behind the kitchen. There was a pass-through and a doorway, so you could cook and look out into the rest of the apartment, but they wouldn't be able to see him. He closed his eyes, listening, and heard something else.

What is that?

Sounded like they were carrying something.

I can't be that lucky. God, what do you say, can I be lucky?

The locks chucked back—he'd relocked it without thinking, just to be careful—and whoever it was had a little trouble coaxing the dead bolt. But they had keys, so…

Reese checked his watch and kept breathing, soft and slow. The door opened wide, and he could smell them. Male, sweat, an edge of weaponry and violence, a breath of rain and exhaust from the city outside…

…and also, a familiar scent that tightened every nerve in his body. He could hear her breathing, slow and torturous.

She was alive.

She was being half carried down a familiar hall. Holly's head lolled—her arm was over someone's shoulders, and her legs worked slowly, as if she was running in a dream.

"That's a good girl." Unfamiliar male voice, hushed and amused. "We'll just get you home and you can play Sleeping Beauty."

"Yeah, for the rest of her life." Second man. "I hate these jobs."

What the hell was going on?

A familiar door reared up. Someone was carrying her home. What had happened? The jumbled, confused pieces refused to fit together. Everything blurred, as if she'd had too much to drink, or...

The familiar squeak of her front door, creak of hallway. She let out a sobbing sigh of relief and a gush of sweat broke out all over her. Her legs firmed up, and she tried to raise her head.

"I think she's waking up."

"Hurry, then. Find the bed." Sounds of movement. She blinked, caught a glimpse of her kitchen, moving shadows. "Oh, for God's sake, she's a hippie. Look for a pillow, anyth—*ulp*!"

The world turned over, and her entire body met hardwood—she'd taken this place because of the floor and the light—with stunning force. Her head bounced a bit, and she let out a hurt little cry, her body curling around itself just like a snail's. More confusion, shuffling and a snap, like breaking a branch.

Holly just closed her eyes. Why was she on the floor? Food poisoning? It couldn't be alcohol, she didn't drink...

Was her time up? She'd planned, but it was still a surprise.

"Holly." This voice was half-familiar. "Christ. What

did they give you?" He sniffed, deeply. "Ah. Lucky your heart didn't shut down. Come on, open your eyes again, honey. Let me have a look at you."

She did her best to obey.

There, silhouetted with sunlight, was a familiar face. Dark eyes, a baseball cap shielding them. Nose slightly too long, cheekbones slightly too high, the charcoal shading on his cheeks from stubble answering one question—he did get a shadow well before five o'clock.

Wait, what time is it? "Reese?" she croaked, her throat too dry and a metallic taste filling her, from teeth all the way down to stomach.

He examined her critically, staring into her eyes for what seemed like forever. Nodded, slightly, as if he'd found what he expected. "Come on, let's stand up. How do you feel?"

"Drunk. Did I drink? I never drink." *Not enough to get blasted, at least.*

"How did they get you? Where were you when you were taken?"

Taken? Her arms were heavy, but she managed to rub at her eyes. He pulled her up, wiry strength evident in his grip on her arm. Despite that, he was gentle, and she was glad, because she ached all over. "I...there was a van. I was... I was going for coffee. With you." The fog in her head was breaking up, but not nearly quickly enough. "Why are you in my house?"

"I'm rescuing you." He eased her down onto the futon. "We don't have a lot of time. Do you have a bag, a backpack, a suitcase? Backpack's best."

"I...in the closet. Why?" She peered past him, and her heart gave a strange thump, filling up her throat. "What are...oh, God."

Two slumped shapes on the floor, both in dark charcoal suits. Heavyset men, both with crewcuts, and under one's jacket a gun butt peeped out. The sight made her woozy, because it was obvious they weren't sleeping.

They were definitely, indisputably dead. And it smelled awful in here, like a plugged-up toilet. Now that her nose was clearing up, the reek was almost too much to handle.

Her heart tried to pound, but could only manage a fast walk. She stared. "What's going on?"

He ripped aside the curtain over her closet; she'd found the cloth cheap at the fabric store and sewn it herself. "You were picked up, drugged and questioned. They brought you back, probably to arrange you on your bed and put a pillow over your face. It would be ruled suicide or overdose, because of whatever they doped you with." He grabbed the navy-blue Eastpak she used for shopping or laundry trips and started going through her dresser.

"What are you *doing*?" She hopped to her feet—or tried to, sat down hard as her recalcitrant body informed her that she wasn't going to be standing up unassisted anytime soon.

"Getting you out of here. Unless you want to stick around for them to send someone to finish the job of killing you."

"Why would…" The world had gone mad. *That wasn't a dream. That really happened. Someone…but why?* "Why would anyone want to—"

"I told you, I'm in security. These guys are the other side." He closed the bottom dresser drawer, firmly. "Stay there. I'm going to get your bathroom stuff. If you want a book, now's the time to get it. Think about that."

"A…a book? Why are you… Hey. Hey. That's my backpack!"

"With your clothes in it, yes. Pick a book, Holly. I'd hate to pick the wrong one."

"What are you even doing?"

"Weren't you listening? Getting us out of here. We have five minutes, probably less."

She tried to push herself up again. "Wait. They were carrying me up the stairs. You…you killed them?"

"It's them or you. I don't want it to be you." There was a rattling sound from the bathroom, and he came out, zipping her blue backpack closed. He'd turned the baseball cap around, too, and under the shade of the bill his dark gaze was level and intent.

He was suddenly looming over her, blocking her view of the bodies. "Come on, Holly. We've got to move."

"I…but where?" She couldn't even begin to sort this out. *Was I in the hospital? Is this something to do with Phillip?*

"First step's getting out of here." Reese held out a hand. His jacket was dewed with the leftover dark circles of raindrops, slowly drying. "Come with me."

"The…the police." Holly's mouth didn't want to work quite properly. Maybe because he was staring at her so intently. "We have to…we have to call the police."

"No. In any case, we can't do it from here." A little beckoning motion. His fingers were blunter than hers, and his hand much bigger. Calluses across the fingertips, tendons standing out on the back, and those just-healed scrapes across his knuckles, still livid.

She reached up, tentatively. "How are you even here? I was supposed to meet you."

"And when you didn't show up I got to thinking maybe I should find you." He shook his head. "We have to move. Which book are you going to take?"

It didn't occur to her to protest. Her fingers touched his, and all of a sudden he had her hand and she was up off the futon, the backpack over her shoulder, swaying a little as he walked her over to the bookcase. She blindly grabbed at one, and then he had her arm. A few seconds later he lifted her over the bodies on the floor by simply grabbing her waist and picking her up, then setting her where he wanted her. Outside her door—which he swept closed, without bothering to lock it—he turned the wrong way, toward the end of the hall instead of the stairs.

She managed to dig her heels in. "Wait, my wallet." It was still in her hoodie pocket, despite everything. "My keys, where are my keys?"

"You don't need them." He all but dragged her. "Time to go. I can hear them."

"Hear what?"

Reese slid the chain free of the emergency exit, popped the door open and glanced out. "Footsteps that don't belong, baby. This way."

She still smelled flat-out delicious, even though there was a scrim of acridity as her body tried its best to get rid of the sedative cocktail someone had jabbed her with. He had to find a place to break their trail—get the beacon out of his hip and give her some rest. Right now she was easy to handle, disoriented and vulnerable. He could have told her the sky was made of frogs and she'd have accepted it, those smoky eyes huge in her wan little face.

The passivity wouldn't last. As soon as she realized she couldn't go back to her tiny little apartment, or her job, or anything else about her life, there were going to be problems.

There are already problems. Am I degrading? How long do I have to keep her awake to make sure she won't go into shock or coma? She still smells good.

More than good.

There was one potential hiding spot close by. It was a good one, tucked in half an abandoned warehouse, water and electricity still running because the squatters in the other half kept it jury-rigged. The power lines overhead fuzzed out a lot of things, and said squatters— different ones each time—kept away from strangers asking questions.

"What are you doing?" she whispered. He had to tear his mind off of her distracting nearness.

"Something I've got to get rid of." He inhaled, and pushed the scalpel in. It hurt, but the pain was easily shelved.

Her hissing sound of sympathy was not. "You're *bleeding.*"

"Got to get this thing out, Holly. Just sit there."

She perched on a stool, the effort of keeping upright and talking probably keeping her conscious. He didn't like the way whatever they'd dosed her with smelled as it worked its way out through her skin. Not as candy sweet as barbiturate, probably a variant of benzo. Hallucinogenic, nervous depressant…he was lucky she wasn't screaming and clawing at her own face. This was probably enough to give anyone a bad trip. It also made her smell sick, but that was probably just a gloss.

"Oh." A soft, wondering little sound. "God, doesn't that hurt?"

He tried not to sound amused. "Only a little." *Pain suppression. One more benefit from the little buggers. How long, though? I'd probably start showing symptoms. Feel clear enough. Might be okay.*

He wouldn't really relax for another seventy-two hours, though. If he made it that far with no degrade, he might conceivably be safe.

Funny how now he was feeling pretty charitable toward the virus. Damn near proprietary. The invaders were his now, and they wanted to stay alive. Just like he did.

Got to keep her alive, too.

Funny how that was all of a sudden right up there with his own survival as a priority.

Yeah, funny. Focus on what you're doing.

The little silver capsule squirted free, blood greased. Forceps were clumsy, but he caught it, popped it in his mouth in case it needed body heat, and from there it was just temporary sutures and bandaging. By tomorrow the incision should be sealed up nice and tight.

If he wasn't losing the virus even now.

Holly watched this, her eyelids at half-mast. How fast would her body work through the stuff? She was awfully thin, and they'd given her far too much.

That wasn't the real question, though. Just how the hell was he going to keep them both alive? Living on the run was fine for an agent, but she was a civilian, and she had a life. People who might miss her. Maybe even family, though it would have been in the file, wouldn't it? He hadn't had time to dig too deeply in the background stuff.

She swayed on the stool. He finished applying the semisutures, more disinfectant for the small wound—it barely burned at all. Then a gauze pad and medical tape.

She held grimly to the sides of the seat, her knuckles white. Behind her, an unfinished concrete wall reared, naked of graffiti. The other side of the warehouse was a shambles, but this one was a bare, well-insulated shell. The squatters had either been incurious or unable to get in. He'd stashed a few supplies here. One of the reasons it was such a great hole to go to ground was the car sitting not ten feet to Holly's right.

A nice, respectable Taurus, an indeterminate shade between black and gray, with fresh plates, a cache of ID and a weapon or two, as well as a few more welcome rolls of cash.

Couldn't run without money.

Cleaning up the blood was a few minutes' worth of work, but the plastic wrap he'd taped down had kept his clothes from getting more than a drop or two. He balled everything up and tossed it in an overflowing metal rubbish can, glanced at the pale, swaying Holly and stripped the gloves off as well. "Hey."

She didn't even respond, just stared blankly. He smelled another drift of that weird chemical and its stench of illness, caught her as she almost went over. The beacon, tucked between his cheek and gum, had to be dealt with soon.

He held her upright, looking at the top of her head. Tangled, inky hair, the heat of her mixing with the copper tang of his own blood and her, that delicious, maddening, shapechanging smell that fused every circuit in his head and hit everywhere he wasn't aching. And quite a few places he was, too.

"Shh," he said, though she hadn't made another sound. She tipped forward, her head resting against his shoulder, and Reese closed his eyes. Just for a second. Pretending. "It's okay. You're safe, you're with me, it's all right."

"I don't know...what's happening." She sounded so forlorn.

"It's okay." He searched for something to say. "All you need to know is that you're safe."

"I want to go home."

He winced inwardly. "I know."

"I want to sleep." A breath of petulance. Well, she'd had a hard day, right?

Understatement of the year, Reese. "You can't yet. Until I know you'll wake up."

"I don't care."

"I do." *Don't ask me why. Not clear on that myself.* Oh, but he was. Lying to himself about it, though. "Let's get you into the car, Holly. You can rest, but you can't sleep yet."

Unfortunately, she wasn't listening. She'd passed out, and he still had the beacon tucked between his cheek and gum.

"Damn," he muttered, with feeling, and carried her to the car.

The dreams were awful. The doctor's office, with Dr. Gregory's salt-and-pepper beard moving as he told her, *No need for a lot of concern, we just want to make sure.* Arriving home, sitting in the car for a moment, bracing herself for telling Phillip...walking in and seeing his set face. For a moment she thought he already knew, then the moment at the kitchen table when he told her, *I want a divorce, Holl,* as calmly as someone else might say, *It's sunny out today.* She hadn't even set her car keys down or taken her coat off. Then, sitting in the courtroom, hearing her divorce proclaimed final, seeing Phillip hand in hand with *her*—the blonde, bubbly med school student, one of his classmates. All those study dates, and Holly working two jobs to see him through school.

Her lawyer, almost in tears—*why won't you fight? You can have alimony, the judge will practically throw it at you!* Not wanting to explain—it didn't matter, she would be dead soon anyway, why make more trouble for anyone?

Faces warping, her nylons running, looking down and realizing she was naked, and then the dreams were less memory and more nightmare. Running through dark corridors, hearing the woman's soft, inflectionless voice. *Collateral.* And the tenor. *Put her back.*

Someone talking to her. Her hand in a bruising grip, a cool washcloth against her forehead. "It's all right. I'm here."

The realization that she was probably sick calmed her somewhat, and she woke in stages, thoughts swirling and settling and finally making sense. *Am I in the hospital? Fever dreams, maybe. Wow. That's unpleasant. Did I collapse? What happened?*

Who knows I'm sick? God.

She ached pretty much all over. The sheets were damp, and she was in a T-shirt. Which meant maybe not a hospital.

Was it a hangover? Or had she buckled, her body finally deciding whatever was growing in it was too much to work past? She hadn't felt any different that morning, but that was life.

It always bit when you weren't looking.

The jumbled pieces in her memory refused to jell together. The last thing she was sure of was walking down the street toward a coffee date with Reese. No, wait. Something about a van.

Was I run over? How ironic would that be?

"Welcome back." His face loomed over hers, and she blinked rapidly. Her throat was cotton dry, and she let out a little croak of surprise. It was Reese, dark eyed and too big for the suddenly crowded space. There was a slice of white ceiling behind him. It wasn't her apartment, and for a second she was confused at the relief she felt. "Take it easy. Here."

What the hell?

His arm under her shoulders, there was a cup at her lips. She drank, gratefully—mineral-tasting tap water, tepid, with a side of chlorine. Her nose wrinkled, but she was thirsty. He took it away before she'd had enough, but after a moment or two her stomach rumbled and she was glad. Any more and she'd likely spew it right back out.

"You're out of the woods." He looked a little tired, faint circles under his dark eyes and his stubble having a field day. He hadn't shaved in a day or two, and his T-shirt was rumpled, damp under his arms. "Whatever they dosed you with is out of your system."

"Reese?" *Someone roofied me?* "What. The hell." She licked her cracked lips, wished she hadn't, because his gaze dropped to her mouth. "Where—"

"We're in a hotel. Safe for the moment."

For the moment? Her brain kicked into gear, everything inside her skull suddenly functioning the way it should. "For the moment?"

"Yeah. Look, Holly…" He sank down on the bed beside her. "You're going to have a little trouble with this."

"With what?" She tested her arms and legs, warily. They worked. Not the best they ever had, but they still worked. She wasn't in a hospital, so she hadn't collapsed. Which meant there were things to be done. Had she passed out at their coffee date, or—

Figure that out later. Right now, get up and get dressed. "I…oh, God, what day is it? I've got to get to work."

His mouth firmed up, became a straight line. "You can't go back there."

"I *what*?" *Great, Holly. Start screaming. That'll work wonders.*

"It's dangerous. They had a file on you—"

"A file? Dangerous? What?" She pushed herself up on her elbows and froze.

There was nothing on under her T-shirt, and she was in this bed, and the only person around was him.

He didn't seem to notice her sudden stillness. "I told you I was in security. Which is sort of true. I work for some…dangerous people. They tried to kill me."

"They scooped you off the street, drugged you and probably questioned you about me. You didn't know anything, but I've hung around you once too often, I guess."

"Hung around…oh, damn, I knew it. I *knew* it." She flopped back down on the bed. The pillows were squooshed and a little damp. How much had she sweated? "I knew those tips weren't for real!"

"I'm sorry. They…these people don't play nice, Holly. I'm not sure why they wanted to retire me, but—"

Oh, hell *no.* "*Retire* you? What exactly do you do for a living, Reese with a first name nobody uses, huh?"

He was looking at her oddly, one eyebrow lifted, somewhere between puzzled and unsurprised. "Holly—"

"Get away from me. I'm calling the cops." She lunged for the bedside table, but his hand closed around her wrist.

He pushed her back down, and she was either painfully weak or he was freakishly strong. "You *want* them to find you? Want to get scooped up and drugged again, or just shot? Those guys in your apartment were going to suffocate you on your little futon there, and you wouldn't have put up any fight. It would've been easy with the drugs in your system."

Drugs? Futon? How does he know I… She stared at him. His fingers were warm and oddly familiar.

"You want to call the cops? Fine. The instant you do, I'm gone, and I'm your best chance of staying alive." He reached over to the night table. Under the fugly 1970s amber-glass lamp, there was a chunky, cheap phone and two manila folders. "But look at these first. They're target files. One's for you." He took a deep breath. "The other one's for me. Look at them, and if you still want to call the cops, fine." The bed squeaked as he levered himself up, and he tossed the folders into her lap. "We're safe for probably another twelve hours here. If you're with me, I'll keep you alive. I suggest you do some reading and then take a shower."

Holly realized her mouth was hanging open. She shut it, looked down at the folders.

Embossed on the covers, down on the lower right corner, was something she'd seen a million times on all Dad's paperwork. Even the refusals for treatment, and the settlement papers, saying they didn't believe the wartime chemicals had given him the big C— PROPERTY OF US ARMY.

And there was another stamp, this one full of terrifying meaning to any military kid.

CLASSIFIED.

Her heart started to hammer. Her palms were wet. *Dear God. What the hell is happening to me?*

She opened the first one with tentative fingers, and something inside Reese relaxed a fraction. Not very much, because he'd expected her to have trouble with believing him. He was a stranger, and he'd just told her something off the unbelievable charts. Not to mention she was recovering from a benzo overdose—and how could he tell her that?

I can lick your sweat and taste the drug in it. I can hear your heartbeat. I can go straight up a brick wall if I have to, and your entire life has exploded because I thought you smelled good. Better than good, and you're the last person to deserve anything like this.

Goddamn it.

She blinked at the contents. He couldn't tell if it was his file or hers. The thought that she might be reading his made his skin tighten all over, in a not entirely unpleasant way.

"What is this?" She sounded baffled. Maybe he should have fed her first, or given her more water.

She looked up, those smoky eyes huge, her eyelashes matted, her cheeks flushed with remaining fever heat, and his mouth went dry.

My God. She's so pretty.

She was, in fact, beautiful. He hadn't seen it before, or had he? Was it just that smell, drenching him, working inside his skin? Thin and tired-looking, she was still gorgeous. Maybe he could just admit it to himself now.

If not for the sourness of the drug tinting her scent, he could think she was sitting there all mussed and flushed after an entirely different chain of events.

He cleared his throat. "It's, ah, a target file. Name, vitals, other information. Photos so you can zero them. The other's stuff background, so you can…anticipate."

"Anticipate." She looked back down at the papers in her lap. "Target."

"Yeah." *Euphemisms. Trade talk to make it easier to do nasty things for your goddamn country.*

Lies.

"My God." The flush paled, and he had to stop looking at that mouth of hers. His focus was slipping. Was it degradation, or was it the persistent pressure below the belt? It was hard to think, looking at her sitting in a bed. Especially when she was wearing one of his shirts, and he knew exactly what was under it. He'd had to search, really, because there could have been a telltale in her clothes, and besides, she'd been thrashing with the aftereffects of overdose. Sweated right through her jeans.

"What do you *really* do? No, wait." She shook her head, pushing the first file away. It fell open, and he saw it was hers. "Don't tell me. Or you'll have to kill me, right?"

"No." *The whole point of this was to keep you alive.*

I didn't even blow town, not that you'd know how easy it would have been. "Look, I was—"

"Shut up." She flipped the second file open, almost angrily. Stared down at it. "Oh."

Was she seeing the CV? His service record? "I went into the Army because the only other place to go was back into a state home or halfway house." The words were ashes. "Then there was the program. It turned me into…what I am. I did my job, served my country."

"Good for you." Pearly little teeth sank into her lower lip, and her paleness was alarming. She was damn close to transparent. "Why do they…who are *they*, exactly?"

He doubted she really wanted to know. "Are you going to call the cops?" Deliberately harsh. "Because if you are, I am not going to waste time explaining. If you're not, you should probably take a shower, and we can get something to eat. You're hungry—you'll fall over if you don't get something in you soon."

He saw the betraying little twitch. Her right hand, probably tempted to reach for the phone. Waited, trying not to breathe, because every time he inhaled it was like getting a mouthful of something too good to be true.

Then she looked up at him, blinking rapidly. Those marvelous, smoky blue eyes brimmed with tears, but she swallowed, hard. Her shoulders came up a little, as if she was used to settling burdens on them. "One of these for me, right. And one for you. They…did someone try to…"

"Yeah."

"Why? What did you do?"

"I don't know." *Don't care, either.* But he probably should. Were they winding the program down? Were other agents being liquidated, or just him? Nothing had seemed off until the tomboy nurse had locked him in that room—and the fact that there had only been a flimsy lock on the door meant that they'd expected whatever was pumped in through the vents to disable him in a matter of seconds, right? "I followed my god-damn orders. The only thing I did that they didn't tell me to was ask you to coffee."

As soon as it was out of his mouth, he regretted it.

A single tear brimmed over. She wiped it away, roughly, with the back of one hand. Stared at him as if he was something slimy that had just crawled out from under a rock.

Well, he was, wasn't he. And even now she was try-ing to understand, instead of being screaming-furious at him. Christ. Too smart for her own good, and too soft, as well. She didn't deserve this.

"Is this some sort of joke?" Hoarse now. She shook her head, violently. "No, it isn't. Because it's not funny, and there's no reason…there's jobs on here I didn't even remember *applying* for. God. And the…oh, God. Medi-cal… God. God."

"Holly—" What could he say? He'd already stuck his foot—hell, his entire leg—in his mouth, and kept chewing.

"No. Just…no." She scrambled out of the bed, and the sight of those long, bare dancer's legs damn near starved his brain of blood. He even stepped toward her, expecting her to have a little trouble walking, but she grabbed the wall and hauled herself along with grim determination. "Stay *away* from me!" Even her bare feet were pretty, but the cheap avocado shag carpet here probably made her skin crawl.

She deserved so much better. The bathroom door

was another flimsy piece of work; she slammed it and spent a few seconds fiddling with the lock. He let her, listening intently.

The shower turned on, and he heard her hitching breath. The sobs went right through him, and he spread his hand against the door, because even though he knew it wasn't a good idea to go in there he wanted to.

Badly.

He didn't. If she was ambulatory, she needed food and fluids. Just because they were probably safe here for another twelve hours wasn't a good reason to stay.

Oh, quit lying to yourself, Reese. You want her dependent on you, because she's safest that way. And you're a monster, because deep down you're feeling a little grateful, aren't you. Now that she doesn't have any choice.

His nape itched, again. If he started going downhill, she wouldn't stand a chance of surviving. He had to hope the little invaders were still happy and comfortable swimming around inside him.

Reese turned on his heel, surveying the room. He'd have to clean up and get her out of here.

No matter *what* she thought of him.

It felt like a hangover. At least washing the dried sweat and guck off her skin helped steady her. The headache receded a little, but her bones felt rickety. Like they'd turn to rubber at any moment and spill her onto the indifferently cleaned tile floor.

It made her long for her own bathroom, spick-and-span and familiar. Unfortunately, the fog inside her head was clearing, and there were a couple things standing out like rocks on a seashore.

Things like two twisted, dark lumps on her living room floor. Like Reese's voice, calm and firm. *You're with me. You're safe.* Reese's dark eyes hot and distant as he sliced open a long scar on the outside of his hip, digging out what looked like a little silver bullet.

And a woman's voice. *We either keep subject until she metabolizes, or we return her. We watch, and see if Six bites... I calculate ten percent odds he may.*

Collateral.

As in *damage.*

The water never got very hot, but at least there was soap and the towels weren't mildewed. The flyspecked mirror showed her a pale, trembling woman with dark circles under her eyes, and even though her entire body ached she could tell nothing...that he hadn't...

At least she hadn't been...molested. Not that it mattered, but it was nice to know.

Her mouth tasted like a rancid subway car and she kept having to grab at the counter or the wall to stay upright. She probably looked drunk.

There, set neatly on the peeling yellow counter, was her toothbrush and a tiny minitube of Crest, the same flavor she had at home. And her comb—black plastic, wide toothed, the chips on it familiar as her own hands.

She had a foggy memory of Reese packing a backpack while she sat on her futon and tried not to pass out.

You're with me...you're safe.

The image of him sitting at his regular table, clutching a cup of cold coffee and staring at her, wouldn't go away either. The thought that maybe he'd planned this, or...but how would he get all that information?

Just thinking about the target file made her feel sick. Lists of jobs she'd applied for, her last five places of employment, Phillip's name and an address that was probably current, pictures of her—including her state ID photo. You couldn't get that unless you were official. And medical records, Dr. Gregory's name and address, and copies of scrawls that were his notes on her medical charts. Who would bother to go to this trouble? Sure, considering how he tipped, Reese was maybe rich... but what rich guy would go to these lengths and make a fake file on *himself*, too?

On the other hand, she'd been drugged. Could she trust anything she remembered, even?

The last thing she remembered with any certainty was being bundled into that black van. And that was thought provoking, wasn't it? Because she'd seen the van twice before, while she was walking. Hadn't paid attention, but she was sure she'd seen it. Or its twin. That was the trouble with black vans, they all looked the same.

The thing about working food service was, you saw a lot of people. You got a feel for them. After Phillip, she'd sworn never to be taken in again. Reese was a little...weird...but he'd seemed pretty...well, nonthreatening. Even asking her out to coffee had been shy, and awkward, and completely note perfect.

The people I work for aren't very nice.

I work security.

They tried to kill me.

She had nothing but the towel and the T-shirt to wear, so she wrapped herself tightly in the towel and closed her eyes, her hand curling around the doorknob. She thumbed the lock, twisted and took a deep breath.

When I open my eyes, I'll be in my own bedroom. I'll be looking into the kitchen, and the first thing I'm going

*to do is go to the kitchen sink and get that big green cup
Ginny gave me for St. Patty's, and I'm going to drink
so much water I'll have to go straight back to the bathroom. Then I'll call Tony and tell him I can't come in
today because I'm busy having a nervous breakdown.
I'll go to the bodega, get a newspaper and start looking for a new job just in case.*

It was a great plan. She swept the door open and
stepped out, her feet not finding hardwood but slightly
oily carpet. When she opened her eyes, she saw a run-
down, seedy motel room with horrible pineapple-
colored curtains and a bed that looked as though it had
been used as a trampoline. Her backpack was on the
twisted-up comforter, and peeking out of its top was a
familiar battered paperback.

A copy of *Come, Love, Sleep.*

Now she remembered blindly grabbing it, and everything inside her turned over with a sick thump.

It's true. It's all true.

Reese was nowhere in sight.

It was, Trinity thought, rather instructive to see just
how frantic people could become once the window for
effective action had passed and they were playing catch-
up. There were more efficient ways to catch a rogue
operative, certainly.

She had simply decided to follow Bronson's ill-
tempered order and cease informing him of such things.

An interesting quandary: Did one obey the *letter* or
the *spirit* of the order? Such a consideration had never
been of overriding import before. Each scenario pre-
sented to her before the last forty-eight hours had been

clear-cut in the extreme. Or had she simply not seen the complexities under the surface?

As it was, Bronson placed her in the office, at the smaller, glass-topped desk, and returned with a box of file folders. "Look through these, start calculating," was all he said, before retreating to his own desk and getting on the phone to continue requisitioning resources, in between barking sharp orders at Caldwell whenever that unhappy major returned to this nerve center. It was Caldwell who'd brought more military assets into the equation, which was wasted effort, since any program agent would know to stay away from any installation—but Trinity didn't say a word. Instead, she leafed through Division's files on the program participants.

At least, the agents. The ones who had survived infection and had not been subject to induction. Was her own file somewhere in this box of red-jacketed statistics and numbers?

Perhaps. There was no reason to hurry, though. The longer she could keep Bronson unaware of her current mental state, the better.

And just what is your current mental state?

Six's file was familiar; she had already calculated the percentages Bronson wanted. He wasn't even asking for the *important* ones.

The door banged open, but it was just Caldwell, out of breath.

Bronson settled back in his chair. "Christ, knock next time, will you?"

"It's Eight," Caldwell panted, sweat on his forehead turning his blond high-and-tight a little darker. His fatigues, usually ironed and starched to the picture of perfection, had suffered a bit.

Trinity's own clothes needed laundering. Bronson seemed to have forgotten her requirements.

"What *now*?" Bronson reached for the empty box of tissues. "God*damn* it."

"They bungled the civilian erasure." Caldwell half bent, his breath coming in huge shuddering gasps. "It's a *mess*. We have him, we're bringing him in, but we had seventy-five percent casualties, and—"

"And?"

"The news is on it. A house fire, but they'll find shell casings, and—"

"Crap. You *moron*. You let the cops onto that site?"

"I don't appreciate—"

"Never mind. We have resources in place. Dean Thackeray's plane lands in forty-five minutes. Get out there and bring him up to speed."

"Thackeray?" Caldwell looked like an eager young basset hound, just aching to scramble after an interesting smell.

Bronson pinched the bridge of his nose, as if his head hurt as well. "Civilian egghead to run the medical tests. What about the grids?"

"Up and running, as well as the sweeps."

Six isn't in the city anymore. Trinity closed his file, set it aside. The only thing troubling her was why Six had bothered to return to the woman's apartment. A drugged civilian could not have taken out two of an Alt-Sec team.

Not without help.

What would make Six return? He had grown adept, it seemed, at hiding his emotional noise. Eight had not, but the civilian entanglement there…

The next file was Eight's. She opened it carefully,

scanned the first page. Paper clipped to the second was a black-and-white photo—the same nose, the same tousled blond hair, the same smile, the same flat disdain hiding behind his expression.

Trinity found herself tracing the line of that jaw, the glossy paper slick under her fingertip. Something about Eight…bothered…her.

Bronson and Caldwell were still talking. Pointless jabber, all of it.

What is happening to me? Trinity found her throat dry, again. Her physical senses were as sharp as ever, her body functioning at peak, every system running smoothly. It was her head that was the problem. *Am I degrading?*

If she was, sooner or later Bronson would notice. There was an eighty percent chance she would be slated for liquidation in that eventuality. If the agents kept behaving like this, soon the program would be closed down and the loose ends tidied, and there was a fifty percent chance Trinity herself would be seen as a loose end even if she wasn't degrading. The longer this went on, the more that particular percentage would tick upward.

How strange. Trinity turned the page. *I do not want to die.*

Well, then. It was time to plan. And it was high time to start considering everyone else, especially Bronson, as a hostile element.

Reese pushed the door open with his foot, the plastic bag heavy in his left hand. Protein, fruit, whole-wheat bagels for carbs. Light stuff, Gatorade to balance her electrolytes, some Emetrol in case she was still nauseous and—   .

Holly whirled, strings of damp hair flying, clutching a pale pink T-shirt to her chest. He'd picked the clothes that smelled most strongly of her, figuring they were likely to be the most comfortable; she was wearing a cream-colored underwire that had obviously seen better days.

All the blood rushed out of his head, and he hoped he was wearing a neutral expression. Just looking at those pale bare shoulders, thinking about the bra straps digging in a little, imagining loosening them up or unhooking the back, sliding his hands down her arms, maybe daring to feel along her ribs, cup the soft heaviness of her—

"I thought you'd gone." Breathless, and her eyes were huge. Baking bread, ripe apples and vulnerability, that's what she smelled like now. The room was thick with it. Under it was the lingering of sickness, a strange burned-metal taste, but it could have been the benzo or even just an incipient cold.

He swept the door closed. "Just, ah, getting something to eat. And some, you know, bottled water." *I sound like an idiot.* It was hard to talk, looking at those bare shoulders. A slice of hip disappearing into her jeans, perfect as a seashell. The contrast between rough denim and her skin made his fingers itch to touch.

She nodded, and the transparent relief and fresh apprehension mixing on her face filled his head with the rushing sough of high winds. The vulnerability threaded through her scent reached all the way down and yanked on something blind and instinctive.

Something *protective.*

He almost dropped the bag, but she'd already turned away, presenting him with her bare back, the bra strap a straight bar across flawless pale skin. The shirt was over her head in a trice, and he had to take a deep breath. Which didn't help as much as it could, because it filled his lungs with that smell, and everything below his belt was either numb or aching stiff.

He shifted, trying to relieve some of the pressure, and found out he was still carrying the bag. *Jesus. Am I going to lose my mind every time she shows a little skin?*

There were worse things, but still, he needed his head clear. There was a flimsy table in front of the curtains. He set the groceries down and twitched the fabric aside a little, checking the parking lot. Still clear.

If he was still smelling her, it was confirmation the little invaders were still working. Physically, he felt fine, except for the embarrassing fact that his body seemed to be stuck at teenage boy around her. Having a semipermanent hard-on was not conducive to thinking straight.

If she let him get close enough, he was either going to go off like the Fourth of July or embarrass himself with wilting. Again. Not to mention if he tried to explain Tangiers to her, and how afterward the only time he could even come close to getting it up was when he caught a whiff of her—he'd sound like a pervert.

He wanted, very much, to sound like a real human being to her. Even if he wasn't. His nape itched, tingling. "How soon can you be ready to go?"

"I thought you said we had twelve hours." She bent over her backpack, the tremor in her hands either hypoglycemia or fear. Or both.

"We probably do. That's not a reason to stay here, though."

"Where are we even going?"

"South." *And you're taking this a little too well.*

Her head dropped. She stared down at the backpack. "Oh."

"You should eat something."

"Why me?"

Why should you eat? Or why am I doing this to you? Is that what you're asking? He cleared his throat. That was no help, but it gave him a few seconds to maybe think about what he should say. "Um. You mean, why did I…"

"Why did you even come into the Crossroads? I can't remember when you started coming in."

Ten months ago, give or take a few weeks. Right after the second time I was in Venezuela. I only started coming in regularly after Tangiers, though. Because I couldn't stay away. "It was just chance," he heard himself say. "Then I kept going back to see you."

"But *why*?"

What did she want to hear? If he could guess that, he could guess how to get her into the place he wanted her.

"It was a Sunday," he heard himself say, and swore internally. Looked like he was going to tell her part of the truth. "I, uh, I had my coffee. There was an old man at the counter. Red suspenders. Looked like he'd done some trucking when he was younger, just the way he sat. A Bulls baseball cap. He called you honey a lot. Middle of the day, he stiffened and fell off the stool." *First I thought he'd been shot, and was looking for angles.*

"Ernie," she whispered. "Always tipped in quarters. He'd had a heart attack."

I know. "You got everyone away from him, shouted

for that tattooed girl to call 911." *She snapped to attention, too, because you looked ready to take her face off if she dragged her feet.* "You asked if anyone knew CPR. There was an orderly there from Cat General, on his lunch break. He started doing chest compressions and mouth to mouth. You…" He was staring at the grocery bag, he realized, at the apples he'd carefully sniffed and examined for blemishes, the wrapped block of Colby Jack, the bagels with their flecked tops. "You were down on the floor with him. You were holding the man's hand, and telling him it was going to be all right."

It didn't do any good. The orderly hadn't been doing CPR hard enough to crack ribs, and that was the only way to do it. But something else had bothered Reese ever since—what sort of woman would hold a dead man's hand like that? Maybe the sort of woman who could… Christ.

The sort of woman who could overlook the fact that Reese was a ghost. A dog trained to dig. An agent, not a…

Not a man.

She sniffed now, too, and wiped at her nose with the back of one hand.

His arms ached, just like they had on that rainy night as he followed her home, wanting to help. Wanting to touch. "He was dead as soon as he hit the floor." Why was he hoarse? "But you kept holding his hand. I just… I kept coming back. I couldn't stay away. I'm sorry."

Holly half turned. Now she faced him, hugging her blue backpack, and he didn't know how to quantify her expression. "That was a long time ago."

Less than a year. He shrugged. "I'm sorry I brought all this down on you. We'd better get moving."

He'd been about to say, *I'd take it back if I could*, but that would have been a lie. He had no problem with lying; it was part of every agent's arsenal…but still.

The uncomfortable thought that maybe he should lie to her, just to keep her calm and safe, wouldn't go away. He'd told her to go ahead and call the cops, and Reese had to be glad she hadn't matched that bluff.

Even if he threatened it, he wasn't going to leave Holly to them. He had what he wanted, and even if it wasn't optimal, well, making the best of it was on the agenda. One more reason why he wasn't even close to being anything she could…like.

She nodded, sniffed again. Clutched at the backpack as if it was a life raft. "Okay."

He'd been prepared for anything but simple acceptance. Of course, right now she was still weak and shaky, and it was good strategy on her part to play nice with him. Had she noticed he'd left her alone in here with the phone? Maybe he'd been hoping she'd do something, call someone, force his hand.

"Okay," he echoed. He hitched his own backpack higher on his shoulders and grabbed the plastic bag again. A single toss had the room key on the tangled bed, and he reached for the doorknob. "You got everything?"

Good work, agent. We've got her acting complicit. Keep it up.

He told that cold, calculating little voice to shut the hell up, and got going.

Holly was too hungry to care what he'd brought, really, but it was still better than anything fried or greasy.

The apples were just right—crisp, not mealy—and the cheese wasn't her favorite, but the instant she saw it craving hit her hard. The bagels weren't toasted, but that was okay. Even the Gatorade tasted like manna. For once, she could eat. Maybe she just had to get hungry enough.

She realized she was stuffing her face and tried to slow down, tearing off a hunk of cheese and nibbling at it. "Do you... I mean, are you hungry?"

They were heading through suburbs now, each mile clicking over taking Holly farther away from her life. Minimalls, residential areas, Gas Food Lodging signs. The car ran smoothly; it was always weird to be driven around when you usually took the bus or the subway. Sort of magical, the pavement slipping away effortlessly.

Reese shook his head, frowning slightly at the freeway. Thin midafternoon sunshine struggled through rainclouds, not very successfully. Speckles of drizzle hit the windshield, smearing when he flicked the wipers on. Seen from this angle, his profile was a little ugly. Nose too long, and his mouth too tight, and he really should have shaved. Right now all he needed was a glower and a cigarette to look like a villain. "I'm okay. I tried to get light stuff, easy to digest. Good for you."

So, you work for the Army, and you're a health nut. Okay. "Are you vegetarian?" The clouds were thickening. Autumn rains coming in. You could see them approaching from a long way away once you got outside the city's tall buildings. That's why she liked this part of the country—nothing to sneak up on you. Not like Boston, where divorce and...other things...could show up out of the blue.

"What? No." He sounded baffled, but that frowning expression didn't change. "Why?"

"I just wondered." Now she could remember him getting breakfast at the diner, and bacon. *Stupid question, Holly. Pick another one.* "Why are we going south?"

"Warmer. Besides, easier to hide once we're over the border."

"Over the…" She cracked another bottle of Gatorade, even if she was going to have to pee in ten miles. Her throat felt as though she'd swallowed a belt sander, and the headache just would not quit. Her back didn't hurt, though. At least, not much. "Why?"

His frown didn't intensify, but it didn't fade, either. "Safer. Easier to hide."

"Is that your plan?" *Because I'm hoping you have a plan.*

Now he glanced at her, a shadow of amusement crossing his face before vanishing. "Pretty much."

"Oh." She couldn't tell whether she should be reassured or not. The rain intensified, and he turned the wipers on low. Brake lights glared against the wet road. "Some plan."

"Do you have a better one?"

"I'm not a…what exactly are you? Security consultant. Uh-huh." It probably wasn't a good idea to sound so sarcastic, but her bravery was going up with her blood sugar. "You work for the Army, or…?"

"For the government. A division you've never heard of, let's say. I started out in the Army. Then…there was an accident."

"What kind of accident?"

"IED. Roadside bomb. I'd never walk again, they said. Then they told me about the program."

He'd never walk again? Funny, he seems to be doing okay. "What program?"

"Experimental. It would get me back on my feet, and there were...other benefits. In return, I'd work intelligence. I suppose that's what you'd call it."

No way. "You're a *spy*?"

"I'm an agent. I solve problems, I troubleshoot, I gather intel, I liquidate—"

Wait a second. "Liquidate?"

He was silent.

Everything she'd eaten settled in a cold lump, her stomach suddenly informing her that enough was enough, thank you. The nausea, an old familiar friend, filled her throat. She capped the Gatorade, very carefully. "So...am I a problem? Something to...troubleshoot? To liquidate?"

"No."

She waited, but that was it. He turned the dial for the heater, touched the defroster. Left it alone.

"So what am I, then? Collateral? As in damage? That's what she said."

"Who?" Sharp interest now, and he was stealing little glances at her without turning his head.

I can't even begin to explain. "I don't know. I just... voices. I wasn't... I couldn't think. It was too bright." *Return the subject...paperwork for a cremation...see if he bites.* She shuddered. The pressure in her stomach drained away.

"It's the drugs." Casually, as if it didn't matter. Maybe this sort of stuff happened to him all the time. "If you remember more, tell me. It might help."

"Help what?" *How is there any helping this?*

"I don't know if they've liquidated the program itself or just me. Either way, they're going to look for me, and for you, too. Those target files mean they have deep pockets and access to all the systems any government uses to keep track of people. Probably running grids and cores right now—"

"Can you please slow down and use English?"

He took a deep breath, his hands tightening on the steering wheel. "It means that if we stay in the country, sooner or later they're going to catch us. I want you safe, so we're going over the border."

Nice to know you're concerned. "Aren't I safer if you just drop me off? They'll question me and figure out I don't know anything—"

"That's not the way they see it."

"How do they see it?" *And who is they, really? Government? This is just...* She couldn't even find a word that fit.

"You're a liability, one they were willing to suffocate in her own bed. They don't know what I've told you. They don't know what I might do."

"Since they tried to...to kill you."

"Yeah."

She waited for him to add more. He didn't. So she took another tack. "What about going to the police? The media? I mean, if you go public they *have* to leave you alone—"

"God, you're naive." Now he was smiling. "It's pretty adorable."

Holly's jaw dropped. She stared at him, clutching the Gatorade bottle. Liquid sloshed. "I don't think I—"

"You're what's referred to as emotional noise. Keeps an agent from thinking clearly, makes things messy.

Maybe that's why they wanted to retire me, I don't know. I'll figure it out when I can, but right now all I'm concerned about is getting us over the state line and finding someplace to sleep. Collecting you was a high-risk maneuver—running with a civilian in tow is a tall order even for a program agent. I'll tell you what you need to know, when you need to know it. Clear?"

She stared at the bag in her lap. *Emotional noise.* What did that even mean? "You could have just left me there." *I wouldn't have known the difference.* "Why didn't you?" *Because all that stuff about Ernie wasn't a reason. It wasn't even an explanation.*

Another deep breath, and his knuckles were white. He was squeezing the wheel like it had personally offended him.

Maybe that was one of the questions she wasn't supposed to ask.

The silence stretched out, thinner and thinner, a balloon filling with dangerous gas. She busied herself with tidying up the ravaged remains of groceries, every rustle of the bag now incredibly loud. The song of the tires against blacktop was familiar, but this time it failed to soothe her.

"Forget it," she finally said to her feet, arranging the bag carefully between the pair of blue trainers he'd produced from somewhere, in her size. New shoes, their bottoms barely touched with grime. "I'm just glad to be alive, I guess. This is…pretty weird." *And that's the understatement of the year. What would Dad think about this?* It hurt to think of her father, an old familiar pain.

He said nothing. Holly settled back in the seat and stared out the window while the miles rolled away.

* * *

She drifted into sleep a little later, her breathing evening out and her pulse nice and strong. He kept his eyes on the road.

Why didn't you? Was she serious?

The freeway dipped slightly, then rose. Once they were out of the orbiting belt of suburban sprawl, the road would be arrow straight, heading for the horizon. Lots of time to think while following that line.

Lots of time for her to get accustomed to him. And lots of goddamn time for things to go wrong.

That smell of hers was too distracting. He shouldn't have told her she was emotional noise. Things just fell out of his mouth the wrong way whenever he thought he was finally doing okay with her. Still, she'd end up falling his way eventually. She'd have no choice, now that it was survival.

He glanced over, just to make sure. Still there, still in the seat next to him. Breathing deeply, a real sleeping beauty. He checked the rearview, frowned slightly.

It wasn't time to worry just yet. The cop car three units back was simply pacing traffic, looking for a wrong note. He tasted a little adrenaline, exhaled softly. Control of autonomic functions wasn't perfect, but it was a damn sight better than a civilian's.

If he could get close enough to Holly, if he didn't wilt when the time came…well. The thought raised a pleasant sweat at the small of his back, a tightening all through him. *Stand down, soldier. You're not out of the zone yet.*

Now that he was bathing in it, the smell was intensely…comforting. Soothing, even as it revved his hormones up. He checked his speed again, checked the rearview. Something about the cop car was off.

Sun broke through low-hanging clouds, misty spots on the windshield. Just when he was beginning to get a little concerned, the cop three cars behind him lit up like a Christmas tree. A cold wave passed down Reese's entire body.

I haven't even prepped her for casual interrogation yet. Dammit. Too busy being careful, trying not to upset her even more.

The cruiser leaped forward, a shark in the shoal of suburban traffic…and passed by as Reese hit the turn signal and slowed. It whooshed past, and he was suddenly aware of a slight groaning sound as his tension communicated itself through the steering wheel.

Don't ruin the car, idiot.

Still, it was a comfort. Dodged a bullet and found out he was still enhanced. The longer he went without losing function, the better he felt about the whole damn thing.

Of course, would he be able to tell if he was losing cognitive enhancement? Now *there* was a riddle.

Traffic decreased, and another set of city limits were left in the dust. The road went through a couple long, shallow curves, then straightened. By the time Holly made a small murmuring sound, dreaming about something—*hope it's pleasant, honey*—he had taken the peel-off to the other south-going interstate he wanted, and even turned the radio on, very low. Just enough to keep him alert as the scenery changed to rural and the miles slipped away under the tires.

She woke up, alert and curious, in a motel over the state line, and immediately the questions started afresh.

Reese set another plastic bag down carefully on the

bed. More apples, more bagels and more cheese. He'd have to get her something more substantial in a bit.

Holly, rumpled and just awakened, accepted the latte in its white paper cup with a sigh of gratitude. "Oh, God, you're an angel. So, who are we running from? I might as well know."

"Bad people." He tried not to look at her bare shoulder, pale and fascinating. Those baby blues were wide and impossibly pretty—it wasn't goddamn fair for her to look so good first thing in the morning, for God's sake. Or to be so cheerful and uncomplaining.

The tired smudges under her eyes were gone. Of course, she'd gotten some solid rest, even if she was too thin. Her collarbones stood out, starkly. She settled in the bed, her back propped on the pillows, and if her expression hadn't been so plainly unsatisfied it might have been one of his little dreams come true.

As it was, he'd slept on the floor and could tell there was something brewing in her head.

"Government. The…the files, they were stamped by the Army. Right? And *classified*—I was a military brat. I know what that really means."

Anything from "above your pay grade" to "they'll chop your fingers off if they find you peeking." Reese strangled the urge to sigh. "I'm property of the US Army, yes. I'm technically on loan to the program, codename Division. At least, that's what they call it. The medical stuff, the poking and prodding, the experiments." He exhaled, sharply, and dug in the bag for an apple. He'd want a protein load later, but he didn't want to take her to a restaurant yet. It was probably good her father had been in the service—she'd take to him a little easier. "You should have some breakfast. Checkout time's coming up."

"Is that another euphemism?"

What? "No." *Although if you want me to, I can come up with a few. Starting with that pretty little mouth of yours.*

Said mouth pursed a little. "Are we going to keep living in hotels, or…?"

"There's a destination. Until then, yeah." Trying not to think of how delicious she looked wasn't working.

"Ooh, a destination." Maybe she didn't mean to sound sarcastic, but he didn't think so. "And that would be?"

Not yet, cutie. "You want to settle down and decide what you want to know first?"

"How about who's trying to kill me?"

"Who's trying to kill *us*." The sooner he could get her thinking with an "us," the better. "There's a list."

"Just like Christmas."

He decided that particular kind of sarcasm wasn't good for either of them. "Where the present is a bullet in your brain, sure. The Army probably doesn't want us dead, because I'm a significant investment of resources, but orders are orders. The program? Same thing, probably, unless there was something in my bloodwork or my psych evals that changed the ground. Which leaves the hush-hush, the intelligence agencies that don't have initials in public. They've got the clout to give the other two orders, and they could have decided to close up shop. Because agents like me, well. You train us to go dig and nose around, and then you find out maybe that wasn't such a good idea. Because we do what we're trained to." He took a deep breath, watching her as thoughts moved across that transparent, heartbreakingly naive face. She still smelled mouthwatering, probably because she hadn't showered yet. Reese was soaking her up like summer hills during the first good rain.

It's interesting how the smell changes. Food when I'm hungry, and other things when I'm—

"What did you do? Are you…" She gulped, and paled a little. "Are you a double agent? Or—"

"I'm a good old red-blooded American, honey. I did what they ordered me to do. The only thing I did without their say-so was asking you to coffee."

Now there was a flare of anger. "Do you think I somehow—"

"Of course not. If I thought that you'd be dead."

Silence. She stared at him; he straightened. The apple, carefully cupped in his hand, was cold and hard. *Well. That was the wrong way to put things.*

"Nice to know where I stand," she said, finally. "Why are you even bothering, Reese? I mean, what did I ever do to you?"

Nothing. It's all about how you smell. How you're too patient and kind for your own goddamn good. And how even now, she wasn't screaming or deconstructing.

Does she have to be so goddamn perfect?

His temper rose, just a little. "I guess I just… I don't know." *I followed you home. I wanted to knock on your door.* "Look, I could have just vanished. I didn't. I came back to your apartment because I thought whoever was sent to toss it might know where you were."

"Very chivalrous." She took another sip of latte. "So, if I called the police…"

"You won't."

"Why not?" A challenge, now, lifting her chin, and

he wondered how anyone could have divorced her. She could burn a man down with that look, and he'd thank her through the flames.

"Because that would be stupid, and you're a lot smarter than you want anyone to know, Holly."

For some reason that was the wrong thing to say. Or at least, she frowned, and it was time to admit he was in trouble.

Because he wanted to make her smile, and this wasn't doing it. How stupid was that urge? She didn't have to be happy; she just had to stay near him, right?

Was he going downhill? Would she have to do the thinking for both of them? A degrade was possible, though he didn't feel it physically. Without a battery of tests, he couldn't be sure. There was a margin either way, a really uncomfortable one.

"Then can you tell me where we're going?"

"South."

The frown deepened. "Our destination, Reese."

"No."

"Why won't you tell me?"

"Because if I get taken, I don't want to know where you'll head for."

"And if I get…taken…you don't want me to know. Okay."

Well, he called her smart—he had to realize she'd figure that out. "You're not going to get taken."

"Oh? I'm the weak link here, right? The civilian. The emotional noise."

I shouldn't have said that. "So I'm not going to let them take you. If it comes down to you or me, Holly, you'll run and I'll hold them."

That managed to ease the frown, but it was replaced

by puzzlement. She stared at him like he was speaking Esperanto.

Reese's back prickled with sudden awareness.

I don't like how that feels.

Time to move.

He stiffened, and Holly braced herself. Whatever she was expecting, it wasn't his quick turn, crossing the room and peering out between the curtains glowing with morning sunlight. They were open just a little, and she realized it was so he could look out without moving them.

"Get dressed," he said, quietly. "Now."

She sat there and gawped, the latte in her hands.

"Did you hear me? Get up and get dressed, Holly."

"What is it?" *I sound like I've been punched.* Breathless, and her hand began to tremble.

"Get moving." His face changed, just a little.

If she asked any more stupid questions, he might decide to leave her behind. Holly scrambled off the bed, almost dropping the latte.

He was still there when she tore the bathroom door open, buttoning up her jeans. Sunlight striped half his face; he glanced at her and she couldn't decipher his expression. Was he irritated? Was this a game?

"Brush your teeth and use the restroom, Holly." His left hand had turned into a fist. He shook it out, relaxing slightly. "We have a few minutes. I just don't like the way it looks out there."

You don't like... She shook her head. He was probably crazy. She was probably crazy, too.

Collateral. As in damage.

Seven minutes later he pressed the latte back into her hands. "You need the caffeine. Let's go."

"Will you even tell me what's going on?"

"We might be blown, I don't know."

"Blown? What is blown?" She realized what a dumb-ass question it was about two seconds too late.

He paused for just a second, opened the door. "The only thing you need to worry about is doing what I tell you."

"Great." *Given the alternative, though...*

That was just it. She didn't have any alternative. Right? At least, not one she could arrive at without a whole lot of heavy-duty thinking.

"I'm going to take care of you."

There's a lot of things that could mean. She looked at the carpet—cheap nylon, again, but a slightly higher grade. Blue, with little flecks of gold and brown. "Okay."

"You have no idea what that means, I guess." He wasn't looking at her; he was giving the hall a good once-over.

I guess not. She set the coffee down on the little table by the door. Hitched her backpack, with its small assortment of hurriedly packed stuff, higher on her shoulder. Followed him out and tried not to let the logical extension of that line of thought loose inside her head.

Do what I tell you, it'll all be fine. She'd heard that before. From Dad, sometimes, when he didn't want her to worry, even when he started losing weight and the sickness crept over him in inches, his body consuming itself and the stack of medical bills growing higher and higher. At least Holly was avoiding that. She wouldn't leave a single debt behind.

No, what bothered her was that she'd heard it most recently from Phillip. *After we get me through med school, it'll all come together. I'll take care of you.*

They took the stairs, and it wasn't until they were in the car and driving away that Reese seemed to relax a little, checking the rearview every few seconds. Holly's hands clenched together in her lap, tighter and tighter, especially when the cop cars, their lights on but sirens silent, zoomed past them going the opposite direction.

"Sloppy," Reese muttered. "No grid, I'll bet."

She could barely get the air in to talk. "Is that...is that good?"

"Could mean they're grasping at straws. Could be a convenience store robbery in the area. They go silent for those. Maybe I'm just paranoid, but better safe than sorry, right?"

"Right." *How would anyone know where we are?* She tried to make her fingers unclench.

They wouldn't, unless they have ways of finding out, and that...

"Calm down, Holly. We'll stop in a couple towns to get you more coffee. Caffeine withdrawal headaches aren't fun." He checked the rearview again, following signs for the freeway. "I'm not going to let anything happen to you."

"That's awfully nice." What was she supposed to say, to that? "But, you know, it already has. Happened, I mean." *More than you know.*

"True." He sighed. It seemed to catch him by surprise, too. His right hand reached over, and he threaded his warm fingers into the knot her hands had become. "I'm...sorry. I mean, I'm not sorry you're with me. I..."

I would have kept working, and coming to see you, as long as I could."

The silence between them was a balloon again, this time full of crowding, jostling, whirling. Her stomach flipped once, and again. Was she going to start another round of dry heaving?

"Holly. Breathe."

I'm trying *to.* It wasn't happening, though. Was this it? All the stress finally swooping down to finish her off?

Ironic. Really ironic.

He hit the turn signal, plunging off the main road, and a residential section full of autumn-painted trees in long rows swallowed them. The houses were small; this wasn't quite a city, and the hotel was only there because the interstate ran right nearby—

Her brain refused to work. There wasn't enough air, she kept making a funny little whistling sound when she tried to inhale.

"Crap." The car swerved up to the curb; he popped it into park and hit his seat belt. "Holly. Breathe."

His hand slid free of hers. She shut her eyes, trying to figure out where all the air had gone. A burst of cold from her left side—he'd opened the car door.

When he opened hers, she almost had her lungs back under control. His fingers pressed against her forehead, and the smell of autumn and cold dampness swirled around her.

"Shh, sweetheart." He had her seat belt off, too, and Holly was glad, because she leaned over and retched.

There was nothing in her stomach but a swallow of coffee. Bile scorched the back of her throat. She gasped, tears welling between her eyelids, and Reese was talking to her. Low and urgent.

"It's all right, baby. I'm right here, nothing's going to hurt you. Try to breathe. I'm right here, Holly. I'm not going anywhere. It's okay. Everything's okay."

No, it's not. She hadn't had one of these since the divorce papers arrived, the blank-faced process server mumbling and shoving them into her hands—

She grabbed onto the thought. *Panic attack. You know what to do.* She brought her hand up to her mouth, got a good grip on the skin on the back of her wrist, and bit down, hard.

"Christ!" Now he sounded worried. "Holly? Don't, Jesus, don't hurt yourself!"

The pain jolted her, interrupted the spiraling panic. It broke in a gush of sweat, her heart thundering in her ears so hard she could barely hear him. At least she could breathe, even though the world had narrowed to a single fuzzy point of light.

We're worried about your tests, the doctor had said. *We want to run a few more.* The walls were paper thin in that medical suite; she'd already heard him and the tall, queenly female doctor passing back and forth terms that weren't cryptic when you'd helped your husband prep for med school tests. Or when you'd heard the same thing from the doctors as your father died by inches in front of you.

Things like *elevated counts* and *swollen lymph nodes* and *prejaundice* and *insulinomas, too, look at this*. Holly listening, alternately hot and cold, the knowledge burning inside her. *Pancreas. Virtually asymptomatic in the beginning.* The nausea, the back pain, the digestive problems when she *could* eat—she was lucky to have escaped jaundice, really, you couldn't hide turning yellow.

She came back to herself slowly, leaning forward. Her forehead was against something warm, and someone was holding her. It felt nice.

Safe.

He smelled good. No cologne, just clean male. She hadn't been this close to anyone in a long, long time. He was still talking, low and soothing.

"—sweetheart, I promise it'll be better. I'll make it better. Just relax. Just breathe nice and easy, baby, and everything will get better. I'm right here."

How does he know what to say? The truth was, she'd been waiting all her life to hear that sort of thing. It was a damn shame it had to come from him. He probably wasn't a bad person, but her life was gone. Completely thrown out the window.

Again. How much bad luck could one woman have before she decided to just step away from it all? Like leaving your slippers next to the bed. Goodbye, so long, don't write, don't call, just forget there had ever been a Holly Rachel Candless.

"I…" She coughed. Her mouth tasted awful. He had her upright, somehow, and they were under a giant oak that had lost its leaves already. The houses here didn't have fenced yards, merging their greenery in companionable tangles. Were there people inside, wondering what these strangers were doing? "Reese." A croak. Had she thrown up? She didn't taste it, but her abdomen ached so badly.

"I'm right here. You're safe."

No, I'm not. She straightened. Found her balance. He didn't want to let go of her, maybe thinking she'd fall over, but she pushed until he did. "You should just leave me here." She sounded surprisingly steady, she supposed. "It doesn't matter. I'm sick, Reese. Really sick, and it won't matter if they do…whatever it is they're going to do to me. I should have told you earlier. I'm… I'm sorry."

"What?" He glanced up, checking the street behind her. "I'm not going to let them catch either of us." A level gaze, and—of all the things he could do, he chose to brush a few damp strands of hair out of her face. "What makes you think you're sick?"

"I…" She was shaky and exhausted now, even though she'd slept so heavily. "Look, just leave me here. Okay? I just—"

"No." His eyebrows drew together. He inhaled, sniffing, and she stared. "Nothing wrong with your charts but some anemia and severe stress. Panic attacks are normal—you have anxiety spikes. Your blood pressure's low, too. You shouldn't be on your feet all day."

How do you know? Do you have medical training, too? It was probably in that stupid file he had, her life pinned on the wall like a butterfly. "Look, I—"

"Get in the car." He pushed her, gently but irresistibly, and she half fell into her seat. "You start feeling like that again, we'll pull over again. Drink some of the Gatorade. Your electrolytes are all out of whack." He locked the door, closed it and went around the front of the car. A high blush from the chill on his cheeks, he looked like a young professional out for a Sunday drive with a nauseous friend, she supposed.

Was it even Sunday? She didn't even know what day of the *week* it was.

He dropped down into the driver's seat, buckled

himself in and the car roused softly. He stared out the windshield for a few moments, and Holly was suddenly certain he was going to say, *You're right, you're weight I don't need, get out.*

It would serve her right, too. All of this had happened because she'd selfishly wanted to feel normal and go out to coffee. She should have turned him down, shut him off, found another job, pulled away, done what she knew she was going to have to eventually do.

"I want you to listen to me," he said, finally, very quietly. "Are you?"

There's nobody else talking. "Yes."

"I couldn't stay away from you. I'm selfish. I should have left you alone, but I didn't." He nodded slightly, as if she'd agreed. "I'm not going to. Drink something. We're going far today."

He wasn't going to listen. Holly slumped in the seat, her head throbbing.

We want to do some more tests, the doctor had said. She'd agreed, nodded through scheduling them and never gone back. Paid the bill for the initial visit when it arrived, even though it took her down to quarters for the rest of that month. *No insurance* meant *couldn't afford it.*

It's expensive, Phillip had said, even though he was covered through his school. *Why bother when I can just treat you? We can use the money elsewhere.*

You didn't need a weathervane to know about the wind, Dad always said. She knew what she had. And when she got home, there was Phillip at the table, just waiting to drop the bombshell. How he must have nerved himself up to it.

It didn't matter. Nothing mattered. Even being selfish

over a goddamn coffee date didn't matter. It all ended up in the same place, and her condition had been steadily worsening for a while now. She didn't have much time left, and Reese was bound to have a weapon handy, if a woman got desperate enough.

So Holly just closed her eyes, and let him drive.

That was close. In any number of ways.

What did she think she had? Her medsheet showed nothing but low blood pressure and mild anemia, though there were notations about her bloodwork being off. He hadn't smelled anything off in her in all this time, except the drugs and that deep-yellow metallic tang, the only thing about her that didn't smell delicious. He'd also studied the financials and figured out that she'd put her ex through med school, which was a waste since Holly had no doubt been the bright one in that marriage.

Any man who would divorce her was an idiot.

Maybe it was just rabbit talk. If you weren't trained to handle it, the stress would get to you. Hell, it got to you even if you were trained, which was why he was worrying about her ex instead of trying to pin down what had felt so off this morning.

If he had deep pockets and government resources, he'd have hit the airwaves with APBs and some sort of cover story by now. Nothing in the papers, nothing on the radio, nothing on the television this morning while Holly slept and he kept the sound turned all the way down.

That was distracting, too. The blue flicker of the television playing over her peaceful face, and imagining her waking up and smiling at him.

Just didn't smell right. That's all.

Maybe it was the lobby, where the kid at the desk had looked at him just a little too long. Maybe it was the distant sirens cutting off as they got closer, silent as sharks while Reese and his little minnow swam out of the net. Was he just being paranoid? If he started deconstructing, they were both dead in the water.

He was sweating lightly. His pulse kept wanting to spike. Holding her while she shuddered and tried to breathe, helpless even with the little invaders still working in his bloodstream making him stronger and faster…it was enough to give him a serious case of the wind-ups. He needed to clear his head.

There was a good way to do that, but he didn't think she'd go for it. Not to mention the fact that he'd probably wilt before takeoff, given his luck.

Stop. Calm. Think.

She was silent, slumped in the passenger seat with her eyes closed, but at least her breathing had evened out. She wasn't shaking with distress, or making that soft choked sound that turned him inside out. The freeway was unreeling under them, nothing was likely to explode in the next few minutes, so maybe he could start making her a little more comfortable.

Just how are you gonna do that, soldier?

Any way he could. "Holly."

She stirred, a little. "What?" One colorless little word.

"I told you I was in an accident, right? Bomb in the road." He waited for the light to turn green, accelerated onto the on-ramp. "Broke my spine in two places, ribs, legs…for a while they weren't sure I'd live. But I did. Woke up quadriplegic and they said, *Wouldn't you like to walk again?*" A short, chopped-up laugh;

he merged onto the freeway. Traffic was light, nothing out of place. Just one car among many on the American road veins, moving along. "I knew I couldn't. But they asked, so I… I just didn't want them to send me back to the state home the recruiter found me in. I hated it there." He stole a glance at her. She was pale, shaking a little, her eyes still closed. An arc of charcoal lashes against her cheek.

So he went on. "They scraped and prodded and poked me. I wasn't too bright, but I was an ideal candidate in…other ways. So they…they injected me. I didn't know with what. Then I got sick. Really sick."

He'd picked up little bits of information while he burned with fever, unable even to thrash. Screaming about fire until his voice gave way, every nerve ending frayed, tearing an inch at a time. No relief, no letup, just the burning and the pain. "The casualty rate for that phase of the program was about ninety percent. I made it, though. Lay in bed for another two weeks, eating everything they gave me, and one day my legs started twitching. Then my arms. It hurt." *Regrowing nerve tissue is a bitch.* "I had to learn how to walk again. How to run. How to do other things."

"That's pretty impossible," she whispered.

You're telling me. "The best part was cognitive. Neuroplasticity. Learning new things. Repairing damage. Sensory acuity, pain suppression. I can hear your heartbeat. I can smell aspirin metabolizing in people, for God's sake." *And other things.* "The physical's pretty nice. I'm a lot stronger than I look. Cellular respiration's up, flexibility and endurance, you get the idea." He took a deep breath. "That's why I'm valuable. That sort of enhancement doesn't come cheap."

"How did—"

"I'm telling you this because I want you to know. If you were sick, really sick, I'd smell it on you." *Like that yellow-metal tang, because you're coming down with something.* It bothered him, but so did everything else about this. "I'd *know*. You're just stressed by being placed in a…a situation." *Being drugged, kidnapped and dragged around like baggage. Time to start treating you a little nicer. Once I'm sure we're not blown or dogged.*

"How did they do all this? Like, you're some kind of bionic man, or something?"

"I have no trouble with metal detectors, babe." *All flesh. I'll show you sometime.* Now *that* was the wrong thing to say, but it was pleasant to contemplate.

"Then how do you know I'm not sick?"

Are you really going to tell her? "It doesn't matter. What matters is that I could tell you if you had something bad. I would smell it on you, and I don't."

"What do I smell like?" A jagged sigh. "I can't believe I'm even asking this sort of question."

I can't believe I'm almost ready to tell you. "You smell…good."

"Good? That's it?" Now she sounded irritated, and it was a welcome change. Maybe if he got her flat-out angry she'd cope better.

Not a lot of traffic now, and a little subconscious muscle relaxed, easing all at once.

The problem was, he didn't want her angry, either. He wanted her…happy. Or at least reasonably content.

That's not what you want.

"You smell *more* than good."

"Oh." The irritation had drained away. "How do I

know you…well, it's useless to be asking questions now, right? Once I've gotten over the fact that I was kidnapped by government psychos, a bionic spy is small potatoes."

Just keep thinking that way. Of course, when she eventually saw what he was capable of, what would she do?

It was a little late to be having any sort of qualm. So he took a deep breath. This one was freighted with apples and spice, a familiar heat below the belt. Goddamn distracting with her so close, warm and breathing. What could he tell her?

"It's not useless. You want to understand what you're in. It's reasonable."

"And you're a reasonable guy, right?"

He was ready to agree, but something in her tone warned him. Still with her eyes closed, slumped there, her pulse hiking a little and a slight undertone of nervous smoke to that glorious scent of hers, making the yellow-metal tang that much more prominent.

Keyed up with panic and adrenaline, and ready to let it all out on someone. He was the closest target.

The *only* target. If it made her feel better, fine. If she wanted to scream and punch, he didn't mind.

So he just shrugged. "No, Holly. I'm not reasonable. Never would have gotten into the program otherwise. I'll tell you what I am, though."

"Scary?"

You could say that. "Yeah. And determined, and resourceful, and capable of just about anything when it comes to you."

"Not to mention crazy," she muttered.

"Got any more adjectives to throw on the pile?" If

she was going to blow up at him, now would be a good time, when he had her under wraps and still vulnerable.

"Tons." She let out a shaky sigh, her hands lying limp and discarded in her lap. "Reese?"

"What?" His knuckles were white on the steering wheel. *Don't wreck the car.*

"Thank you. I… I haven't had a panic attack since the…the divorce."

Now that was pure Holly. *Thanking* him, as if he hadn't destroyed her life. "Must have been stressful. I'm sorry."

"You can't smell cancer, Reese."

"Mmh." An easy, noncommittal answer. Was that what she thought she had? Why? It brought up other interesting questions, ones he had no answer for.

Could he smell cancer? And just what was that yellowish component to her smell, the only shade that wasn't flat-out delicious? If she'd been sick when he met her…

Don't borrow trouble. Just keep moving.

"They were just coming to pick you up." The aspirin Bronson had taken just before entering this glare-lit, linoleum-floored room wasn't kicking in nearly soon enough. His head was pounding, and being in a room with one of the damn subjects was always nerve-racking. Eight was zipped to the metal chair, the chair was bolted to the floor and the new head of the medical staff swore the massive dose of tranquilizer was still working its way through Eight's system.

The blond guy, reeking of smoke and covered with soot, dirt and probably dried blood from the capture team, stared at him, his nostrils flaring a little. He said nothing.

"You escalated, Eight. This is bad. I can't help you if you don't tell me something. Anything." *Make him think you're on his side.* His own shirt was none too fresh, he couldn't even send Three to get him a new one. Christ alone knew what would happen if they lost *her.*

Besides, he didn't want that computer brain in his apartment.

Eight sighed. It was a deep, heavy sound, and Bronson braced himself.

"What. Do you. Want." Each word as flat and uninflected as if Three was speaking.

Three was in the safe room, watching through the video feed. She hadn't corrected him in a whole twelve hours or so, which had to be some kind of record. Which reminded him, he should probably send her to residence soon. She was looking a little wilted.

Not that it mattered. She'd never win any goddamn prizes.

His head would not quit pounding. That bottle of Chivas in the filing cabinet was sounding better and better the longer this went on. Plus, the light in here hurt his eyes. The cinder-block walls weren't comforting at all, either. "Another agent's gone off the reservation." It was Bronson's turn to sigh. "I've talked to the higher-ups. Told them you could track him, especially since it's domestic. I think I've got them ready to give you another chance." He kept his hands loose and dangling empty, wishing he could stick them in his pockets or even carry a file. A pencil, a paper clip, anything.

The autopsy had confirmed the civilian girl Eight had been banging didn't have any hint of the original virus *or* Gemini. Eight's bloodwork from two days ago was solid, but the eggheads were muttering something about core load and stress factors. Control had checked in—some of the other agents had been brought back in, fat, dumb and happy, and they were slated for the induction process, even though there was a near-zero survival rating for that. If they did survive, they'd be like Three.

No trouble at all.

Eight's head tilted slightly, his eyes as bright blue and direct as ever. He was in rags of civilian dress—jeans, a sweatshirt, his filthy socks since they would have taken his boots as a matter of course—but he didn't look nearly as battered as a man who had just been through a house fire and rendition should.

Even secured to the chair with zip ties and handcuffs, it was best not to underestimate *them*. Which was why Bronson stayed near the door, and why Caldwell was right outside and teams stationed at either end of the hall this interrogation room sat off of.

"Did you change your cologne?" Eight asked.

"What? I don't wear—come on, soldier. Don't be a smart-ass. I *just* got chewed out for sticking up for you. Are you going to be reasonable or not?" *Because if you don't, you're liquidated. You idiots can't survive a shot to the head, no, sir.*

Ten minutes later, Bronson stepped out into the hall. Caldwell, sweat drying and flaking on his forehead, snapped to attention. He had blue eyes, too, just like Eight, but they were bloodshot and blinking now. "Sir?"

"He'll play ball. Take a six-man team in, untie him and give him something to eat. Get him some kit. I'll pull the target file together."

"You think he'll—"

"He doesn't have a lot of options." Bronson massaged his temples. "In any case, we've got him chipped, and we've got grids and cores from here to Florida."

"Yessir. You're doing a good job, sir."

Like you *can tell.* But Bronson nodded. "I'm going to go home and get some clothes. Call me if anything happens, and for God's sake, don't let Three offbase."

"Wasn't planning on it, sir. Um, should we… I mean, um, should I feed her?"

"Feed her, water her, whatever. Just keep her on the damn base, and be careful with Eight." Bronson glanced at the door. "By the book, nice and slow, don't cut any corners."

"Yessir."

By the time Bronson reached the end of the hall, his headache was starting to fade. He decided not to ask Three what she thought of Eight's calm, steady agreement to do what needed to be done. He had a handle on this himself, and all of a sudden, his entire body itched. He couldn't wait to get into clean clothes.

Another evening, another motel, a dispirited brick lump right at the edge of another city. A truck-stop diner crouched across the parking lot, a vast expanse of pavement behind it studded with diesel pumps and dozing semis. The headlights were stars, taillights rubies, or maybe it was just that she was hungry and tired.

"Are we stopping for the night?" She sounded whiny, she realized, and sighed deeply. He was quiet and thoughtful, a good traveling companion, but he wouldn't let her drive. *I'm fine*, he kept saying. *You just rest.*

"Maybe. Mostly I thought you could use something warm, and to stretch your legs a little." He cut the engine, set the parking brake, and his gaze roved over the lot. "Not sure I like the idea of sleeping here."

"Still not going to tell me where we're going?"

"I don't want you to—"

"—know where you're headed, right. But you can easily go somewhere *else* if they end up catching us. So can I. So give."

"South. We'll slip over the border at a likely place—"

"Without passports?"

"You'll have one by then. Once over, we'll vanish. Probably live in a city, nice and anonymous. Get to know each other, rent a little house."

"That takes money." That was just the first flaw in the plan that she could see. There was a whole cavalcade of others, ones she was too tired to list. Sleeping in a car all day was oddly exhausting.

"Money's easy." He scratched at his stubble, frowning at the diner's gold-glowing windows. Incandescents always made the light so warm. "You can learn Spanish."

"How is money *easy*?"

"Think about what I'm trained for, Holly. Anyway, it'll be nice. You'll get a tan."

"If I don't keel over and die first." Her chin settled. She was sulling up, as her father would have put it.

Dad might have liked Reese. At least, they would get along, in that military-man way. Not when Dad was sick, though.

Before. When he'd still been the brawny, gruff linchpin of the world. Now Holly wondered if he'd ever felt this kind of fear, struggling through the chemo. Maybe his withdrawal hadn't been strength, closing himself off from the world that had treated him so shabbily.

Maybe he'd just been scared.

"You're not going to keel over." Endlessly patient. What would it take to make him angry?

Did she want to know? She'd better find out, soon. Just in case. "You can't smell cancer."

"Some dogs can."

"You're not a dog." *You keep calling yourself one, but you're not.*

"Mmh." That noncommittal sound again. "Why don't you go in and get us a table. I'm going to check the motel."

"Okay." She reached for her backpack, felt for the doorhandle. Was he just trying to get rid of her? Probably.

"Holly." Very quietly.

"What?" *Why can't I look at him?* At least the diner was bound to have something good on its menu, even though hoping for a decent salad or some pasta was foolish in the extreme. On the other hand, maybe truckers were health nuts. Barb had worked at a truck stop once—*good tips*, she'd said, *but be ready to smack a few hands away from your rear.*

She would never see Barb again. Tony was probably pulling his hair out in fistfuls, bemoaning her lack of reliability. They would think something had happened to her…which, really, something had, but they'd forget her soon enough.

She probably wouldn't even be able to eat here anyway.

"I am not going to let anything happen to you." He said it quietly, almost as if he meant it.

That's a nice thought. "Okay." She scrambled to get out of the car, inhaling sharply as the cold hit her.

Shouldn't south be warmer? Of course, they were tending westward, too, for whatever reason Reese had in his weird little head.

Her stomach growled, so she closed the car door carefully and headed for the diner.

It was all too familiar—a hum of conversation, clinking dishes, something hitting the grill with a steaming hiss, hurrying feet. It even smelled just the same, grease and heat and overcooked coffee and a faint tang of chlorine from the bleach rinse. Holly's knees almost buckled, but she told herself it was just from spending so long in the car.

"Hep ya?" the waitress on greet duty said, blinking sleepily. Her graying hair, pulled back under a net, was still neatly braided, and though she sounded halfway to dreamland there was a sharp twinkle in her hazel gaze.

"Hello. Two, please."

"Where's the other?"

What? "At the motel. He sent me to get a table."

"Just passin' through?" She fished out a couple of plastic-covered menus, and slight unease began under Holly's hair, right at her nape.

"We're on vacation." Holly's tone plainly said, *Is it normal to get the third degree when asking for a booth?* Maybe she looked shabby, or just too tired.

Or maybe this was a truckers-only place? Who knew?

In any case, it must have been the right response, because the waitress nodded. "Ah. We get all types here. Smoking or non?"

Holly dredged up a smile. "I prefer non, but whatever you have free. It looks busy." *You need someone to wipe your board, too. I could have that done in a hot minute, if you'd hire me.* Was here far enough away to hide?

"It is." The woman paused. "Most people go straight on into the city from here, except for the boys. They like to stop."

"The boys? Oh, we saw the truck stop." She followed, nice and docile, and asked for decaf.

The smoking side was packed, and the counter on the nonsmoking side, too. Broad backs, T-shirts and heavy jackets, male laughter. The booths were empty, just a sprinkling of heavyset men, very few women. A bright spill of jukebox music ricocheted from the smoking side, and Holly settled on cracked mauve vinyl, keeping her back stiffly away from the needlepoint cushion. Nothing was going to make this sad little place look new again, and she put her backpack on the window side of the booth just to be safe.

The decaf came, half-burned by the smell of it, and she had just picked it up when a shadow fell over her.

It wasn't Reese. It was a burly man in a flannel shirt, his blue baseball cap settled firmly enough that it might have been glued on and his beard neatly trimmed. His eyes were bloodshot, his jeans were worn and he looked as though he was having some trouble staying upright.

"Hello there, sweet thing," he slurred, and the intense, inappropriate desire to laugh burbled up inside of Holly.

"I'm sorry?" she managed, politely, frozen with her coffee cup halfway to her mouth.

"How much?" He leaned over, and she caught a breath of unwashed, sweaty man with a little more fat than muscle, but still plenty of both. It wasn't like Reese's clean healthy scent.

I could smell it on you. What else could he smell?

"I'm sorry?" she repeated. "You seem a little confused."

He rested his elbow on the back of her booth, effectively trapping her, and the unease was full-blown now. "Give you fifty for a blow," he semiwhispered. "Pretty mouth of yours, and all. I got a nice truck. Private."

Several pieces fell together at once. Truck stop. Motel. The waitress's questioning.

Oh, God, he thinks I'm a hooker. "I think you've mistaken me for someone else," she managed, with just the right tone—not overly amused, not overly offended— even though her heart had started hammering and sweat prickled under her arms.

Out of nowhere, help appeared. "Hey, sweetheart." Reese, tall and a little rumpled, smiled benignly at the heavyset man, but he didn't slide into the other half of the booth. "Who's your friend?"

"I think he's confused," she began, diplomatically.

"Really." Reese's open, pleasant expression didn't change, but something in the set of his shoulders made the other man straighten self-consciously, taking his arm away from the back of the booth. "Can we help you, sir?"

"Just asking," the man mumbled, darting another glance at Holly. "Pretty girl there."

"That's one reason I married her." Reese's hands were loose and easy, but she suddenly had the idea he was about to do something silly. "What did you want?"

"Nothin'." Thankfully, he backed off, with one last lingering look.

Holly's skin crawled. She set the coffee cup down

carefully, as if it was porcelain instead of thick heavy industrial china.

Reese lowered himself into the other half of the booth, cautiously. "You okay?"

"I think…" She coughed a little, and managed something slightly above a whisper. "He thought I was a lot lizard."

"A…" A curious expression drifted over Reese's face. "Oh." His dark eyes narrowed fractionally. That was all.

Fifty for a blow. "I'm having all sorts of new experiences nowadays." She managed a nervous half laugh. "I just…do I look that bad?"

"Of course not. You're too pretty for a place like this. The motel's a dump. Rents hourly."

"Oh." Her skin was crawling even more now. "I… Reese, I'm not hungry."

He was already reaching for his wallet. "I don't blame you. We can find someplace nicer."

"God, yes." She all but scrambled for the edge of the seat. The waitress was shuffling back, bright interest all over her avid little face. "I, um… I need to use the restroom."

"Me, too." A tight smile, and he motioned to the shuffling hag. "I'll wait for you, okay?"

"Okay." She made it away, and just as she reached the front she saw her erstwhile suitor heading into the men's room.

Oh, God. It took a little while, locked in an indifferently cleaned stall, for the shaking to stop. *I want to go home.*

She couldn't. She knew she couldn't, but still. It wouldn't be that hard to find a pay phone, would it?

He couldn't stay with her all the time. Just to hear Barb's scratchy voice again, or just to tell someone, anyone, that Holly Candless still existed and wasn't a truck-stop prostitute.

Funny, I wanted to vanish, but not like this.

At least the water from the sink was hot, and there was industrial-grade soap. She scrubbed at her hands a long time, staring at the wan blue-eyed woman in the mirror, and found herself hoping Reese would leave her behind.

If he did, though, what might she be reduced to just to stay fed? Or to get home?

And what might be waiting for her there?

He paid for the overcooked coffee and was pleasant enough, but every nerve in him was a wire brush standing straight up. Her distress was still ringing in his head, that acrid undertone to her smell, fear and adrenaline all over again. He knew the man was in the bathroom, maybe taking another hit of whatever metallic drug he jacked himself on to stay awake on the road. It was too harsh to be bennies, so probably meth.

What are you thinking, Reese?

Except he wasn't. He was very far from thinking.

He couldn't let her out of his sight for thirty seconds, for God's sake. Maybe it was the vulnerability on her drawing predators to the water hole. It was more likely his fault, bringing her here. They stuck out like sore thumbs, her more than him, and the waitress's knowing little smile mounted his fury another notch.

He palmed the bathroom door open and found himself in a sorry hole with three urinals and a boxed-in stall, its walls and door cut off at ankle instead of knee height. It could be hosed down with little trouble, and the half-formed idea in the back of his head subsumed under a hum of alertness.

The stall was closed, and he could smell the man through a reek made up of every other nastiness crawling through this room. A silver box attached to the tiled wall promised condoms and cologne, for just a few quarters per.

She didn't belong here, and he'd put her right in harm's way.

Again.

There was a sniff, a heaving snort, a sound like a lowing cow, and the stall door swung open.

The man in the blue baseball cap blinked at him, rolling down his sleeve. He'd develop track marks before long if he was shooting instead of snorting now, and lose a lot of that pudge. Reese's lips pulled back from his teeth.

It took so little. Weight dropping, his booted foot flicking forward, hooked behind the trucker's knee and yanked forward just enough, a blurted sound from the man's wet shapeless mouth lost under the formless noise of the jukebox in the smoking section. Another light strike, open palm on the chest, to get him to fall correctly. Backward, the angle gauged just right, and the man's head hit sturdy porcelain with a sickening crack. Another crack underneath was the shearing of a neck snapping, and the drug-fueled kicking of the empty body was easily avoided.

Death by toilet. Fitting.

Reese pushed the stall door closed with the tip of his boot. The diner outside made its usual, normal hum.

He ran his hands through his hair, checked himself

in the mirror. Just fine. The next person to come in here would assume the trucker had slipped and fallen, if they noticed him at all. Autopsy would chalk it up to a drug-fueled accident. Clean, untraceable and proof positive that he was still functioning at peak.

Good work, agent. Now collect your civvie and get out of here.

When Holly came out of the little girls' room, pale and huge eyed, he had his thumbs hooked in his pockets and turned from the rack of newspapers near the door. Winter Storm Approaching, the headlines screamed, and wasn't that the truth. They might outpace it, but the smell of impending snow outside was thick enough to cut with a spoon.

"Let's go." He got close enough to put an arm over her shoulders, and the hostess smirked behind the counter. For a moment the urge to step over, fold his hand just right and give the old woman a knuckle strike to the throat drifted through him.

Holly sniffed, as if she'd been crying in the bathroom, and the small sound cut through everything else.

You're safe now, he wanted to tell her.

Even if it was a lie.

Two hours later she pulled back the covers, staring at the hotel bed as if she couldn't quite figure out what to do with it. This place was much nicer, on the other side of the damn city, and there had even been mints on the plump pillows. She'd carefully set them aside on the nightstand and then just stopped, looking down at the crisp white sheets.

She was exhausted, and he was starting to get foggy after being too painfully, hurtfully awake for too goddamn long. Even the little bastards in his blood couldn't keep him going much longer, not with this sort of stress. He was now reasonably sure they hadn't been killed off by the gas, whatever it had been.

Lucky him.

Once she fell asleep he could settle.

She stared at the pillow for a long moment, and when she spoke, the words didn't make sense immediately. Soft and flat, her pretty voice a monotone.

"I can't do this."

What? "Sure you can." So tired. *I made it safe for you. Safe as possible, at least, and that jackass will never bother another woman again. Probably made the freeways a little safer, too.* "Brush your teeth and lie down. Sorry about the fast food, but I thought you wouldn't want to get out of the car." *You didn't eat much, anyway.*

"No." She turned, and there was a glint in her beautiful smoky eyes he didn't like the look of. "It just… Reese, I'm sorry, but I can't do this."

"Just lie down. Sleep will—"

"I don't want to." She picked up the backpack, and he heaved an internal sigh. This was going to get difficult. "I want to go home."

He reached for patience. "That's not a good—"

"I don't care what they do to me. I don't care what happens." She skirted the bed, and yes, friends and neighbors, she was heading for the door. Hitching the backpack onto her shoulder. Did she have a plan? Not likely. "I just want to go home."

"That's rabbit talk, Holly." His nerves pulled taut as guitar strings, he took a deep breath and stayed where he was, next to the table. There was no way she was getting out of this room, but if he could avoid upsetting her, if he could just defuse her verbally, maybe—

"I don't care. I'm going home."

"You think you can just hop on a bus and go back to working at the diner? They'll nab you before you cross the state line, Holly, and then—"

She just shook her head, a tendril of black hair falling in her face, and she was almost in the critical zone, passing the door to the bathroom.

Stop it, he pleaded, silently. *Don't make me do this.*

"I won't tell them anything, Reese. Just—"

Moving, sliding past her faster than a normal human being could even think of moving. The thing about moving that fast was how it made the rest of the world seem so goddamn slow.

She gasped, staring at him—now with his back to the door, his hands loose and easy. The look of frank openmouthed surprise might have even been funny, in another situation. "How did you *do* that?"

"Weren't you listening?" Another deep breath, struggling to bring his pulse down. "I can do a lot of things, babe. You are not leaving this room."

"You can't watch me all the time." Scowling, a line between her eyebrows, and with her mouth puckered up that way all he could think of was getting his hands on her and—

She flinched, because he'd moved again. Her backpack slid, he caught it, snapping her hand down neatly as she grabbed for it, and they ended up nose to nose, Reese holding the goddamn pack and mirroring her stumbling steps as she backed up.

"Try me," he answered, very softly. Her smell wrapped around him, delicious and warm and comforting. "I am not going to let you do anything stupid. You're with me now, and it's going to stay that way."

Those big, smoky blue eyes, now full of crystalline tears. The faint lines beginning at the corners of her eyes—even her wrinkles were pretty, goddamn it all, and she was shivering again. Not with cold; he'd turned the heat on in here.

Probably with fear.

"I'm going to have to teach you to trust me," he continued, searching for the right thing to say. "I'm sorry I left you alone in there, but I won't do it again. I have never..."

What was he trying to say?

I have never really had anything in my entire life. Maybe he could say that. Or, *They made me. I was a lump of meat and they turned me into this. I'm not even human.* He could follow it up with *The only time I feel like a human being at all is when I look at you, for Christ's sake. Because you're so goddamn naive and sweet, and you're more than worth fighting for. More than worth protecting.*

How would she take that? It balled up inside his chest, all the things he wanted to say, and he lost his chance when she shut her eyes and inhaled as if to scream.

The backpack hit the floor, he clapped his hand over her mouth, and her frantic backward motion to escape him turned into him pushing her just enough to tip her balance.

They landed on the bed, Holly suddenly struggling, and it ended with both her wrists pinned over her head and his other hand still over her mouth. His knees on either side of her thighs, and her thrashing softness underneath him threatened to blow every circuit in the mess his head had become.

How in the hell did I get here? He went still, just letting her strain against his hold and his greater weight. That smell all over him, bathing him, and the physical contact had its effect. An iron bar with its roots sunk into the lowest part of his belly, everything that could make him a man instead of a killing machine narrowing to a single still point—she was sweating now and the urge to lean down and flick his tongue against her throat to taste it almost drowned him.

"Calm down," he whispered. *Please. I don't want to hurt you.*

That was the problem, though. He probably would before this was over.

He already had.

When she finally went limp, tears sliding down and soaking into her tangled hair against the twisted pillow crammed sideways under her head, it got a little easier.

Only a little.

He peeled his hand away from her mouth, cautiously. Hopefully he hadn't suffocated her. "Let it out," he managed, his voice a husk of itself. "Let it out, Holl. Go ahead and cry."

"I w-want to go home," she whispered.

It was enough to break a man's heart, if he had one. Was that why his chest felt so tight? The exhaustion made it difficult to think, and God, if she moved the wrong way he might add another goddamn reason for her to want to do something stupid to escape him.

"I know." His throat, desert dry, all but clicked as he swallowed, hard, searching for control. "I know, baby. I'll make you a home. A nice one, whatever you want.

We just have to get through this, and I'll make you everything you've ever wanted. I know I can." *I'd better. It's the only way to make up for all this.*

Will I feel human then?

Her eyes flew open, and she stared up at him through that welling screen of tears. Her lips, reddened by the pressure—Christ, had he bruised her?—parted just slightly, and she twitched as if to try to throw him off.

Reese lost the battle. His hand tightened around her wrists, his entire body threatened to explode…and his mouth met hers.

She couldn't breathe. Somehow the air must have been getting in, though, because she didn't pass out. He kissed her like he was drowning, as if he wanted to crawl inside her, and the confusion added to everything else inside her skull, turning it into a whirlpool.

It had been so long since someone had…well, at least she hadn't forgotten how. He was heavy, way heavier than he looked, but braced on knees and elbows he didn't crush her. A weird, undeniable feeling of safety swamped her, utterly crazy, but her body wouldn't listen. Heat all through her, concentrating way down low, but it was Reese who tore himself away, sliding to her left, landing on the bed and going still. He let go of one of her wrists but kept the right one, his fingers gentle but undeniable. That slight contact sent buzzing electricity down her arm.

Holly gasped. The ceiling sparkled in places, acoustic tile full of little bits of glitter. Slowly, her breathing evened out. The tears kept trickling, hot and shameful.

"I'm sorry." Hoarse, rough, as if he'd just finished running a marathon.

Maybe he had.

Her mouth felt full. Ripe. It had been forever since she'd done that. Why did it have to happen now?

"Why..." She couldn't even find a reasonable question to ask. "Why do you..."

"Do you really not know?" A bitterness to the scraping in his tone, and it took all Holly's courage to turn her head against the pillow.

He stared at the ceiling, too, a high flush along his stubbled cheeks, and he looked...

Well, tired. That was some of it. But underneath the exhaustion and the usual set expression, there was something else.

He looked sad.

Oh, dammit, Holly, you already have a bad track record and no time for this, don't do it. She'd survived Phillip, but only just, right? And only delayed the inevitable. The desire to leave had all but evaporated. She had thought it over. Down to the front desk, get a cab to the bus station, use her debit card to buy a ticket, go home to her shattered apartment and sleep for a week.

As a plan, it kind of sucked, but it had seemed reasonable at the time.

"This is messed up." He swallowed, hard, his Adam's apple bobbing, a strangely vulnerable little movement above his shirt collar. "I thought, you know, maybe I could get you into a nice apartment. Money isn't an issue, but keeping you secret would be. Coming to see you whenever it was safe. Even if...even if nothing happened."

That is really bizarre. "So...sort of like a kept woman?"

"No, just... Maybe. I don't know. So you didn't have

to worry. You worried too much, I could see it. And you were too good for that diner. I wanted to…look, I was institutionalized growing up, okay? I never had a girlfriend. I never…"

"Institutionalized?" *Girlfriend? Is that what he wants? I thought I was just baggage.*

"Slow. Developmentally delayed." A pause. "A moron, that's what the kids might call it these days. That's the nicest thing they call you when you just stand there and smile."

"Reese—" So much more about him made sense now.

"I hit eighteen and the streets, sleeping in a state home when I could. The recruiter wanted to get his quota, and he did me a favor. I was smart enough to figure out they'd feed me there, and the rules made it easy. I even liked basic training, being useful. Being worth something. Then…the accident. They made me into…what I am."

"Bionic." The sheer unreality of the situation could have been laughable, if she'd felt any amusement at all. The image of Reese as a young man, struggling to deal with all this, was…well, it was pretty heartbreaking, when you thought about it.

You and your strays, Phillip had said once. *I won't keep buying cat food when we're starving, Holl.*

Had he ever wondered where she went after he told her he wanted a divorce? Had he come back to the house and looked for her? She'd been moving so steadily from one thing to the next, she'd never even thought about it before.

Reese swallowed hard, again. "You keep saying that. I'm all flesh, Holly."

I'll just bet you are. All things considered, they were having a very calm conversation. Ignoring the soaked crotch of her panties—good God, it had been a long time, but still, she didn't have enough laundry to have this sort of response to a man—was working out really well. Could he hear the way her heart was trip-hammering?

Could he maybe smell arousal, too? God.

She gathered what was left of her brainpower and her courage, so to speak, and plunged ahead. "You're not…developmentally delayed…now."

"Nope. They fixed that. I'm tired, though, haven't been sleeping. The little bastards help, but…"

Wait, what? "Little bastards?"

He rolled his head to the side, looked at her. "I'm sorry because I'm *not* sorry, goddammit. I'm glad you're with me. I'm a selfish little jerk and I have you, and you can't even run away from me because you'll end up dead. I'm not above using that to keep you here, and after a while you'll get used to me. I can't even be sorry about that. It's all I wanted from the first time I walked into that diner, and now I have it, and I'm not giving it up."

"Well." She searched for something to say. "That's, uh. Not very romantic." *And I'm not going to be around very long. It doesn't matter.*

Of course, if it didn't matter, maybe she could… what? Just go with the flow? One last hurrah before the curtain call?

What would he do when the inevitable happened? At least one person would miss her, and though it was awful to think of him feeling the same sharp grief she'd felt when Dad died, it was still…well, sort of comforting. She'd worked so hard to pull away so that nobody would miss her at all, nobody would feel that kind of pain on her account. Because it was unutterably greedy to want someone to miss you, wasn't it? Compared to that, his own admission of selfishness didn't seem so bad.

He blinked a little, and the open surprise crossing his face would have been hilarious, too, if she'd felt like laughing. "I'll do romantic if you want, Holly. Candlelight, roses, everything. Just…all you have to do is tell me, you know, but you have to work with me, I've never done it before. And they're not going to give up on looking for us. I've got a bad feeling."

When you say that, I'll bet it means something really bad indeed. "That's why you came back to my apartment?"

"Why did you think?"

"I thought maybe you felt… I don't know, *sorry* for me."

"I messed up your entire life, so it was just the least I could do, is that it? Maybe a normal person would feel that way. I can't tell." His mouth compressed, and when he spoke again it was very softly. "I'm not normal. But I wasn't about to leave you there."

"Why?"

"You seriously can't figure out why?"

"Maybe it would go a little easier if you just said it." *Oh, my God, am I really having this conversation with him? With a bionic spy?*

"What else do you want me to say?" Now there was a hint of anger. "I'm not normal. I'm not a real person. The only time I feel real at all is when I'm looking at you, when I'm around you, okay? You're everything

I thought I was protecting when I went out to do my duty for my goddamn country, and I'm barely keeping us both alive. I'm not a hero, goddammit, I'm not even human. I'm a fake, I'm selfish, I'm an agent, I'm unreasonable and hair-trigger and goddamn dangerous, and I'm also going to take care of you. So do me a favor and stop with the rabbit talk and the not trusting me." He let go of her wrist and levered himself off the bed in one clean, economical motion.

How fast could he move? One second he'd been by the window, the next in front of her with his back to the door. It was eerie. It was downright terrifying.

Still…

I'm not a real person. Was that what he thought? The same man who'd come back to get her, the same man who'd held her and told her it was going to be all right, the same man who had tipped so well probably because he didn't know what else to do?

He was inside a shell of his own, except somehow she was in there with him.

Holly pushed herself up on her elbows, cautiously. Her entire body tingled. It was a nice change. "Reese?"

He was over at the window again, not peering out at whatever it showed. He just stood there with his head down, and for a guy who had just had a serious chubby pressed up against her just a few minutes ago, he looked a little…lost. "What?" Struggling for patience, maybe.

"You're real to me." It sounded unhelpful now that it was out of her head. "I mean, really real." *Like that's better. Goddammit, Holly Rachel, can't you say something useful for once?*

His shoulders dropped, too. The silence between

them, no longer dangerous, was still full of something…
uncomfortable.

"I hope so," he said quietly. "Brush your teeth and
get some sleep."

"Are…are you going to sleep too?"

"Maybe."

"You can… I mean, there's the bed, here. You can…
we could share." *Oh, Lord. Well, I've been divorced for
two and a half years. This probably isn't a rebound.* The
weird, irrational desire to laugh swamped her again;
she pushed it down.

"If you want." Offhand, like it didn't matter.

I need sleep if I'm going to sort this out. "I, ah, think
it would be good. For you. Okay?"

"Okay, Holly. Whatever you want."

Oh, Jesus. She grabbed for her backpack and padded toward the bathroom. Halfway there, she looked
back over her shoulder.

He just stood there. Waiting, maybe. For what?

Whatever you want.

Was it really that simple?

Why couldn't I have met you before I got sick?

That might not have made anything any better,
though. Because of Phillip, because of…everything.
Holly shook her head, wiped at her wet cheeks and escaped into the bathroom before anything else happened.

He waited until she was asleep. Eased himself onto
the bed, a millimeter at a time. Clothes still on, boots
still on, belt still in place and backpack right on the
floor.

You're real to me. Really real.

Maybe she even meant it. The beginning stages of

dependence on him. He should have been overjoyed. He was, in a way. When he wasn't feeling like the lowest worm on the goddamn planet.

She moved restlessly; he froze. Waited until she settled again. Warm and safe, under the covers. Her inky hair spilling over the pillows, and maybe he could roll over and smell her up close. Maybe even slide an arm around her, just to make sure she wouldn't get any damn rabbit ideas while he slept.

So tired. And the weather wasn't giving him anything but worry. First real serious storm of winter—things were going to get dicey. Add his growing certainty that they were being tracked somehow, and he was a ball of nerves just when he needed clarity and control most.

Pushed her. Held her down. It didn't help that her response had been immediate, and pretty goddamn volcanic. Smelling the sudden wash of coppermusk heat from her had just about made him embarrass himself.

Which made him think about Tangiers.

Don't. He found himself edging closer, hardly daring to breathe, moving up slowly as if she was a target.

She muttered something formless, moved again, and as his arm curled over her waist, she sighed and scooted backward, settling against him with an absolutely scorching little wiggle of those hips of hers.

Reese let out a soft breath into her hair, closing his eyes.

It was just as good as he'd thought it would be.

No.

Better.

He could finally inhale and fill himself with her. It wasn't as close as he wanted to be, but it was a start.

She sighed again, made a tiny sleepy sound and was gone into boneless unconsciousness.

You're real to me.

Even if she didn't mean it...well, it was a kind thing to say. Just the sort of thing you'd expect from a woman who would hold a dying man's hand or give every single child an extra peppermint. Christ, of all the reactions he'd expected, that had to be last on the list. She was downright amazing. How could anyone ever have let her go?

Sometimes, in his head, the kid he had been still showed up. The dopey, happy, stupid little idiot. Hadn't even realized when he was being hazed, taken advantage of, picked on. Just sailing through the world with everything around him so baffling that the only response was stupid deadness and a wide uncertain grin.

What would that kid say, if he could get close enough to the woman Reese held?

It ain't just the way you smell. It's that when you smile all of you lights up, and when you sad the whole world goes black. You a pure miracle, miss. You even feel bad for puppies and kittens.

No, that wasn't what that kid would say. That kid would probably just stare gapmouthed at Holly, unable to even leave a tip to make her backsore waitress days easier. That kid would never even know she existed.

Not the way he did now. Maybe he should thank them for that, the whole goddamn clutch of them, from the program architects on down.

Another deep breath, and he was floating. Relaxing, to just pretend she was there because she wanted to be, was sleeping next to him because he was...

Nothing, then. Sleep.

* * *

White light. An unfamiliar sound. He was off the bed in a heartbeat, the knife yanked free and ready for play.

Holly, at the window, turned slowly. It was her opening the drapes and eerie directionless snowlight pouring into the room, not any threat, and she looked slow because he was moving much faster than even an agent should.

Reese stopped dead. Blinked, orienting himself.

Her hair, wet from the shower, was raveled silk along her damp shoulders. Wrapped in a towel, she was still steaming from warm water, and the clean lines of her long bare legs threatened to leave him breathless. Milky pale, glowing under the pale light, smoky blue eyes wide, it was as if she'd just appeared, angelic, offering water to a dying man.

"It snowed." Childlike wonder. "Look at that."

Uh-oh. "Get out of the window." He stowed the knife, made it across the room in quick strides and yanked the curtains closed without bothering with the chain pull on either side. The mechanism resisted, and something pinged off in a different direction, hitting the wall with a metallic click. He ignored it. The parking lot below was full of featureless humps of white. It looked bad.

The storm had run faster than they could. If he hadn't been so tired last night, they would have had a chance. *Goddammit.* "Great."

She tightened the towel with a quick casual motion, the terry cloth compressing her breasts. Looked up at him, still wide-eyed, her collarbones so fragile and her neck so thin. Her hair was brittle, too. He had to feed her more. "Oh. I suppose it's bad for driving, isn't it."

"Yeah." He stalked for the flat-screen television

above the useless dresser—did anyone ever actually put their clothes in that thing, for God's sake?—and tried to ignore the fact that she was incredibly, softly naked under a hotel towel. It didn't help that he could see her in the mirror set to the right of the TV, or that her smell was all over him.

Small consolation that he felt fully sharp now, too, in more ways than one. Mental and physical both clicking along nicely, now that he'd had some rest. He and the virus were still getting along.

Holly paused. "So...what do we do?"

It was jungle warm in here, maybe from the hot water. Or maybe it was just her, heating up everything inside him. Still, she'd said *we*.

That was good.

"I'm going to check the weather report, clean up. If it's bad for driving, we'll see. This part of the country gets snowplows out regularly, so that might be okay. We can't stay here."

"Oh." She absorbed this. "If we can't drive, then what?"

"I've been through this way before. There's options." His throat had gone dry, because the temptation to turn around and fill up his hands with her was well-nigh irresistible. "Put some clothes on. It's cold, and you're distracting me."

"Distracting?" It wasn't fair, she sounded honestly baffled. Did she not get it? He'd done everything but hit her on the head and drag her into a cave.

"*Incredibly* distracting." He found the remote, clicked the television on, clamped down on his pulse. *If you don't want me tossing you in that bed a second time, get dressed.*

The sudden détente was still fragile, so he couldn't say anything like that yet. But he could think it all he wanted, couldn't he?

Down, boy.

The sound came on with a roar; he winced and turned it down.

"—gripped by a sudden winter storm. The National Weather Service has issued a severe warning, asking you to stay home if you possibly can. With the forecast for tonight calling for freezing rain and two feet of snow reported in the metropolitan area—"

He hit mute. The blonde reporter continued, blithely silent, her trained expressions flickering. School closures, power outages, all sorts of fun and games outside this calm little bubble.

Damn.

The percentages were bad either way. Staying here was risky; he wanted to be moving. Crawling along in the snow with a civilian to keep alive was bound to be worse, though, and the chance of a fender-bender or even getting stuck was uncomfortably high. Weighed against that was the persistent unease, lingering even now, when he was fully rested.

He kept watching, hearing Holly move in the bathroom. No APBs saturating the airwaves. Of course, there could be one on the cop scanners, but the press would get hold of that. Which meant either they thought him dead—the gas, whatever it was, still might have some sort of effect—or they hadn't halted the program and liquidated agents.

If they hadn't, well, guess who would be hunting him? Which made moving even more imperative.

Most of the available options were bad. Time to pick one and hope for the best.

"Holly?"

"Hmm?" She peered out of the bathroom, a comb in her hand. Jeans again, and that same well-loved bra. No shirt yet.

Christ. He told his hormones to settle down, hoped they'd listen. "Do you like camping?"

"In this weather? Not really. But my dad used to take me out hunting with him."

Better than he'd hoped. "We're not going to be in a tent, sweetheart." *Though that might be nice—you'd have to snuggle up to me.*

"Then where are we going to be?" A little defiance, as if she expected him to resist telling her.

It was probably too late, but he could at least try to ease some of the tension. He tried for an easy grin, and found one. "Out with the wolves, little girl. Finish up, I want a shower."

Fat, fuzzy flakes whirred down, clumping on the windshield wipers. Chains bit a layer of compacted and double-scraped snow, digging in—she hadn't even asked why he had them in the back of the car. Being a bionic spy was being like a Boy Scout, maybe—always be prepared.

In a whirlwind they had become a newly married couple from Hawaii, stuck in the storm and needing appropriate clothing. The concierge beamed at them and wrote down directions to a decent sporting-goods store in the same mall complex as a grocer's. Reese put his arm over Holly's shoulders and nuzzled her hair, and Holly's confused blush was taken for something else entirely.

The two-story hulk of sporting goods was full of camo—pink camo for the ladies—taxidermy displays, racks of guns behind a long glassy counter, tents, bicycles and everything else, and it was doing land-office business. She would have thought that the people in this part of the country would have already been prepared. She'd ventured to say as much to Reese, who had actually briefly smiled. "The locals are probably all getting toilet paper and French toast," he'd said, glancing at a display of parkas before choosing a nice dark blue one with a fur-lined hood for her. "Eggs, bread, milk."

Her own laugh had taken her by surprise. He'd looked outright pleased for a moment before putting a pile of clothes in her arms and telling her to try them on.

He paid with cash, and afterward the grocery store was pure havoc. Still, they made it out with six bags of supplies, and she was beginning to get the idea camping meant something different to him.

Maybe she needed a lexicon to keep up.

Finally, creeping away from the edge of the city along the freeway, Reese's expression intent and serious, she decided to push a little more. "So you've been here before?"

"Mmh." Either neutral or affirmative, no way to tell. Concentrating on driving, he looked completely different from the smiling, obviously in love almost-klutz he'd shown the sporting goods employees. He'd done such a pitch-perfect imitation even Holly had fallen into the game.

Which one was the real Reese?

Or the real Holly? It would be kind of ironic if she

was just finding out who she was *now*, with so little time left.

"And we're going where?" She fingered the new gloves, lying in her lap. The car was jammed with supplies—where did the money come from?

Money's easy.

She'd suspect he was some sort of con man if she hadn't seen him move so fast. Almost blinking through space, and so quiet. He was heavier than a man should be, even a muscle-heavy one, and she had the bruises on the outsides of her thighs to prove it. High up, where he'd crouched over her, skin fever warm and his fingers clamped around her wrists.

She bruised more and more easily nowadays. And this morning, combing her hair, more of it was falling out.

Reese had a knife, and she hadn't even *known* before she woke him up. Plus, the unsettling vision of two dark blots on her apartment floor, souls fled and that awful reek, sort of put paid to the notion of con man, too.

Or gave it a more disturbing edge. Which would be better—con man or superspy?

Jeez, Holly, you sure know how to pick them. First Phillip, now this. Except they were as different as night and day.

Reese glanced at her, a brief flick of dark eyes, and returned his attention to the road. "There's a cabin."

"A cabin." She flipped the gloves over, ran her fingers along the stitching. "Okay."

"We should get there before the freezing rain hits. The approaches are pretty easy to cover out there, and there's—"

Just hold on a second. "Wait. Whose cabin is it?"

"Mine."

"Yours? Then why were we—"

"Or more precisely, one of my identities'. They trained us to stick our noses in, cover contingencies, make plans—"

Us. "So there's more like you." *Great.*

"Probably not nearly as nice as me."

"Or as charming. You outright flirted with that girl at the register."

"Which one?"

The one with the nose ring. "Can you tell them apart?"

"Are you jealous?"

It was almost like trading wisecracks over the counter. At least he could keep up. "Well, we *are* supposed to be married."

A ghost of a smile. "Holly, I'm trying to drive. You're distracting me."

"In what way?"

"Pretty much every way."

Good. She tried not to feel pleased. "How many are there like you?"

"I don't know."

"You don't—"

"The last thing they'd want was us comparing notes, especially with that casualty rate for the infection."

Now there was something new. "Infection?" And he'd said something about *the little bastards.*

Was he…sick…too?

"Holly, please."

No, I'm not going to let that one go. "What kind of infection?"

"I'm trying to drive."

"What kind of infection?"

He eased down an exit, a snowplow rearing in front of them and sliding away, heading majestically for what looked like a ditch. Miraculously, the huge machine labored and chugged over a bridge that looked built of stone matchsticks, and a gorge opened up on either side of it. Fortunately, Reese turned off on another scraped road, creeping around a long slow curve that was probably a lot of fun when it wasn't snowing so fast the windshield almost clotted up. His mouth thinned a little. "I will tell you everything you want to know when we get to the cabin. For right now, just let me work. Please."

You didn't mention "infection" before. "Are you contagious?"

"What? Of course not, you think they'd let me live offbase if I was? Dammit, Holly, please."

At least he didn't sound too irritated. Now she had a little more information, too. *Infection. Little buggers. He changes the subject whenever it comes up, whatever they did to him. You don't walk again after your spine gets broken, but he can go through metal detectors.*

It was like quizzing Phillip, trying to put together symptoms and coming up with a diagnosis.

Was Reese sick? He seemed pretty healthy. Except maybe emotionally, but she was one to talk, right? As a coping mechanism, isolating herself hadn't worked very well at all. People kept creeping in, even when you built yourself a shell.

She decided to try another tack. "What do I smell like?"

"Hmm? Oh. It changes. When I'm hungry, it's food. When I'm not, it's…other things. But always good. You smell…good."

"Like food?" *Well, yeah, working in a diner will do that to you.*

"Not just any food. You know cravings, right? They hit, and all you can think of is how you want, oh, maybe a slice of pie. Cherry pie, not any other kind, you know?"

"I smell like cherry pie?"

"No, you smell like…" He feathered the brake as the car glided around a corner. The houses spaced themselves farther and farther apart, barns and barbed-wire fences hunching against the cold. It was amazing, how soon city fell away. Maybe they just built them smaller this far west.

Keep him talking, Holly. "How many identities do you have?"

"A few."

"How many is a few?"

He goosed the accelerator as they started to slide, chains making a hissing rasp. The car righted itself, as if it had never meant to stumble. "Enough to keep you safe, but I do need you to let me drive."

Well. It was more than she'd had before. Holly gazed out the window. The infinite sky that meant snow was changing, shading by degrees into a dull beaten-iron pall. It looked nasty.

Enough to keep you safe. He kept saying things like that. It was enough to make a woman feel charitable.

Waking up this morning, finding his arm around her and him stretched out on top of the covers, realizing just how strong he was…and that he hadn't, well, *done* anything. He'd even still had his shoes on this morning, for God's sake.

I'm not a hero...the only time I feel real is when I'm looking at you.

How could someone so competent be so inwardly shy and clumsy? Of course, if he had grown up in institutions, he was probably lacking a lot of Real Life Experience. She probably had enough for both of them, though. Who was really the naive one here?

The houses became just dots, the barns more ramshackle. The road worsened, and they crept onto a two-lane highway behind a snowplow that lit the windshield with flashing amber. It wasn't even noon yet, but the light was failing. That gray pall was moving in quickly. There was nothing to stop it but the mountains bunching up in the distance, and it occurred to her that maybe he'd been making for this place all along.

"Were you heading here from the beginning?"

"I chose this route because it had options along the way, and this weather's been threatening for a couple days now. We're going to get over the border, just not as soon as I'd hoped. This is the next best thing."

"Are you sure?" *After all, you are the expert here.* Her nose itched, and she was heartily tired of fast food.

"Absolutely." He sounded very definite, so she relaxed fractionally. The radio burbled softly, an AM weather station giving passionless reports with a list of unfamiliar place-names. Reese touched the volume knob, turning it up just a little, and Holly took a deep breath.

There was, really, nothing else she could do.

His memory was still good; he stayed on the road more by feel than anything else. The place was defensible, and the road up to it was a bit dicey, but the sedan gave it a good shot. At least they didn't have to hike in—after the freeze hit, he didn't want to be trekking back and forth carrying supplies.

They bounced to a stop just as the chain on the front left tire gave up and flung itself free with a metallic squeal that made Holly start, and the sudden jolt of fear through her glands was enough to make his stomach turn over. Being so close for so long made him sensitive to every small change in her.

So he tried to sound reassuring. "It's all right. Just a chain. Doesn't feel like it popped the tire. Stay here."

"Is that the cabin?" Did she sound disappointed? What had she expected?

It was small, with a steeply pitched roof, and under a cap of heavy wet snow that was going to freeze solid soon its dark windows were empty holes. All glass intact, though, that was good. A shack of a shed would be leaning against the north side, ready to hide the car if he could get it back there. The pumphouse tucked in the angle right next to it was also hidden, and the cabin was longer than it looked, but still. Maybe she was disappointed. There was a whole lot for her to be disappointed about, starting with Reese and the mess he'd made of her quiet little life and beautiful apartment.

Doesn't matter. It's safe, at least until the thaw hits. "It doesn't look like much." His shoulders were tight, and his neck ached from the tension. Driving in this mess was not his idea of a good time. "Once the fire gets going it'll be fine. Better than a tent."

"It looks like a fairy tale." She reached for the doorhandle. "I'll help you—"

His fingers closed around her wrist. Gently, but she

froze. The engine was still humming right along, blowing warm air into the car's tiny bubble of civilization. No need for her to get cold yet.

"You'll stay right here." Very quietly. "Just in case."

"Just in case what?"

"Just stay here, Holly. Okay?" He almost said *trust me* or even the crowning absurdity, *humor me.*

"Fine." She stared at the cabin as if it would turn into a billboard any moment, giving her a set of directions. "I should help you, though."

"You will." *Stay where it's warm for right now, sweetheart.* He couldn't say that to her, though. It was entirely too…intimate.

The trees up the hill had broken the force of the wind, and the snow wasn't too bad here yet. He could taste the iron tang of more on the way, and the darkness of freezing rain would spread up as the system curled against the mountains. This hollow was pretty sheltered, and the fast-falling snow would drift up over the tire tracks. If a layer of ice accumulated, all the better.

He shut the car door gently, pulling his gloves on. Balsam and pine, a rill of cold dampness from the creek to the west, the grit of stone close to the surface. Deer, an oily dry scent, very fresh. Other animals, including a thread of acrid weasel musk he almost wrinkled his nose at. No hint of humans, except the exhaust from the idling car.

That was partly why he wanted her closed up, so he could get a good lungful of all this without her distracting, maddening, wonderful proximity.

The shed was still in good shape, and the hulking shape in the corner, covered with canvas, was another insurance—if mice hadn't been at the wires. He'd check that out later. For right now, the chain had just torn, and there was another set on a listing wooden shelf. "Nice," he congratulated himself, even though there wasn't enough wood. He could fix that easily.

As soon as he stepped out, kicking the wedge firmly under the shed door, he knew Holly hadn't listened. Clumping around the side of the house was enough time for him to take a deep breath, that thread of her on the cold air like champagne.

He was opening his mouth to say something a little sharper than was really necessary when she came into view.

She'd stepped away from the car, tipping her head back. A new knitted cap, a fur-collared coat, the new boots and her gloves tugged on, she stood in the snow, staring up at the sky. Her mouth was open and her little pink tongue out, catching snowflakes.

Just like a kid.

The cold blushed her cheeks, visible even in the failing light, and her charcoal lashes blinking rapidly, gemmed with melting snowflakes. Her hands turned out, cupped to gather more of the falling flakes, and Reese's heart gave a sudden, violent, painful lunge inside his chest.

God, please... He didn't even know how to finish the thought.

She might have heard him crunching through the snow, drier now that the temperature had started to drop, because she laughed, a low pretty sound, and brought her chin back down. Biting her lower lip now, a little shyly, then the smile broke out over her face like sunrise. It was the first unguarded one he'd seen from her, and it walloped the air right out of him.

"It's beautiful," she said, hushed in this cathedral of trees and ice. "I love snow."

"Yeah." He sounded hoarse, and sharp. What could he say? Nothing he was thinking.

I will do anything for you, just don't go anywhere. Just don't leave. Stand there and smile at me, and I'll do anything you want. It wasn't precisely pain. Was this what cardiac arrest felt like? *Just let me get close. Just please, please don't go anywhere.*

It was coming down faster, gathering on her shoulders and her cap. He had to get her inside. He cleared his throat, and her smile faded, bit by bit. "Let me get the key. I have to dig it up. You can go in—it's pretty bare, but it's shelter. There's water, and… I, uh…"

"Okay." She hugged herself, cupping her elbows. Was it the cold, or had his traitorous face showed something? "I'm sorry, I just wanted out of the car. I know you said—"

Christ. "It's all right." Nothing in his throat would work right. "Really. Let me grab the key."

Enough wood to get them through the night, and the deep pump was still functional. It only took a bit of monkeying around and waking the thing up before he was rewarded with a low hum. The former owner of this place had been a survivalist and had sunk plenty of cash into getting a source of weak but useful off-the-grid electricity. The geothermal would even heat the shower water; no doubt Holly would be glad about that.

He locked everything up nice and snug. It would take a little while for the power to steady out, and they'd have to run the water for a bit to clear the pipes, but all in all, it wasn't bad.

Inside, Holly had lit a candle in the kitchen and was rummaging in the grocery bags. "You have a fridge, but I suppose with the power out we can put stuff outside to—"

He flicked the switch, and the pale glow from a single overhead bulb made her laugh with delight, the sound shivering all over him. Her breath plumed, mostly because the door was open to stage the rest of the supplies in. The car was safely in the shed, and next was the goddamn fire and warming her up. The geothermal would also raise the temperature in here, but too slowly. Plus, why make it work that hard?

"You're a magician." She actually grinned, and the aforesaid fridge—a small antique white enamel number—clicked into humming life. "This is amazing."

"Good place to go to ground." *Once we leave we can't come back, if there's an agent tracking us.* "Where'd you put the matches?"

"Oh, right here—" When she turned around again, she flinched, probably because he'd moved too quickly.

Again.

"Wow." She held up the cardboard box, shook it a little. "This means I can actually cook, too. If that range is functioning."

"Should be. There's no oven, though." The goddamn rock was back in his throat. "Sorry. I don't mean to scare you." *That's the last thing I want.*

"You don't." Very softly. She probably wasn't aware she was lying, but he could smell the fear on her. Keyed up and nervous, adrenaline a copper thread. "I mean… I trust you."

The yellow-metallic tang rasped against his palate, and that made him uneasy. His gloved fingers touched hers, sliding the matches free. "Good." So close he could feel the heat she gave off, the warm draft of her breath, hear her pulse rise again. A pleasant rasp of arousal sliding through her scent; she leaned over that invisible line, judged by fingertips and skin response, that separated *friend* from *more than friend*.

If it hadn't been so cold he might have lost it right there, again. Instead, he froze, trying to think of what to do next.

She went up on tiptoes, her gloved hand sliding around the back of his neck, and her gentle irresistible pressure made him bend forward. Her lips pressed against his scratchy cheek, a soft fiery kiss.

Her fingers slid away, and she sank back onto her heels. The shakes going through him made it hard to straighten, and the ache below the belt wasn't going to go away anytime soon.

"I, ah." He had to search for words. "Should get a fire started."

"Yeah." She turned away, peering into the closest grocery bag. "I should wash some dishes. You have dishes here, too?"

"I... I don't know." About all he'd done was sleep on the couch and chew an energy bar after he'd signed the papers and gotten the key. It had been a full four days off the grid to close the sale, and it had been worth the stern talking-to Bronson dished out and the double round of ridiculous tolerance tests afterward. "I'm, um. Yeah. Just going to get us closed up and a fire."

"Okay." She kept digging in the bags and opening cupboard doors. Playing house. Another woman might be snotty about the lack of comfort, or angry at him, or any of a thousand things. Holly just got to work.

It took another few seconds for his head to clear. The shaking went down, and he told the ache in his pants to go away. It probably wouldn't listen, but at least he was making the effort.

She kissed me. It wasn't until he had nursed a handful of tinder into a respectable flame and started building a proper fire up that he realized he was grinning like an idiot.

Trinity kept her head down, pacing behind Bronson and Caldwell. The tension had broken, and the reek of relief spreading from both of them was matched only by the smell of a bacon double cheeseburger pumping out through the older man's skin. They thought they had a reason to celebrate.

She could have told them otherwise, but they didn't ask. So she simply followed along, a ghost in a woman's body, her face a mask. It was becoming more difficult to guard against flickers of expression. Just four hours ago she had stared into the slice of mirror over an indifferently scrubbed bathroom sink in the lowest, most secured part of the base, and watched her face move as she thought. Strange, how concentrating could change the architecture of that collection of muscles and bone.

"There's a storm moving over, things have fuzzed out a little. Eight's working like a charm, though."

Only temporarily. She could have said it, didn't. It had been…nice, she supposed, to get into clean clothes. Who had bought them? The gold hoops she'd been wearing in her ears since she woke up after the induction process, whose were they? Her own?

She'd never been able to hold her own file. She was perhaps the only person who had noticed several *other* files, not just the doctored ones, missing after Eight was cleared for release. It was, after all, her job to bring them when Bronson wanted them. He had not asked for any, but perhaps he would, soon?

"Good. What about that goddamn doctor?"

"Tied off." Caldwell sounded happy about that. He had a fresh crewcut on his sandy head, and his uniform was ironed, as well.

Trinity watched her shoes, diligently carrying her forward. *Tied off* could mean any of a number of things. The odds favored a staged suicide at said doctor's apartment. The doctor had taken Trinity's vital signs more than once, asked her questions. Now he was gone.

It…bothered…her. More than it should. How many casualties had she reported on since the induction?

Had she *really* signed up for this? Without her memory, who could tell?

"Thank God." Bronson slowed down. He sweated, even at this pace. It was amazing, how his body kept going through all the cholesterol abuse he piled on it.

The guard at the double doors saluted; they plunged into the nerve center. Grids running, cores being checked, screens everywhere, people running back and forth with papers and clearances, phones softly beeping. They thought they were hunting a terrorist. The patriotism was astonishing. You could almost *smell* it, bright and shiny but with a rancid undertone.

Caldwell was immediately swarmed, Bronson reduced to tagging along and listening. Trinity glanced over the room once, collating information. *Ah. Eight has made his move. Too late, though. Assuming he did not wish to catch Six.* It would take them, she calculated, approximately six more hours to realize they had lost him for good, unless someone here noticed one or two small things. Perhaps she should help them?

Why?

It was such an elementary question. Terrifying, in all its implications. Why do anything? Control over her autonomic functions was not complete, but she could perhaps, with enough concentration, stop her own heart. Why bother continuing, especially if she was to be used in this fashion?

Illogical, Trinity. What did it matter how she was *used*?

She stopped, head down, swaying slightly. Caldwell and Bronson kept going, information they didn't need being thrown at them from all angles. Trinity could have told them ninety-eight percent of what they were taking in and collating was useless now that they had sent Eight out, that removing Eight's civilian entanglement would simply intensify a certain dangerous sector of the emotional noise. How had he talked them into it? Fatigue and Bronson's arrogance no doubt had given him an opening, but—

"Three?"

She replayed the last few moments of mental footage. What was that rasp against her nerves? It wasn't physical at all.

Irritation. She was *irritated* at being disturbed.

"Sir?" A single word, uninflected. Sweat prickled along her lower back before she brought that system under control.

"The chances Eight will bring Six and the civilian in alive."

Calculations tangled inside her head. *Zero. He doesn't want to retrieve them.* She had a choice, now.

Was this what other people felt? How did they stand the uncertainty?

Answer as if his assumptions are correct. Immediately the pressure eased, and she found answers. "Both alive, forty percent. Six alive, thirty-three percent. Civilian alive, sixty-eight percent. Civilian alive and uninjured, seventy-four percent."

"Why is Six's survival chance so low?"

Assuming he and Eight engage in combat, and Eight wins. It was much easier when she simply added their inaccurate assumptions to what she was supposed to answer. "Six will ensure the civilian survives, even at the cost of his own life."

"That goddamn emotional noise," Bronson muttered. "At least you're still working, Three."

Am I? She had *felt*. Only mild irritation, true, but still…she was to report any oddity, no matter how slight.

If I do, odds of my own survival go down drastically. She gazed over his head at the screens—traffic feeds, information flashing by rapidly, grainy surveillance footage of Six and the civilian. Her long black hair, distinctive, and her pinched, pale face when they had brought her in reeking of sedation. Why had Six settled his attention on the woman? Candless, that was her name.

Irrelevant.

The only relevant thing, Trinity decided, as a harried-looking brunette woman brought in a fresh pot of coffee and Bronson quizzed one of the engineers about draining satellite platforms to track the car they thought Six was driving, was her own chance of survival. If she began showing signs of emotional noise, there was an unacceptable risk of them seeking to imprison or liquidate her.

Or to try the induction process again.

"Three." It was Caldwell. He'd had a chance to shower, too, and he held out a cup of coffee. "Here. As soon as we find them we're going to scramble copters."

She took the mug and thought about her odds of escaping, as both Six and Eight had done. As Fourteen had done before they liquidated him, as some of the others were showing signs of doing.

It was not enough to calculate.

Trinity began to plan.

Holly's back didn't ache for once, and the quiet was full of tiny sounds—the snow, deadening all outside noise, just underlined the crackling of a fire and the faint static-rubbing sound of the AM radio station. Reese cocked his head to listen to the recital of air pressure, place-names, precipitation, forecast, but at least he ate. It wasn't much—pancakes, bacon, eggs— but it wasn't industrial food, and a glass of orange juice convinced Holly she wasn't dreaming. She managed a few bites of bacon and at least two pancakes, a banner event. The orange juice even stayed down.

The dinette set—two plastic chairs and a table left-over from the '50s, to judge by its pink top—was rickety but adequate. The cabin was one large room except for the tiny bathroom, a burlap-covered couch that folded down into a twin bed and one ratty old armchair with a dusty afghan flung across it. Other than that and the stove, there was nothing but a collection of woolen rugs over a hardwood floor, polished silky smooth but gritty with accumulated dust.

Her nose kept itching, and her throat was a little scratchy. Probably just the change in the weather, and

God knew she'd itched all over, relentlessly, for months now anyway. Holly snuggled deeper into the blankets— everything was new and full of store and packaging smell, and while that was distracting it was better than dusty and nasty—and tried to get comfortable on the lumpy couch. He'd even thought of flannel pajamas for her, but not for himself. Did he ever relax?

They probably trained him not to.

The flickering from the stove was soothing. Reese, by the front window, stood in what she was beginning to see as a habitual posture—head tilted to listen, hands loose, shoulders back.

"Hey," she finally whispered. "Reese?"

He didn't move. "Are you warm enough?"

"Sure. Can you…can you come over here?" *Why am I nervous all of a sudden?*

There were lots of reasons, she supposed. Here she was with this stranger in the middle of nowhere. They wouldn't find her body until spring, if he had ideas. Of course, he wouldn't have dragged her out all this way and…she could just go on and on in circles until she dropped. It wasn't like she was going to survive this anyway. Each time she used the restroom there were traces of bright red in her urine. She couldn't eat, her hair was falling out, and really…it was going to be all downhill from here.

So it didn't matter. At all.

Except even when you were dying, some things did. Even if you were in an exotic—to say the least—situation, on the run with a bionic agent who looked so lost and forlorn, standing there watching, that her heart lit up inside her with a sweet aching.

He glided silently across the floor, not even a betraying squeak from the boards. "What's wrong?" Dark eyes a glimmer in the dimness—did he have a cat's vision now? Just how strong and fast was he?

I don't have a lot of time left. So why not make it count? "Nothing's wrong." She snaked her arm out from under the pile of blankets, the couch creaking as her weight shifted, and felt blindly in the cooler air outside. You could tell it was cold, that it was freezing outside, even if it was warm enough in here. The air just felt different.

His fingers threaded through hers, warm and rough. "Holly…" Was he going to start making excuses? Or telling her, *I was wrong, sorry, you're not what I thought you were*?

That was the thing about staying out of the dating pool. When you were thrown in, you found out you'd forgotten how to swim. "I don't think anyone's going to be out there. Why don't you come to bed?"

If that didn't get the point across, nothing would.

"I, uh… I thought, the floor…"

"I don't want you to freeze to death." She tugged on his hand. He'd gone so still he probably wasn't even breathing.

"Well, you know, the couch, it's not very big. I don't want—"

"Reese." As if she was talking to Doug when he was on one of his rampages, nice and firm. "Take your shoes off and get under the blankets with me. Please." *So I can do at least one nice thing before I go.*

"Holly…"

"Unless you don't want to, in which case I'll just be really embarrassed, but that never killed anyone." She could have kicked herself. Joking about killing someone with a bionic spy. Infection, but he wasn't contagious. It wasn't like it mattered, even if he was. What was one more thing to weigh her ailing body down?

"I just…if I do, Holly, I might not want to stop."

"Oh." *That's all right then.* "I might not want you to."

He made a sort of strangled sound. She couldn't tell if it was a despairing groan or a disbelieving laugh.

She had to let go of his hand so he could get his shoes off. The couch accepted his weight with a slight protesting noise, and it was like being in high school again, close quarters and giggling and trying to be quiet. He didn't smell like Phillip, though, thank God.

No, he smelled familiar. Safe. Cleaner than Phillip, and more intense.

He was almost fever warm, and he settled her head on his shoulder as if it was a china egg. That was okay, because while he was settling the blankets with finicky care she slid her hand down his chest to his stomach, hard even under the thermal and flannel, and by the time he realized what she was doing she'd worked the button of his jeans free.

"Holly," he whispered.

Holly paused. "Do you not want to? I mean, I thought you'd like to." Wriggling a little closer to breathe in his ear. *I'm seducing a superspy. What a way to go.* "I really hope you'd like to."

"I, uh. I have some problems—"

Sounded like they were bloodflow problems. "Me, too." She got the zipper down, slid her hand in and found soft flesh over iron. "Hmm. Is this a problem?"

Was he sweating? He seemed to be having trouble breathing, too. At least, he gasped as she worked her hand a little farther in. *My, that's very respectable. A hidden treasure, you could say.*

"I haven't, you know, for a long time—"

Thought you said you never had a girlfriend. "That's okay," she whispered. "We have all night, right?"

"Holly..." He was shaking, so she made a little shushing noise.

"I think I'd like it if you kissed me." *Help me out here a little, superspy.* She freed her hand, a little regretfully, tried to move so she could get her elbow down and lift herself enough to look at him.

That set him off. His free hand tangled in her brittle hair, and he kissed the corner of her mouth before he got oriented, and it was just like it had been in the hotel room. As if he was drowning, and it wasn't at all like Phillip or the few run-ins with the male species afterward, before she decided she was better off not getting that close to anyone.

He kept kissing her, so it was up to Holly to start getting their clothes off, and the first shock was the amount of muscle on him. The second was how it moved, fluid and more heavy than flesh had any right to be. Most men felt smaller in the dark, but he most definitely didn't, and the fever heat of his skin might have made her cautious if his hands hadn't started roaming. There was a ripping of material—*this is a brand-new top*— and he was sweating, enough to print on her own cool skin.

Am I cold? I can't be, he's just so warm—

The next shock was just how strong he really was. He moved and Holly found herself pinned, the blankets sliding as he kissed down the line of her throat and nipped, lightly, just where it was most sensitive.

She gasped and realized he was saying her name, over and over again.

Her legs were tangled with the pajama pants; his mouth moved onto her breast, tongue teasing at her nipple, sending a bolt through her, teeth scraping lightly, her legs suddenly free and one of those too-quick movements. He had her wrists again, she slid her knees up and he...

Stopped.

Right there, she could feel him between her legs, a hard probing. But he'd frozen, and she wriggled a little. "Don't *stop*!" *That's the worst. And I might not have the energy to try this again tomorrow, superspy. Come on.*

"I...have some...problems." He was fighting for breath.

Maybe this wasn't such a good idea. "Reese—"

He slid into her with a convulsive movement, almost painful, stretching. Holly's head tipped back, she tilted her hips, and amazingly, frustratingly, he stopped *again*.

"What are you *doing*?" She wriggled a little bit, sighing as he sank down onto her a little more.

An experimental nudge. Her breath caught. Pulsing, stretching, on the thin edge of pain before he moved again, a long slow stroke that just about turned her inside out. He made another sound, this time more purr than groan, and she might have thought he wasn't enjoying himself except for the sudden fact of his mouth on hers again, his hands loosening from her wrists. The sudden rhythm, slow at first but building, her breathless little cry as he stiffened in her arms and went rigid.

Well. That was quick. She swallowed the usual disappointment. It took a while for them to learn, if they were interested. Female biology was complex. It was okay—

she probably wasn't going to ever feel that again. As it was, she was just glad she'd given him something nice.

His breath came harsh and ragged. "Sorry," he gasped into her throat. He really did sound chagrined.

"Hmm? Oh." Holly tried not to make the restless little movement that would mean rejection. *Well, for the last one, I suppose that was okay.* "It's pretty normal. It's okay."

"Normal." A low laugh, and he inhaled sharply, nuzzling her cheek. Kissed the corner of her mouth.

"Move a little." She twitched, wanting to push him to the side. Now that he was done he'd probably sleep. She could, too. The fire crackled, painting every edge with soft, leaping light.

"Why?" Now he sounded amused. "What if I like it where I am?"

"It's okay—" Holly began, but there was a definite stirring. He didn't feel so fever hot now, and when she eased her hips a little to check, the hypothesis, so to speak, was verified. Things were definitely looking up. Her stomach had calmed down, too, and she actually…

Well, she actually felt *interested.*

"All *sorts* of physical benefits." It was his turn to whisper in her ear. "You didn't think it was over, did you?"

In the middle of the storm, under layers of ice and packed snow, the cabin was a warm dark kernel. A layer of blankets, and then him, curled around a sleeping glow, the heart of the entire night. Soft and warm and so deeply relaxed she was barely breathing. Pulse nice and slow, her scent all over him in layers of memory and flash impressions, her, all her, closing around

him, tight hot velvet, the taste of her sweet and a little strawberry-acid, her soft little noises and delicious
slight movements. He'd gone over pretty much every
inch of her, learning, discovering, and if she hadn't been
sleeping he would have done it again. And again. That
metal tang to her scent, the yellow-sharpness, made the
rest of it just that much more enticing.

She was so thin, though. He had to get her to eat
more.

Reese lay in the dark, the fire in the stove banked
and the fire in his blood a comfortable, comforting heat.
Sticky, glued to her in a web of scent, he could finally
think about Tangiers.

Heat. Dust. The smell of the sea, a thick cloud of
pollution. The call to prayer echoing through narrow
hot streets as the knife slid in. Twisted, wrenched free,
and he was on to the next. Five men in the room, blood
spraying as he bent impossibly far back, spine crackling, foot flicking out to catch the only one who had
time to react under the jaw with a sickening snap. On
that last man to make sure, knife dragging through
flesh, and instinct knew before the rest of him, because he was already whirling.

The knife didn't leave his hand. It clattered to the
floor, his fingers at the last moment refusing the direc-
tive from his cold, active brain.

There, in the doorway, the children. A black-haired
girl, her dark eyes wide and horrified, holding the
brown, pudgy hand of a toddler. Boy, his nose told
him. Naked except for the white of the diaper, the toddler stuck its other fist in its mouth and regarded him
solemnly.

The girl was inhaling to scream. She couldn't be

more than nine, and her print cotton dress moved a little as she began to tremble, shock releasing a flood of chemicals he could taste into her bloodstream. If she howled now it would alert the rest of the compound.

Mission compromised. Silence the incidentals.

The moment stretched like taffy, mind and body straining, two dogs and he was the bone in the middle. Cold logic told him that the girl was dead anyway, or she'd be traumatized the rest of her life by this sudden eruption of violence. Was one of the men here her father? Brother? Uncle? Who knew?

They didn't tell me about killing kids.

The trouble with the memory the virus gave him was that it was like being there all over again. He buried his face in Holly's tangled hair and inhaled, deeply.

The girl didn't scream after all, just made a whispering, mewling sound. Maybe she thought she was screaming, but her little body couldn't catch up. Reese's hand flicked out as he bent, and he had the knife. Cocked it and threw; it arrowed through dapples of sunshine robbed of its force by stone lattice and waving draperies...

...and the knife thudded into the wall beside the arched doorway, stuck there quivering. By the time the children looked away from its black hilt, he was gone, out the window and up, scrabbling across heat-simmering rooftops. They had a description of him now, and the city had closed itself against him. Shot twice, blown out of every hide he could find, he'd barely made it even with the virus in his blood.

Afterward, whenever he'd try to visit a girl, those huge accusing eyes. Except sometimes they were Holly's wide smoky gaze, her horrified expression as he tried to touch her.

A man capable of killing kids. Was that what they'd wanted to make? Had something in his psych eval clued them in after Tangiers that he wasn't reliable? He'd given them everything he knew they wanted to hear, playing the part during every interview, every appointment, hiding inside himself even in the apartment. Hiding inside the safe shell of the killer they wanted everywhere.

Except in the diner, where he could fill his lungs with Holly and pretend he was a real human being.

Emotional noise is also a variable, agent.

Missions were easy. You had your briefing and whatever support they saw fit to give you, you went in and *did*. How much easier was it now that he was running? No support but his own wits and the virus, and Holly to keep safe. Of course, running simplified things. When all territory was hostile and the enemy was everyone else, he didn't have to make any hard decisions. His path was laid out, nice and straight. Get her out of the snow and over the border, settle somewhere for a little while and play house. Then, in stages, they'd get somewhere halfway across the world and fall into the expatriate life. He could probably even pick up a few merc jobs—they weren't that hard to find.

Still, what would Holly think of that? She wasn't an agent. She wasn't even close to informant status or training, for Christ's sake. Getting her anywhere near a mission was unacceptable, and if he left her somewhere, in some city, how could he be sure she was safe? It would distract him.

The alternative was a cover and some other kind of job.

Reese sighed. Here he was next to her, right where he needed to be, and he couldn't stop going over and over the next set of problems. At least he'd managed to redeem himself from the first embarrassment. Getting her there took a little patience, but the reward was well worth it. She made such interesting, helpless little sounds—and if he kept her happy, it would make it easier to keep her close.

The closer she was, the more he could feel as if he'd salvaged something from the brutality of a world that could make agents and send them out to kill kids.

He relaxed all at once. Brought his pulse down even farther, lengthened his respiration. If he could get it to match hers, he'd fall asleep. Outside the cabin, the night was alive with the little crackles of ice falling, flash freezing over the massive wet blanket of snow that had erased their tracks. For the moment, they were safe, and she was in his arms, and there was nothing more in the world to want.

Someone moving around, a sizzling and a gurgling. The marvelous, rich smell of coffee fighting with the heavenly aroma of bacon cooking. The low, staticky buzz of the weather station radio. Her mouth tasted awful and her head was stuffed up, and she was sweating under the blankets.

Not to mention pleasantly sore and languorous. Apparently sex still felt good while you were dying. She was achy all over, but no wonder. He was damn patient when he put his mind to it, and that little thing he did with his tongue was just about—

"Hey, Sleeping Beauty." Reese loomed above her, a broad smile on his no-longer-nondescript face. Dark hair wildly mussed, the thermal shirt clinging to his broad chest, he looked very morning after. He also held a blue enamel mug of what had to be coffee. "Breakfast soon, coffee now. I require a kiss before I'll surrender the caffeine."

Holly rubbed at her grainy eyes. Her fingers felt sausage swollen. Her stomach didn't hurt, and her back wasn't too painful. The curative powers of nooky, maybe. "Are you kidding? I have dragon breath."

"Mmh." He bent down, and before she knew it his mouth was on hers. He didn't seem to care about morning mouth, and by the time he finished she'd forgotten morning breath was even a consideration. "Nice. You feeling okay?"

"I might have a cold. All that stress." Her head throbbed. Or something worse. How ironic was that? Just when she'd found…what, precisely?

That was the trouble. She liked him, even though she was deadweight. He'd be better off without her.

Pretty much everyone would. That was why she kept everyone at arm's length. No point in getting cozy if she knew she didn't have long. It was what her father had done, all through the chemo. Mom had packed her bags and left right after Holly was born, so it had fallen to Holly to nurse Dad through the hell of poison dripped into his veins and the long slow fall into choking out his last in the hospice.

Don't think about that.

So she put on a smile and reached for the coffee.

He nodded, thoughtfully, holding the mug handle out and steadying her as she struggled up to sit. Cooler air felt wonderful on her bare back, the fire was merrily crackling away, and she got the blankets settled and accepted the coffee. If the hot mug burned his fingers, he gave no indication.

"Little bit of a fever, tastes like." He felt at her damp forehead. "I think you should stay in bed today."

Oh, really? "Only if you stay with me." *One last really final hurrah? Maybe? Now I'm getting greedy.*

"I'd like that." A boyish, open smile. "Breakfast, though. And we need more wood."

She was about to make a snarky euphemistic comment, but decided against it. Now that she was upright, with the headache twisting up another fraction inside her skull, the coffee was more important. It was even good coffee, not a boiled, pale commercial shadow of itself.

Holly watched him move around the postage stamp of a kitchen. The headache mounted another few notches, and it was warming up quickly in here. He must have built up the fire.

The coffee smelled divine, but her stomach cramped, a bolt of hot pain. Had she pulled something? Not likely. It was the same old nausea, the too-enthusiastic cells floating around her digestive system like tangled tree roots, squeezing. She managed a few sips of scalding liquid before her stomach clenched itself closed and the rest of her demanded a toothbrushing and maybe a shower, not necessarily in that order. She had to cast around for at least her pajama top, found it tangled on the floor, and spent a few wriggling moments trying not to spill her coffee while she got herself a little decent. As long as she could clean herself, she wanted to be clean.

What will happen when I can't, though?

The pajama bottoms were a little torn around the waistband, but not bad. The top was long enough for decency while she shuffled to the bathroom. She got her legs out from under the covers, planted her feet and stood up—or tried to.

A rushing sound filled her head, her knees buckled and she found herself on the floor, the coffee spilling from her nerveless hand. *Have to clean that up*, she thought hazily before Reese arrived.

"Christ. Holly? Holly?" His arm under her shoulders, he didn't so much lift her as just stand up and carry her with him, that strange muscular fluidity of his a little unsettling.

Her head throbbed, as if the sudden change in altitude had kicked at her skull. "I don't feel so good," she managed. "Sorry—"

"Shh." He got her back on the couch, pressed the back of his hand against her forehead. "You're burning up. You weren't a minute ago."

"I…" Her tongue felt funny. The cotton inside her head was thickening. All of a sudden just rolling over and passing out seemed like a good idea. *I guess last night was the last hurrah after all. Good for me.* "I told you, I'm sick." *I'm sorry. I thought maybe I had a little longer.*

"Lie back. Here." He got the covers up over her, though she feebly tried to push them away. It was so hot, maybe the fire was bigger?

I am not thinking quite right.

Reese was saying something, but the words were lost in the roaring filling her skull. Lassitude swamped her, and a crazy sideways slipping sensation. *I'm here, but my body's not. How strange.*

Reese cursed. She wanted to tell him that it was all right, she'd get up in a second and clean up the coffee, get Doug calmed down and wipe down the boards, maybe have a talk with Ginny about her behavior, and…

Is this how it ends? I wanted…wanted to…

The world drew away, smearing like ink on a spinning, oiled plate, and a terribly ironic thought occurred to her just as she plunged into semiconsciousness.

Casualty rate for that is about ninety percent…you think they'd let me walk around if I was contagious?

One second she smelled fine—a little feverish, a little tired, that metallic yellow tang a little deeper, but still delicious. The next, she was on the floor, and the bolt of smoke-sick through her scent twisted his own stomach, hard. As soon as he ran back to the range to get the goddamn bacon set aside, she tried to get up off the couch again. She didn't thrash when he got her back down, but she was sweating even worse now, her half-lidded eyes glassy and her smell flaring unpredictably.

Penicillin? Hospital? He flicked through the alternatives, desperately, and almost didn't notice the subtle change in the sounds outside.

Once he did, though, it was impossible to ignore.

Damn.

"Holly." Soft and inflexible. "Holly, I need you to listen to me."

It could be a deer, or something. Nothing else would be out in this goddamn weather, right? Any animal with sense would stay inside. He could get out to the shed, get the snowmobile fixed up—but if he left her, what was she likely to do?

It wasn't a deer. Or a wolf. He knew what it was.

Holly subsided. Glittering eyes, the fever burning her—he'd have to do something to bring it down. The shock of rolling her in snow wouldn't help. The shower, then.

First he had to take care of outside.

"I have to get something for you." A lie, but a good one if it kept her down. "I need you to stay right here. Right here, okay?" Two guns, the knives and his wits. The hiking boots were all right, and he shrugged into his coat. "Stay on the couch," he told her. Maybe she'd even listen.

The only reply he got was a slurred mutter that might have been his name.

Jesus Christ.

He didn't move right away. Instead, he closed his eyes, listening. Smart was the way to play this one. Advantages were on his side—he knew the ground, and all he had to do was outwait and outthink. The curtains were all drawn, both to save heat and discourage someone with a high-powered rifle from solving a problem or two. Any agent out there had to know he'd hear, and might also know…what?

Holly made a restless movement, and Reese heard the footsteps. Deliberate crunching, breaking an icy crust. Sounded like cleats—not a bad choice for this goddamn weather, but savagely tiring and would make him lose on agility.

The bastard was aiming right for the front door. Making no goddamn attempt to be quiet, even.

What the hell?

The porch shuddered as he clumped up onto it. Crunch, crunch, crunch on the ice, right up to the door.

Knocking, then. Light and authoritative. Shave and a haircut, two bits.

So he's got a sense of humor.

Then, something else. "You gonna pretend you don't notice me?" Male, about Reese's age, and the pulse was perfectly even. Nice and controlled. No bloodlust. "I'm here to help. You might as well let me in."

Here to help? That'll be the day.

It was a ballsy move, walking right up. He could admire the sonofabitch, even if he killed him.

Holly cried out, weakly. Reese still hesitated, barely even breathing. There was no good tactical or strategic reason for the other agent to come right up to the front door and announce himself, for God's sake.

"I won't touch the girl. I just want to talk to you. You're a hard man to catch, you know that?" Amused now. No change in pulse or respiration.

Reese ghosted across the room. A calculated risk, but he already had the gun out. The temperature outside would keep a body from rotting right away, should it become necessary. If all else failed he could rifle the other agent for cash and spare supplies before—

He jerked the door open, gun leveled, nerves stretched tight.

Standing carefully back from the door, his gloved hands raised, the other agent peered out from under a thick knitted cap. He took a deep sniff and nodded slightly, keeping his empty hands up and stock-still. Sandy hair, bright pale blue eyes, a wispy beginning of a beard. Looked as though he'd been roughing it for a few days.

Reese's senses strained. He could hear, smell nothing behind the man. Nothing but pines, deep snow, dry-oily animals hidden in burrows, a hint of smoke from the stove.

"I'm alone," the other agent said. "Been offgrid for a few days now. No tails I can make out."

"Hip?"

"Dug it out first thing, stuck it down a feral cat's throat with some tuna. They'll be chasing it awhile."

"Elegant solution." Reese took another deep breath, searching for any wrong note. "I'm a little busy here."

"I can tell." Those blue eyes narrowed slightly, thoughtfully, though the man's pulse didn't alter. "You poor bastard. I bet you don't even know why she smells so good."

His jaw tightened slightly. "Oh?"

"Relax, Reese. I'm not after your girl." The pack at his feet was snow-spotted and zipped open, so Reese could see inside. How far had he hiked in? There would be a trail, at least until it snowed again. Which, judging by the smell, would be soon. "I'm here because I want to live. Same as you."

There was a slithering sound behind Reese. Blankets, hitting the floor. A creak of springs as Holly tried to lever herself off the couch again. She just wouldn't stay down, but then, he knew that about her, didn't he? A woman that would hold a dying man's hand for a long time, a woman who would tell an agent he was real, a woman who would quietly give extra peppermints to even the worst kids wouldn't stop. It wasn't in her.

Goddammit. "You smell familiar. We went to the same base for blood draws and psych evals."

"Yeah. I'm Cal, by the way. Nice to meet you."

"You might not think that in a little while." Reese was satisfied the man was alone, at least. He knew first-hand just how dangerous an agent could be. He'd have to kill this one the instant a single breath was out of place.

"I'll take my chances. They're not wrapping up the program." Cal's cheeks were roughened with windburn, and a subconscious muscle at the floor of Reese's brain relaxed a little. "Heming went crazy, and you were inci-dental. But they're reconsidering. Two reasons, Reese—emotional noise and possible contagion vectors."

Reese lowered the gun. *Damn.* "Kick that pack over so I can see what's in it. And take those off before you come inside." He backed up a few steps. "You make one wrong move, and you're dead."

"Story of my life, man." The other agent bent, slowly, moving carefully, and something else clicked in Reese's head. The pack wasn't full—and there were manila fold-ers and files in there, spotted with moisture but look-ing pretty legit, mauve ones that looked familiar and red ones that didn't. Knives, a 9mm, ammo clinking, a couple other bits he recognized immediately as agent kit that wouldn't have trace capability.

Which moved this Cal from *active threat* to the *ques-tion mark* category. Reese decided to push a little fur-ther. "What happened to yours? The one that smelled good?" A shot in the dark.

Cal glanced up, his blue gaze flat and cold. "Haven't met her yet. I was friends with a nice enough girl, though, and they dusted her coming for me." Working at the cleats strapped to his hiking boots. He was wet to the thighs—he'd waded through the creek, probably working back and forth to confuse his trail. He smelled hungry, and his cheekbones stood out just like Reese's did after a week or so of hard living. "Is that bacon?"

"You play your cards right, you might get some." *And survive long enough to eat it.*

A soft thump. Holly made another hurt little sound, and Reese decided. The gun went down even farther; he backed up a little more, edging back crabways for her. She'd tried to get up again, and was muttering about someone named Doug.

"Shh, baby." He tucked her in again, despite her irritable pushing the covers away. Glanced at the other agent, who stepped carefully in as if he didn't quite believe his luck. "Shut the goddamn door. And tell me this isn't what I think it is."

First things first. The scar on Cal's hip was pink fresh, and the other agent manipulated the flesh, pulling and stretching so Reese could see there was no telltale bump underneath. He even smelled right. Either the other agent's glandular control was absolutely perfect, or he was telling the truth.

Holly, sweat drenched and tossing, made a low hurt sound. Reese's stomach threatened to clench, and he could smell his own worry. If he could, the other agent could, too.

Cal eyed her, didn't even try to approach. "Yeah. She's got it."

"I infected her." The sick twisting in his stomach wouldn't go away.

"What did you think made her smell so tasty? The little assholes know who they have a chance of surviving in."

Christ. "How do you know?"

"Because they botched coming for me, so I did an infiltrate onbase and snitched some files, just like you might have."

"Smart." *And suicidal.* "You want to burn them as bad as I do?"

"Worse." A flash of dull rage broke through the other man's smiling crust. "If it makes you feel better, she's got a seventy percent chance."

"She'd better." *Because if something...if she...* He refused to even think it.

Holly's eyelids flew up. "Phillip?" she whispered, staring at the ceiling. Thin tracers of steam rose from her forehead; she'd already sweated through her tank top. It clung to her as her hands lifted. "Don't...don't..."

"Shh, sweetheart." He kept an eye on Cal, just in case, slowly sank down to one knee, caught one of her hands. "It's all right. I'm here."

"She'll need fluids and proteins when she wakes up. Vitamin C. You'd better figure out if you can trust me so you don't have to look over your shoulder the whole time."

I know. I'll do what I have to. "It's all right," he soothed, and Holly subsided.

"Reese?" Her hand bit his with surprising, hysterical strength. "It *hurts*..." Ending on a low hiss of breath.

Christ. "I know, honey. It'll be over soon."

"Ninety...ninety percent...collateral, she said...they were... I'm sick..." Faded into a slurring murmur, her eyes half-lidded. Crescents of bruised flesh stood out underneath her glittering eyes, and that wonderful smell of hers came in tsunami waves, underlaid with smoke-burning sickness and that weird metallic note.

"It's going to be okay," he told her. Maybe it was a lie.

Cal shifted his weight, and Reese twitched. The other man stepped back, hands up and loose, very carefully.

"Relax," he said. "Just come down out of the red, okay? I am *here to help*."

You'd better be. Reese didn't bother saying it. "Get some water, and a couple towels. And since you know what the hell, start explaining."

Noah Caldwell watched as Three followed Bronson, her spine completely straight, across the helipad. The old man reeled almost drunkenly, but she simply paced at the same even speed. She made the slippery crunching across deicer pellets look easy, even as Noah's boots slipped and slithered. She didn't bother bending, though the bird's blades roared overhead.

He hurried afterward. Watching her move was like seeing a cat slink along. He'd always liked blondes, but she kept her hair pulled so severely back it did nothing for her. Bronson had a ridiculous parka zipped all the way up, but Three just had her blazer and skirt, pantyhose he'd sent a servicewoman to the PX for. She didn't seem to feel the cold.

None of the agents did. It was enough to make you shiver.

She was the prize, the only one to survive the induction process, and Control wanted an eye kept on her. *Bronson's useless*, Control had wheezed, lighting another cigarette, when he sent Noah out to keep an eye on this part of the project. *But he's connected, and an easy patsy if the whole thing blows up. Your job's to keep track of Three. We don't want to lose that one.*

Thackeray, the civilian doctor, had handed Noah a packet from Control. He knew his orders, and enough about the general situation to make his hands sweat and turn cold while he burned the papers outside the sliding French door of his little crackerbox onbase. Contagion vectors. Liquidation. And above all, keeping Three under wraps. Even if the other agents were going haywire, she was precious.

A country needed soldiers, and if you couldn't tweak them as adults, well, maybe you could *build* them. You could get little wrigglies anywhere, but an egg preloaded with Gibraltar and agents trained from birth? *Those* were precious.

That was for later, though. Right now, there were other considerations, including keeping Three on deck to help catch the others. Control was very clear: Caldwell just had to get the two agents in this part of the country dealt with, tie off any civilian flack, and neutralize Bronson.

Which would be, Noah told himself as he ducked through a heavy steel door into welcome warmth, a distinct pleasure.

The fat jerk was disgusting.

Male voices. Doctors? Hospital? Had she finally collapsed? The thing about knowing you had something terminal was the waiting, God, it just wore across every nerve every damn day.

"Fever's gonna spike and break. All we have to do is keep her below the brain-cook."

A familiar voice, now, and the sound of paper moving. "Says here you were DS-7."

She strained against the delirium. Cold, she was so

cold, and burning at the same time. Slickness every-where, she was covered in slime. Phillip, closing the front door with a small click. "Have a nice life, Holl." Sitting at the kitchen table, right where he had, the warmth of him still in the chair and the numb realiza-tion that she was alone sinking in.

One of the men made a bitter sound, almost a laugh. "Yeah. Serve your country, they said. You've got all the right measurements. Dumb jerk that I was, I went along."

Paper moving. She strained to remember where she was, what was happening to her. "Christ. Is this for real?"

"You really want to ask me that?"

"It was rhetorical, soldier." *Reese. She found the name, clung to it. Tried to speak, produced only a weird shapeless sound.*

"Listen to the vocab on you. Emotional noise went off the charts for every agent sooner or later. You held out longest, it looks like."

"Call me talented." *A familiar touch against her fore-head. It was him, it was Reese, and the thought stead-ied her. If he was here, it would be all right. Or maybe not, because he couldn't fix what was wrong with her. At least she wasn't alone.*

"You gave them everything they wanted to hear in psych eval. Got a future in the theater."

"Like you didn't."

"For a while, I thought being honest was the best way to go."

"Then?"

"Then I wised up on a job, and started thinking."

"Yeah." *A heavy click.* "Here."

"So you trust me?"

"No reason for you to be this forthcoming if you're eventually going to kill me. Unless they want me back in the fold, and I'm pretty sure they—"

"Oh, they might. You were their shining boy—amped mission fidelity, no emotional noise, they want to poke and prod and figure out what the hell. Also, if it's jumped to her, they want her for testing."

"You're not helping your case, Cal." *Reese sounded thoughtful. The world was full of smeared color, pain gathering deep in her twisting, burning body. Confused movement, sudden pressure all through her.* "Shh, baby. It's okay. It's all right. It's going to be all right."

"You smell that?"

Crackling silence, punctuated only by the rasp of cold air against her wet skin. A terrible moment of clarity—something awful was about to happen; it was surging up underneath her, a shark rising through black water.

"What's it smell like to you?"

"Relax, Reese. My little friends don't like her. She's all yours."

"But you can smell it—"

"Christ, will you settle down? She's complementary, you know? Bacon on your cheeseburger—any idiot can sniff and see your swarmies are going to love her. Just like puzzle pieces. You could theoretically infect others, I guess, but their survival rate is going to be closer to two, three percent. That's what the models say. They're scrambling to figure out if any of us have. They're calling it Gemini. A mutation of the original virus."

"Holy crap." *He sounded as though he'd been*

punched. Hard. "And they send us all over the world, right?"

"You're quick on the uptake. Yeah. If there are even a few, the ones who survive will be problems."

"I'll just bet. What's the spread rate?"

"Like I said, all theoretical. They don't know."

"They don't... Jesus. Jesus Christ."

"Add to that the doctor losing his mind. Heming. Thought he was going to be a hero and stop the contagion at ground zero."

"So he botched erasing both of us." *That tone—as if he'd been socked a good one in the gut—was wrong. Reese shouldn't sound like that. Everything was wrong.*

I'm sick, she thought. Very sick, and it's not the cancer. It's something else. *She strained to listen, to remember, but the shark underneath her was losing patience with threatening.*

It wanted to swallow her. Its tail sliced through cold water, and her sobbing breath quickened. She could hear her own heartbeat, racing, pressure building in her temples and throat and lungs.

"Looks like. Aren't we the lucky fellows. Um, Reese? She's heating up."

"I know." *A chill against her forehead—a washcloth? She was dimly aware of more movement, a rising scream, a cracked, hoarse voice.*

Was it hers?

The shark decided to quit playing around and rose with eerie speed. She could almost see it, fins jagged from the chaos of old battles, scars on its sandpaper sides, mouth open and triangular teeth in rows, its dead-glowing eyes fixed on the small struggling human above. It streaked for her, and she screamed, over and

*over, thrashing, struggling, and there was that voice
again, the one she knew.*

"Holly... Holly, shh...come on, baby, it's all right,
you're all right...please, Holly, *Holly*!"

*Jaws closed with a snap, teeth in her flesh, bones
creaking, then, thankfully, the shark swallowed.*

And she was gone.

He had another forty-eight hours before he started
getting tired, but the lump in his throat just wouldn't
go away. He was hoarse, too, from talking to her as she
thrashed. The worst part was when she screamed, or
when she made that low hurt noise, as if she was expecting to get hit.

Cal brought him a bottle of water; he cracked it one-
handed and took a sip. The other agent squatted, easily,
still consciously keeping out of anything approximating
fight range or threat perimeter. "Fever's going down."

I know. Reese didn't say it. This guy liked to talk,
might as well let him.

"So," Cal continued, "I knew you were gone over this
girl. I said to myself, what's the last thing anyone would
expect this guy to do? Which made it easy—all I had to
do was look at your domestic jobs and choose the route
that gave me the most options on my way south, figuring you'd have hidey-holes as a matter of course. Then
it was just following my nose. I wandered around a little before finding this place, had a couple cold camps."

Is he gauging me? Waiting to see if I'm distracted?
It could also be that Cal hadn't had anyone to talk to
in a long, long time. Keeping secrets made for psycho-
logical pressure.

Even for an agent.

"What about your friend?" Reese watched the rise and fall of Holly's chest. "The one they killed."

A long silence. Maybe that would shut the man up.

"Tracy," Cal said, softly. "Nice. Easy. Uncomplicated. No questions. Heming tried to off me, too. I got out and went to pick her up. I… They knew about her, they came for me, I wasn't…she didn't deserve that. I didn't keep her quiet enough, I guess."

Things really could have gone either way. If they had, would it be Reese talking about how he hadn't done enough to keep Holly hidden? *Lots of uncomfortable questions, soldier.* "I'm sorry." It sounded strange, and he realized why.

He actually meant it. It was a kindness, something Holly might say. That empathy of hers. What was it like to swim in the emotional noise all the time, to feel it the way she did?

"Yeah." A drift of changed scent, Cal shifting his weight as well. A blue tinge to him now. Actual sadness. "Me, too."

Thankfully, that shut him up. Holly dozed, her eyelids fluttering every once in a while. She didn't seem to be sweating quite as badly now. Her pulse was slowing, too.

Just let her live. Bargaining. A human response. Who was he asking, though? A god cruel enough to let all this happen? Cruel enough to make Holly suffer?

God didn't do that, Reese. You did.

He flipped through yet another file, his eyelids full of sand. Tox screens, tolerance tests, psych notes. What Cal had grabbed was almost as interesting as what he hadn't managed to get.

Three files on women: two were just autopsy results.

One, a Tracy Moritz, had caught a spray of AK-47 lead. Cal's escape was noted as a failure-to-capture, and he'd left a great deal of his own blood at the scene—Moritz's nice little farmhouse, the mortgage paid up out of foreclosure recently.

Sloppy. But he'd have done the same for Holly, wouldn't he?

Another agent had gotten sticky with a girl; they were both listed as failure-to-capture as well, with possibly-dead notation. The third file on a female was so heavily redacted it was almost useless, but it looked kind of as though the program had found a girl candidate for the little swarmers about the same time they'd found Reese. There were further notes about some other kind of process. *Induction,* it said once.

Intriguing.

Reese's own dual files were thought provoking. Try as he might, he couldn't find a hole in any of Cal's story. The man could be exactly what he said he was. In fact, it was looking like he *had* to be. Just enough suspicion attached to him to be normal.

"So." Reese took another swallow of water. His neck ached, and the floor was cold. He was going to stiffen up if he crouched here much longer, but he didn't want to move. "What's your plan?"

"Ah." Cal nodded, as if he'd said something profound. "Um. Well, you know, I was hoping you had one. I'm geared for on-the-fly tactics—you're more of a long-range guy. You're, um, more strategic. I was hoping you had some ideas."

Maybe I was hoping you *did.* Reese couldn't help it. The laugh burst out of him, swallowed halfway so he didn't wake her, and the momentary flash of rueful surprise crossing the other agent's features convinced Reese that he was, indeed, legit.

The funny side of it hit Cal, too, and their shared, strained laughter brushed tension out of the tiny cabin. Holly stirred, mumbling softly, and subsided when they both shut up.

"Maybe I do," Reese said, very quietly. *Time to come up with one, at least.* "But I'm not going to tell you."

"Fair enough." Cal shrugged. "I'm going to get some sleep." He stood, carefully, backed up until his calves hit the sagging recliner, dropped down into the chair's embrace, and was gone inside seconds. His pulse dropped, breathing evened out, and the smell of glands opening as autonomic control eased into unconsciousness was just right, too. Nervousness, true, but Reese supposed in the other man's shoes he'd be the same. Dealing with a hair-trigger agent who had every reason to doubt you would make anyone a little jumpy.

How long had Cal been running, to pass out like that?

Reese settled himself against the couch, paging through the files more slowly now. Holly's breathing deepened, too, and he started to think maybe she might survive.

If she doesn't, we're going to see how fast two agents can dismantle an entire goddamn government.

It didn't even bother him to think like that. It should have, but it didn't.

Reese turned another page, and settled himself to studying.

Blood warm, soft even though it was lumpy, the bed cradled her. Little creaks and crackles, twitching under her skin. Her head ached, savagely, and it was loud. She turned away, burying her face in the pillow, her greasy hair rasping against cotton. She could feel every single hair, every inch of her skin, crying out for a shower.

Soughing. In and out. She lay there for a long while before she realized it was someone breathing. No—two someones. The thump-thumps she heard weren't bass from a car on Bicknell Avenue; they were…

Heartbeats.

"I think she's coming around," an unfamiliar voice said.

An unfamiliar, *male* voice.

Movement. Bare feet scrabbling for purchase, the sweat-soaked blankets tangled around her trying to trip and send her headlong, the world spinning sideways; her hip barked the pink-topped dinette table and sent it flying. Her back crashed against the cupboard, her heels still scrabbling, and she had inhaled to scream.

His hand clapped over her mouth. "Easy, baby. Easy. I'm here." Familiar dark eyes, and the smell of him—healthy male, deliciously appetizing, her own unwashed reek disappearing into it to make something deep and warm and soft. Comforting. Everything inside her turned over, and she gasped against his hand, her stomach jolting.

The starch went out of her legs. She sagged, Reese caught her, she buried her face in his chest and inhaled. He smelled really, really good—clean and warm, safe and solid. A tinge of something brassy and sharp that made her think worried, a peculiar sharpness that smelled like hunger, too. Her nose was on overdrive, sorting and cataloging, impressions flashing so quickly she almost forgot to breathe.

"You're going to adjust," he said into her hair, his breath a warm spot. "It's all right. You're absolutely going to adjust, everything's okay, you're doing just fine."

I am not! This is not fine! She inhaled again, deeply, shuddering as her brain shivered inside her skull.

Finally, when the shakes had passed, she was able to peel her cheek away from his T-shirt. Her throat was dry, she was gummed all over with crusty, nasty effluvia and she realized her pajamas were in tatters. There was a weird silence outside—snow melting.

She could *smell* it. Pines, and frozen water warming back up to a liquid, and a thousand other little things.

Including another person. Unfamiliar, harsh and strange, and dangerous. Holly froze, but Reese didn't seem to notice.

"See? You're just at threshold, perceptions are shifting. You've got some better senses now, Holly. You can see more and smell more, and do more. Just let it happen—you'll adjust. I promise."

"We all did." That unfamiliar voice. "Welcome to the family, ma'am."

Holly stiffened, but Reese didn't let go of her. He was just as immovable as ever. "That's Cal. He's going to help us."

"N-no—" Her mouth didn't want to work correctly. She could taste the sickness leaving her body, her heart pummeling the inside of her ribs like it wanted to escape. There was a clot of something in her abdomen, high up on the right, but it was swiftly shrinking, starved of nutriment. Another clot behind her stomach, high up and massive, pressing against her heart. The bits of it elsewhere in her body were shrinking, too,

their nasty yellowblack tar taste filling her mouth as she focused. They made tiny sounds as something else ate them, the same warmth smoothing and repairing any damage left behind.

Her back didn't hurt. She felt wobbly, and thirsty, and so hungry she could eat cardboard. To be actually hungry again, without nausea—she'd forgotten what that was like.

What the hell? Her head tilted back. She stared up at Reese, seeing the fine lines at the corners of his eyes again. The individual threads of color in his irises—she could actually see, if she focused, the blocks of cells, the colors, a glint off his pupil—

"Holly." Very quietly, with no trace of anger or fear. "Breathe."

Another walloping hit of scent, but this one wasn't quite so bad. Her head hurt, a swift lance of pain through her temples quickly vanishing. Every inch of her started twitching, individual muscle fibers contracting and releasing at random, but there was a jolt of scent from Reese and that stopped. His heartbeat was nice and even; her own fell into step. She found herself inhaling as he did, and an odd calm swamped her.

"What." She had to cough, her throat was on fire. "The *hell.*"

That got her a smile, and a snort of laughter from behind him. Reese propped her against the counter, one hand at her shoulder. He lifted her arm, and the tremors went down.

"That's right," he soothed. "Just got to get your proprioception down."

What? "Hungry," she managed.

"I know. We're just going to teach your body where it

is in time and space, okay? Your nerves need the feedback, it'll help you adjust." He switched sides, lifted
her right arm. There was a final burst of discomfort as
the clots of malignant cells buried in her rib cage and
abdomen both finished shrinking, and a quiet warmth
began in their places.

*Pancreas. And liver. I guessed the pancreas, I knew I
was sick. I was right.* It wasn't as comforting as it could
have been. She'd been prepared for...what?

To die. I was ready. Only, she hadn't been. What
was she supposed to do now? "I... I want a shower."

"I'll bet you do. Here, your knee. Up here."

Her knee jolted up, almost as if he was a pushy guy
she wanted to hurt. He struck the top of her knee lightly
with the back of his hand, and the touch seemed to snap
the limb into place, all of a sudden bringing it back
into her body instead of just floating off in never-never
land. The other side was the same, and when he slowly
uncurled his fingers from her shoulder, she found she
could stand up, and it didn't seem so...overwhelming.
The world was full of fresh color and detail, but it no
longer slammed into her over and over again like a
baseball bat.

"Interesting," he said, and his mouth quirked a fraction. "Hey, Holly. Let's get some food in you."

Wait. Wait just a second. Her brain finally engaged,
spinning through the last few minutes. And before, but
those memories were curiously...darkened, like old pho-
tographs. "You...wait. Wait. This is...*you* did this to
me."

"It's a virus," that other voice supplied, helpfully,
and she peered around Reese to see a shorter man, built
compact and wide shouldered, sandy haired and with

a beard she could tell he didn't like crawling up his cheeks. His eyes were very blue, and nothing about him was familiar. "CTX-48, if you want to be specific, code-named Gibraltar. It crawls into your mitochondrial DNA and—"

"Breakfast first," Reese said, and Holly slumped against the counter, staring at him. "Explanations can wait."

Ninety percent casualty...infect...thirty percent... little swarmers... I'm all flesh, Holly. You smell good.

"My God," she whispered, and Reese's heartbeat sped up just a fraction. Which meant hers did, too. "What have you done to me?"

The pancakes were vanishing at a good clip, the eggs were all but gone and the oranges had been reduced to peels and seeds. Hungry meant she'd survived, and that was just fine by Reese.

Still, she was too quiet. Eating in starveling bites, those smoky eyes wide and distrustful, and that glorious scent coming in waves. Mixing with the bacon Cal was putting a dent in as well as the richness of coffee, her scent was more intense. More alive.

More like an agent's. And there was something else—that metallic yellow streak, gone. It had been so much a part of her scent before, no wonder he'd thought it intrinsic. Had she been really sick, like she'd feared? Being distracted by her at every turn might have covered something up. She kept folding a hand over the right side of her abdomen, as if it hurt, but nothing sounded wrong, and she didn't smell like pain.

She also wouldn't—quite—meet his gaze. She kept quiet as Cal kept talking about absorption rates and virology, every once in a while throwing the goddamn man a glance just a little too fearful to be inviting or even thoughtful.

When she finally stopped eating and stared into her coffee cup, even Cal seemed to notice something was wrong. At least, his explanations trailed off, and he kept looking at Reese as if asking for direction. Too goddamn late.

It was all right, though. It meant Reese didn't have to explain, and whatever anger surfaced would probably fasten on the interloper.

Finally, the silence turned absolute, and thickened. He poured himself a cup of coffee. There wasn't a third chair at the tiny table, so he leaned against the sink and watched her.

She was alive. Dependent on him, maybe even more thoroughly than before. She still smelled so goddamn good it made his eyes water and his hormones rebel. And he'd been with her long enough to know that there was trouble brewing on the Holly horizon.

She pushed her chair back, gingerly, as if she expected it to fall apart on her. Stood up, with that same finicky care. The tank top did nothing to hide the shape of her breasts, and his own throat had gone dry by now. A crackle glaze of dried sweat all over her, and every fresh drift of her scent made him remember touching her in the dark.

"I think I should take a shower now," she said, very quietly. "Is there hot water?"

"Ah." He had to swallow, twice. His imagination was just too good. "Yeah, there should be plenty. Holly—"

"Okay." She turned, grabbed at the back of the chair as if she was going to overbalance—and he found himself right next to her, his hand closing around her elbow even as she tried to twitch away.

She flinched. Halted, staring at the floor.

Cal cleared his throat. "I, ah…can I use the head before you go in there? Thanks." He scrambled off his own chair with unseemly haste and vanished into the bathroom, slamming the door and turning both the sink faucets at once.

As an attempt to give them privacy, it only half worked. The place was so small he couldn't help but hear them.

"Holly." He wasn't hurting her elbow, he was pretty sure. "Are you…are you okay?"

"Is he your friend?" She was very pale. Her pulse kept wanting to rise, and his, hitched to it, was difficult to keep down.

How did he even begin to explain? "He's…another agent."

"He found us?"

Yeah, I'm going to have to think about that. Predictable is dangerous. "They tried to kill him, too."

"How do you know? Never mind." She tried to pull away, he didn't let her. "Reese, stop it."

Not until I'm sure you're okay. And not going anywhere. "I'm sorry. I should have told you. I just didn't know what you'd do, and…" He ran out of words. *Come on. Say something reasonable. Something she can relate to.*

His brain chased everything he could say around on a hamster wheel, and promptly vaporlocked. It didn't help that he was practically drooling, because the musk of a healthy black-haired woman threatened to dial everything in him over into the red. With that goddamn yellow-metal component gone, it was even more fascinating, and it was a damn good thing her scent hadn't been this intense before. It could knock a man out.

Just like those big blue eyes of hers.

"You kept changing the subject." Her lips were chapped, even though she'd been pouring down the fluids. With her hair mussed and her pajamas incredibly disarranged, it could have been the morning after a completely different set of events.

In a way, it was. "I had to," he mumbled, numbly.

"Let go of me."

He did. She rocked back on her bare heels, as if she hadn't expected that, and a flash of something—was it resignation?—crossed her face so swiftly he almost missed it. The water shut off in the bathroom, and they were running out of any approximation of privacy.

"It fixed the cancer," she said, quietly, almost tonelessly. "I can feel it."

"There wasn't any—"

She shook her head, so quickly her hair made a whispering sound. "I feel it," she repeated, the glint in her eyes daring him to object again.

"Okay. You feel it. Good enough for me." His hands ached to touch her; he had to concentrate to keep them at his sides, nice and easy. *She must have been pretty far gone by the time I caught wind of her. Why wasn't she in treatment? Why wasn't it in her medsheets?* How thin and tired she was, too, and her hair, lusterless not because of stress but because her entire body was starved of nutrients. How had she been able to *walk*, for God's sake?

Reese, you idiot. Maybe he *was* degrading. That would be painfully ironic.

She still stared at him, as if he was a stranger. "Did you know it would do that?"

"If there was anything wrong with you, the virus fixed it, Holly. You survived."

"Guess that makes me lucky. Ninety percent casualty rate, right?"

"That was for me. Not you."

"Not..." Another quick shake of her head. "Reese, look. Did you know? That it would...infect...me?"

He shook his head. *Christ, even if I did I wouldn't tell you now.*

Did she look disappointed? What was it? He couldn't think, not with her standing so close and the last few days crowding the inside of his skull. Digesting that lump of information was going to take a little bit, maybe because he'd been so dumb to start out with.

She's going to end up smarter than me. Maybe Cal is, and that's how he found me. He can't be thinking I'm going to save him, for God's sake.

Except I have to, because it means saving her, too.

"Reese." Hugging herself now, the movement showing even more interesting slices of paleness through her tank top. "Did you know?"

"Does it matter?" Harshly, because the lump in his throat wouldn't retreat. "It's happened. The weather's turned—we have to get out of here."

She tilted her head. Even covered with sweat and sickness, she was still beautiful. "It's all melting out there."

"Warming up. I, ah, I can smell it, too."

"Do I still smell good to you?"

More than good. "Yeah."

"Are you…is this Cal guy…" She pursed her lips, maybe not knowing what she wanted to ask.

Cal chose that moment to step out of the bathroom, the picture of sheepishness, slicking his hair back with damp fingers. "Sorry about that. I'll, uh, just start the dishes."

Holly backed up a step. Two. As though she was waiting for him to say something.

Maybe *I'm sorry*? He opened his mouth to try it, but she whirled and headed toward the couch. She handled the new suitcase carrying her clothes easily and vanished into the bathroom, slamming the door a little harder than necessary. He could probably chalk it up to her not understanding her new strength.

Which brought up an interesting question: How strong was she likely to get? She felt just as soft as ever, without an agent's leashed force. There hadn't been much on the female subject in the files that wasn't crossed out, but—

"She okay?" Cal started stacking plates, and Reese wrestled down the urge to walk over and give the man a shot to the kidneys.

"Don't know. Rough time for her." The bathroom door was a blank face, giving nothing away. Deathly silence before the shower gurgled into life. "Adjusting, I guess."

"That's one word for it." The other agent balanced a pile of sticky plates, and his back was broad under a flannel shirt. It had to be a deliberate movement—you just didn't turn around like that, especially when you knew the other person was armed and twitchy. "She's gonna bolt, man."

As soon as Cal said it, Reese knew he was right.

"I know." *And I'll bring her right back, goddamn it. There's no way she's getting rid of me.*

The stuff was all over her. Crusts of sweat salt and various other effluvia fell away, melting like cotton candy. The water was warm enough, if mineral tasting, and the toiletries smelled kind of familiar—he even knew what soap she liked, for God's sake.

Standing under hot water, the coffee sinking in and her stomach feeling weirdly distended from the sheer amount of food she'd consumed, Holly had to admit she felt…pretty good.

Which was troubling. She'd been really, really sick. Sick enough to die. And now she felt a little shaky, but clear and strong in a way she hadn't since…well, ever. Maybe as a teenager, with her whole life ahead of her and the body and metabolism to meet it head-on. Funny, her memories of that were darkened, too. As if she'd been looking through smoked glass.

She touched her belly, digging her fingertips in. She didn't feel the same thrumming, heavy vitality as Reese's muscles. No six-pack, no sinewy heaviness. Which brought up another interesting point.

We didn't use protection. It hadn't seemed to matter, since she was terminal anyway and he…

Was that what had…infected…her? After a lifetime of being careful. Kind of funny.

You know what else is funny? You're out here in the middle of nowhere with Reese and his buddy.

Except the word for that was *dangerous.* A "fellow agent." It didn't make sense for the man to have found them unless he was somehow Reese's friend.

Now that he had a friend, would he still drag Holly

along? Or would she wake up one morning to find him gone?

"Time for me to start thinking," she murmured, putting her face under the mineral-smelling water. She could taste traces of…copper? Other things, a whole palette of earth and stone, fluid seeping underground, filtering through layers and pipes. Individual water drops on her skin, her heart working steadily, the flashes between her nerves tiny lightning strikes, warming her, building chains of reaction in the dark.

She surfaced with a jolt, shivering even though the water was still perfectly warm. Had she lost track of time?

Mitochondrial DNA…other effects…you heal quicker, more flexible, greater endurance. She'd gotten more over breakfast with Cal than from however long traveling with Reese. *You get smarter, too—damn near genius where you were smart before, but you get some blind spots.*

What were Reese's blind spots?

You run, I'll hold them…the only time I feel human is when I look at you…it's okay, baby, it's all right.

The fractured pieces inside her head weren't helping. They swirled, refusing to coalesce into a reasonable picture. Or maybe she just didn't like the painting she was seeing?

It took her a while to get dressed. She kept stopping, staring into space, while different bits of memory and guesswork fell together. But finally, in jeans and a blue sweater that both reeked of newness, she had to leave the warm, humid little room with its indifferent linoleum and ancient fittings.

They were both at the dinette, and there was a pile of

paper on the newly cleared, rickety little table. Familiar-looking file folders, and her stomach fluttered uneasily.

Whose are those? Other agents? Other "collateral"? The abduction was still a mess of jumbled pieces inside her head, refusing to settle even worse than the rest of the stuff.

Cal pushed his sandy hair back from his forehead. With his broad back to her, he looked just like any other guy on a chair, and if she was waiting on the table she would have thought them both businessmen doing an informal meeting.

A sudden realization shook her.

I'm not ever going home again. And I'm not going to die.

She stood there, a damp towel drooping from her left hand, and afterward she would wonder what she would have said or done if both of them hadn't suddenly tilted their heads, as if hearing something.

She strained, and heard it, too—a low mechanical buzz, very faint, but out of place in the snowbound quiet.

"Damn," Reese said, softly. "We've got incoming."

"Weather eyes?" Falling snow dotted Cal's hair, whirling down in heavy, wet clumps. Ice was falling from creaking branches, and there were spatters of melt *pock*ing through the layer of freezing over everything.

"Dunno." Reese shook his head, cupping his hands behind his ears to focus the sound.

"Where can we go?" Holly, under the porch roof, hugged herself. The blue of the sweater brought out her eyes, and her hair, even wet, looked more vital. She was still too heartbreakingly thin, but that would fix itself if Reese could get enough food in her. "We're trapped up here."

"Not necessarily." Reese took a deep breath. "It's cold. Go back inside."

"Stare at the walls and wait for them to show up? Great." She shivered, hugging herself even harder. "What are we going to *do*?"

At least it was still *we*. "Right now you're going to go inside. It's freezing out here, Holly."

"I'm not going to catch cold and die." Her chin set.

Cal scanned what he could see of the sky, blue eyes narrowed. "I don't like this."

You're not the only one. Inside the cabin, the AM radio had weather reports ticking by, the storm's last spasm moving westward and crashing against the mountains. The warming in its wake would make things sloppy. It could be anything—airlift for lost hikers, weather copter, even just normal air traffic.

Still, there was a rasping tingle against his nerves. It was the same sensation that warned him about Cal.

Could *still* be warning him about Cal.

"It feels hinky," the other agent said, his breath pluming in the cold. "Makes me itch."

Afterward, Reese was never sure if there had been a pause after the words. One moment he was turning over alternatives, the next he had tackled Holly back through the open door. They landed in a heap, her soft little cry mixing with the pop-zing of another bullet, and Cal swearing viciously behind him was a slow groan because Reese was moving fast. Cal kicked the door shut, glass shattering and another popping zing.

Sniper. Probably gone by the time we get out the door. It was the follow-up that would dust them, and

do it pretty handily. Which made it possible careless-
ness—if you were going to take two agents, warning
them like this was a bad idea.

There was no time to think. Holly was struggling
against his hold, thrashing on the floor. Had he hurt
her? Was she hit? He didn't smell blood, but—

"—*off* me!" she yelled, and he had a bare moment
to be relieved before she heaved, almost tossing him
sideways.

Look at that. She is *stronger.* Rolling, staying low in
case more lead came through, Cal was already heading
for his backpack, settled against the chair he'd slept in.
Reese dove for his and Holly's as well as her parka, and
by the time Holly had struggled to her feet—*civilian,
she doesn't know*—he was already barking "Get down!"
and yanking at her arm, planning the next few moves.

The copper scent of blood hit him, and he froze.
God. Oh, God—

"*Hit!*" Cal snarled. "Goddamn it. Got a kit?"

Relief that it wasn't Holly smashed through him as he
dragged her along, an awkward duck scramble. "Back
door. This way."

"What the hell?" Holly, tugging against his grasp.
"Someone's shooting!"

No time to wonder why she wasn't agent strong—did
the virus dilute? As soon as they were behind enough
cover he pulled her up to her feet, hooking down the
first-aid bag—camo green, the Army still did some
things best—and tossing it to Cal. If he was moving, it
couldn't be that bad. "Status?"

"Fine!" The other agent was suddenly all business.
So he shut up when he was under fire.

Good to know.

Snow had drifted high enough to touch the sloped-down roof outside the back door; the resultant tunnel was full of ice-filtered shadowy light. Adrenaline threatened to make his fingers clumsy; he twisted the lock too hard and metal pinged, breaking with a high sweet noise.

"Christ," Holly whispered, hitching her backpack up on her shoulder. "Shooting at us."

Be careful, Reese. Don't give it away. The angle of the slope behind the house made it safer, unless another sniper had worked around during last night. The car could make it out, but instead, he swept the shed with a single glance and pointed at the canvas-shrouded hulk in the corner. "Holly, get Cal bandaged up. We're leaving."

"But…my clothes, the—"

"Everything you need's in the backpack. I put it together while you were in the shower. Get him bandaged."

"You *what*?"

"Clothes can be replaced, ma'am." Cal stepped in to distract her. "Open this up. I'd like to stop bleeding."

"Oh, *God*."

A burst of high brassy fear in the middle of her scent—it almost rocked him back on his heels. But she was already ripping the kit open, and Cal had struggled half-out of his coat.

The canvas fell aside, and the battered snowcat reared up in front of Reese, scratched and scored blotches of green and paleness meant to break up its outline and make it more difficult to see. Of course, the damn thing was as loud as two world wars rolled into one, but it could go places a sedan couldn't.

"Does it still work?" Cal winced as Holly's shaking hands applied antiseptic to the wound—it was messy, but it had only creased him. It was already closing, and Reese hoped Holly wouldn't notice.

"Checked it when we got here." *The mice saw it, but they didn't get anything critical.* "Full tank, extras strapped on."

"A bit of cross-country?" Cal winced again, but Reese suspected it was only for show, to keep the nervous, trembling woman occupied.

"Smart man."

"That car will wallow."

"Like a fat horse."

"Want me to take her?" He could have meant the car—or the woman.

Holly's head snapped up, her eyes wide.

"Holly stays with me," Reese answered, steadily. "You're bait."

"Great. Rendezvous?"

"Your second job in Mexico. Sixteen days from now." Reese shouldered Holly aside; she was having trouble with the compression bandage. A few seconds had everything set right, the white gauze pad pinkening a little as he taped it down. The man still smelled right—peppery adrenaline, the blue sharpness of determination, still no off note. "North side."

"Got it." Cal shrugged back into his coat. "Good luck."

"You, too." It was safe enough to open the shed door, and within a few moments the roar of the 'cat began to seesaw as it slip-slid, gunning for a stand of pines that would provide the best cover.

Holly, numbly pawing at the passenger-side door of the sedan, flinched when he caught her elbow.

"It's all right," he managed around the rock in his throat. He held up her parka and began bundling her into it. "We don't need the car. Come on."

An iron ladder, leading into darkness. Holly clung to the bars, following Reese's steady movement down.

"Guy who built this was a survivalist." His voice echoed oddly—she could hear the dimensions of the slightly sloping shaft, the roughness of the rock walls. Instinct told her the ladder was safe and solid enough, but her breath came in little sips.

It was so *dark*.

"He was sure the government was going to come and take his guns," Reese continued, calmly. "Or that his creditors would show up. It changed from day to day." They had been climbing down for quite some time, and her arms should have been aching.

They weren't.

Her own voice took her by surprise. "What happened to him?" Thin and reedy, as if she was having trouble breathing. Reese had led her behind the big humming thing—*geothermals*, he told her—and heaved up a well-hidden trapdoor. Now it was a climb down and his steady heartbeat, her own going much quicker, thumping in her ears.

"He sold out and went to Peru. Something about a valley somewhere he could hole up in, fight off the rest of the world. He was obsessed with square-foot gardening and panning for gold."

Sounds like a real winner. He sounded, in fact, like

Phillip, only without Phil's determination to get through med school.

Funny, but the thought of her ex-husband didn't hurt anymore. "Is he still there?"

"I don't know. Never wanted to find him."

"But what do you think?"

"I think he got there, but he probably found out it wasn't the place he wanted."

"Oh." More descending, her arms and legs moving like clockwork. *I should be tired. I should be terrified.*

Well, she was plenty scared. The hollow thudding sounds of bullets, Cal's arm soaked with blood, everything left behind again—if she was reasonable at all, she should be screaming. Instead, she was just following Reese. Tagging along, her body moving with dreamlike efficiency. No nausea, no weakness, no hot bar of pain buried in her back. She was still alive.

"Anyway, when they put this in, he had them leave a shaft. For maintenance, but then he came down here over a couple years and did some work. Just in case."

"In case of the government?"

"Yeah, well, ironic, isn't it?"

"Very." Who was the woman using her voice now? Her breath had come back, and Holly realized terror wasn't the problem.

The problem was that she wasn't terrified *enough*. The old Holly—the tired, dying waitress—would still have been screaming her lungs out and quite possibly sobbing after being shot at. This new woman, full of a virus that had shrunk the tumors inside her like sugar lumps under running water, was simply climbing down a ladder and trying not to fall.

Funny, nothing had mattered when she knew she was

terminal. It was so much easier. Now she didn't know what the hell to do, or to think, or to feel.

The end came as a surprise—Reese's hands at her waist, he lifted her down with thought-provokingly casual ease. The darkness was a living thing, pressed against the borders of her body. Reese curled a hand around her nape and pulled her forward slightly. Holly didn't resist, burying her face in his chest and breathing him in. At least he was just the same. *Holly stays with me.* He wasn't going to leave her behind just yet.

She could sense his head tilting, him listening intently.

"Nothing," he whispered. "Bad tactics, to warn two agents in a hide."

"That was a warning?"

"All three of us as pretty targets, lead sprayed everywhere, and only Cal winged by a ricochet? Maybe it was bad luck, I don't know."

Her fingers were numb cold. "God."

"Don't worry. The angle was wrong to hit you. Mostly." His gloved fingers tensed, massaging the back of her neck.

Oh, that's so comforting. The little movement of his fingers did comfort her, though. "Great. Reese?"

"Hmm?"

"Do you... Cal. How did he even get here?"

"By asking himself what he'd do if he was me. If he had to keep someone safe."

"And just like that, he found you?"

"He had files detailing my domestic jobs." A little tension now, invading him bit by bit. Would she have noticed it before?

Domestic jobs? "I don't even want to know." But she

did, she realized. She wanted to know who this man was. The hoarse, gentle voice while she writhed with fever, or a killer?

Oh, sure, he had all sorts of euphemisms for it, and Cal probably did, too. It hadn't hit her before, but getting shot at was probably a good way to concentrate your mind, right? She was in the dark, being hugged by a man who had probably committed murder.

Not probably, Holly. Definitely. The vision of two shapeless lumps on her apartment floor, mercifully darkened like everything before she woke up this morning seemed to be, hit her again. It had been so much easier when nothing mattered.

"Sooner or later, you will." He actually sounded a little sad. "I'm a monster, Holly. But at least I'm on your side."

Well. That's one way to put it. "I don't think you're a monster." *Even if he's killed people, Holl? Really?* "Why are we down here?"

"Because this is another way out. We'll surface a couple klicks from the cabin."

"In the middle of the woods."

"Have some faith in me, baby." His breath was warm in her hair.

I'm not screaming and running away. "Have you… Reese, have you killed people?" *Well, duh, obviously.*

"I served my country." Harsher, now, and he let go of her. Not all the way—he reached down, and his fingers were a loose bracelet on her wrist. "That was part of the deal."

"Did you…do you *like* doing it?"

"What?" Baffled now. He stepped back, and she

wondered if he could see in the dark. "No. Sometimes I had to. But I don't kill children."

"You didn't—"

"Let's go." He set off into the darkness, and she had to stumble after him.

"Children? They...they asked you to hurt children?"

"They sit in offices and make decisions, and the agents do the dirty work. Maybe I shouldn't have tried to stay a little clean. You can hate me all you want."

"I don't—"

"Can you be quiet? I've got to hear what's going on topside."

Can you? She strained her own ears, but heard nothing but heartbeats and her own ragged breathing, Reese's inhales smooth and deep, his exhales long and shallow.

If she made him angry, would he just abandon her? Then what would she do?

You're smart, Holly. You'd figure it out. After all, there was no cancer now. It was like living in a prison, then waking up suddenly to find yourself free in a sunny green field.

God, what I wouldn't give for some sunlight now. Life wasn't about what you wished for, though.

At least she'd learned *that* lesson on her own.

Holly set her chin and followed the tugging on her wrist forward, into the uncertain future.

Of course she'd start asking those sorts of questions now. He'd had all the grace he was allowed, and keeping her around wasn't going to be so easy from here on out. She had every right to run, and what did it say about him that he wasn't going to let her?

It was a long time down in the dark, judging their distance by counting his steps, and when Holly tried to pull away he clamped down on her wrist before he realized she was trying to hold his hand instead.

Why?

Still, with her gloved fingers laced into his, he felt better. Especially when she squeezed. It could have just been easier for her to keep her balance. It could have just been that she didn't want to be left in the dark.

What it probably *wasn't* was any other reason. *Did you kill people?* It was a question he'd been dreading. Was she regretting the other night with him now? Of course she would be.

She was clean, and he was anything but. Still, if he kept her safe, that was a way to balance it out, wasn't it?

Silence, except for her hurrying to keep up. She was much quieter now, not moving as smoothly as an agent, but a normal would think her eerily soundless. The feedback from heightened senses gave you a new baseline for careful. He'd have to teach her how to pass among normals, some of the basic lessons about controlling the autonomics, and other things.

Assuming she'd listen to him.

He slowed as he sensed the end of the steadily rising tunnel approaching. "Almost at the end," he murmured.

"We've been going up." Did she sound tentative? Of course, he'd snapped at her.

Way to go, soldier. "Yeah. The climb up isn't nearly as bad. You're doing great."

A half-choked laugh. "Really?"

Didn't sound like she believed him.

"I'm sorry, Holly. I'm on edge. And I didn't think anyone would find us."

"Maybe they didn't, maybe they followed Cal."

"Don't know yet."

"But you trust him?"

"Only provisionally." *And not with you.*

"Why would they just shoot to warn him?"

"Don't know that they did."

"What *do* you know?"

"Where we're going, what we're going to do and that I'm not going to let anything happen to you."

She was silent. Probably didn't believe him. He had time to change her mind, though. Didn't he?

I hope so.

The end came a little sooner than he'd expected. Fortunately he didn't walk into the goddamn ladder to top everything off. "Okay. We'll climb a bit. There's rest platforms. How are you feeling?"

"Like I just got shot at." A little unsteady. "Like I lost all my clothes. Again."

He squeezed her fingers, gently, before loosening his hand. "I'm sorry, Holly." *And I am. But not enough to let you go.*

"I know."

There was nothing to say to that, so he just pulled her forward, let her find the ladder rungs. "You go up first."

"In case I fall?"

"Yeah."

"You'd catch me?"

"I'd do my best. Or I'd fall with you."

"Oh." Slight sounds—the tips of her boots scraping, hitching against a rung—broader and better anchored than the ones at the other end. She said nothing else, and the tang of iron determination to her marvelous, still-intensifying scent reached in and yanked on something in his gut.

And a little lower. Holly was outright goddamn amazing.

Reese shook his head, waited for her to get a little farther up and began climbing after her.

The rest platform at the top wasn't big enough for both of them, but he braced one foot on the wall behind him, across the tunnel and had a tricky few moments feeling around for the release switch, Holly trapped between him and sheer rock with her feet firmly planted on the iron strip. The close quarters might even have added something if she hadn't been trembling, her breath shorter and shorter and her pulse spiking.

The dark didn't sit well with her. Either that, or reaction to the last few hours was setting in. Could be both. "It's all right," he breathed in her ear. "In a little while we'll be safe and warmed up, and this will be just a memory."

His fingers found the plastic cover; he flipped it up and keyed in the code by feel. If that didn't work there was the killswitch, but luck was with him and there was a low hum. A creaking sound, and he braced himself a little more tightly before lifting his hands to the wheel overhead. No ice, because the exit was just below ground level and incrementally warmed by the same geothermals, so he only had to swear once to get the entire thing moving. A thin crack of light appeared, and Holly's sobbing breath of relief made something in him relax slightly.

"Upsy-daisy, sweetheart."

He watched her going up into the dim light, and when

she finally cleared the entrance he followed. It was, he thought, pretty goddamn symbolic. If there was any light to head for, she was the only one who knew where it was. All he could do was stagger after her.

It looked like a manhole cover in the middle of a shack of a shed that was nevertheless nicely weather-proofed on the inside. A dusty window, one pane rubbed clean, let in pale tree-filtered sunlight through festoons of cobweb.

Wait, a clean pane? That was wrong.

He cleared the entrance and hopped sideways, but not fast enough. A pop, a spear of ice buried in his left glute.

Holly stood with her back to the wall, staring, dead white, hair mussed, and beautiful. He opened his mouth to tell her to run, but whatever was loaded in the tranquilizer dart was potent enough to knock out an agent, and he fell sideways into darkness still trying to say her name.

He'd left orders for Three to wake him up, but it was his phone that did the service instead, buzzing and blurring in his pocket so hard Bronson thought there was a tiny animal in there coming after his family jewels. He jolted out of dreaming, his overworked heart thundering, and for a sleep-fogged second he was back at Shah-i-Kot again, dust in his hair and the stench of gunfire, blood, offal, more dust kicked up by explosives…

Goddammit. She was supposed to wake me up. The phone glowed, spectral in the dimness, and it was a buzz from Control probably asking for updates.

Well, the old man could wait. Bronson was the boots on the ground, and Control had to expect he sometimes didn't have time for little chats.

The worn leather couch he'd been napping on creaked as he hauled himself up. *What I wouldn't give for a nip of bourbon right now.* Washing his face with cold water, swiping his graying hair back, not looking in the mirror any more than he could help it. The blood-shot eyes, the indifferent skin—once he'd been hand-some, but not anymore. He shambled back to the desk, pressed the call button to summon Three and yawned as he rubbed at his eyes again.

A few minutes later, irritated, he shrugged into his suit jacket, slid the phone into his breast pocket and strode for the soundproofed door. He unlocked it with a muttered curse and threw it open, intending to bellow for Three. Instead, the sight of Noah Caldwell, grinning like a maniac and just lifting his hand to knock, greeted him. The major was in fatigues, and he positively reeked of cold, fresh air and gasoline. His baby blues sparkled, and behind him came Three, a high blush in her cheeks from the cold, shouldering a rifle Bronson most definitely hadn't cleared for her use.

"What the hell is this?" Bronson snapped.

"We got them!" Caldwell all but clapped his hands like a three-year-old. "I had Three here calculate routes and vectors. We locked onto them and spooked them, then drove 'em into nets. We've got them all—Six, and Eight, and the woman. She's a damn Gemina. Control will be—"

"You took Three off the rez." *You little prick.* "Do you know what Control's going to do to you when he finds out?"

Caldwell shrugged. His grin faded, but the smug-ness didn't. "Control wanted all assets in place to be turned toward solving the problem. And it's better than you were doing. *Sir*."

For a moment he wasn't sure he'd heard the man right. Maybe it was the smugness, maybe it was sleep-fog, maybe it was Bronson's phone buzzing again in his pocket—this time it didn't feel like a tiny little animal, it felt like a set of tiny claws digging into the top left of his chest.

Maybe it was Three, behind Caldwell, simply studying him as if he was some kind of rare bug. She was in a parka with a fur-lined hood and fatigue pants instead of a skirt and blazer, and they looked good on her, covering up the skinniness. The bags under her eyes were gone; Caldwell had probably ordered her to eat and change her clothes.

Caldwell had probably made sure she had clothes to change *into*. The major was muscling in. Control was already looking to cut deadweight loose, and the big man would be a fool if he hadn't given the little boy a set of orders concerning his immediate superior.

This doesn't look good. Especially not for Ma Bronson boy's Ritchie. "You took a valuable asset off without—" he began.

The major actually *shrugged*. At *him*. At Rich Bronson, who had been here from the beginning. "Three, why don't you rack that and get cleaned up? There's fresh kit prepared for you. We'll debrief over breakfast."

The woman didn't even look at Bronson. She simply said, "Yes, sir," in her usual colorless tone, turned on her heel—even the boots were new—and glided away.

Oh, no, you don't, you pipsqueak. "So, you're the big man now? You're thinking you can—"

"Shut up, Dick." He even said it kindly. "You were making a huge mess of things—I'm going to report as much to Control. Time for you to go out to pasture, old man."

Sonofa... Rich Bronson stepped forward, his fist flashing out. He was old and fat, true, but he'd been a boxer long ago, and he still moved with some lumbering grace. There was a satisfying *crunch*—the major's profile was never going to be Grecian again, and that was just fine. Caldwell's head snapped back, and there was a gusher—bright blood, he'd definitely broken the little snot's nose.

"Now you listen to me," Bronson snarled, shaking his hand out. "I'm still in charge here, until Control arrives himself. I don't take orders from you, and God help me, after I finish talking to Control, you'll be busted down to scrubbing toilets in Leavenworth. Get out of my sight."

He shouldered past the man, stalking for the conn rooms. Time to do some damage control, but first, he was going to tie up a few loose ends. Maybe Caldwell would be one of them.

Had Bronson turned around, he might have seen the major staring at him, bright hate in those already-puffing blue eyes, blood dripping on his uniform from his broken nose and a wide, unsettling smile on those thin lips.

They put a hood over her head, but she could still hear—and smell—just fine. Washed-out scents unlike Reese and Cal's, but male all the same. Metal, pepper, wax—*soldier*, she thought, and a chain of memory detonated inside her head. Her father's uniform, spray starch, nylon webbing, the odor of guns that hung on him when he came back from the range. His aftershave, always with the faint tang of sweat. Engine oil and grease on his callused fingers.

Her father in the hospice bed, and the thin line of the EEG. *Brain death.* He'd fought the cancer hard, but in the end, it hadn't been enough. Nothing in her father's life had been enough.

Oh, Daddy.

There were at least a dozen of them. She stayed limp, not giving them any reason to manhandle her. They weren't brutal, just businesslike, and her arms ached from when she'd struggled, trying to avoid the handcuffs. At least she wasn't cuffed behind her back—that would have been worse.

It had taken more than three of them to overpower her. Even if she wasn't as strong as Reese, there was something to be said for pure desperation.

Metal against their boots, she was carried like a sack of potatoes. They were all nervous, a high rasping edge scraping against her nerves.

Stairs. Her head bumped as she lolled, slung between two of them. Maybe nobody wanted to firemancarry her.

Think, Holly.

The helicopter, hearing military jargon yelled back and forth over the thrum of the rotors. Thin copper thread of blood—she'd scratched and kicked, and one of them had hit her with something that felt suspiciously like a rifle butt. It could have broken her neck, she supposed. She was lucky.

Turns, as they moved along a corridor that echoed

like bare cement. Left, right, two rights, a left. She counted them, wishing her head wasn't spinning so badly. Lost track, restarted. If she got a chance...

What would Dad do? He didn't talk about the war, so she had to guess. He would have known some trick, for when you were captured by the enemy. *Be smart, Holl,* he would always say. *There's my smart girl.* How proud he'd been when she graduated from community college, cradling her diploma in his worn-down hands on the hospice bed. *My smart, smart girl.*

He had loved her, she realized. He'd probably been just as scared as she was, and tried not to show it. Maybe he hadn't been cold at all.

Just terrified.

Finally, a pause, as someone jangled little bits of metal. Soft electronic tones—a keypad, and there was the *chuk* of a heavy lock thrown.

"Rendition?" One of the soldiers, very young from the sound.

"No fun with this one." Older, with the snap of command. "Just set her down."

"What *is* this place?"

"Best not to ask, soldier. Come on, we have to chemwash. Could be biologicals."

A low, collective groan. She was dropped unceremoniously into a chair, and the jolt made her teeth click together painfully. They trooped out, the door closed, and she bent forward, trying to lift her hands high enough to yank the hood free.

It took a little work, since the cuffs at her wrists were chained to the ones at her ankles, but she managed. Just as she did, there was a soft whoosh—another door opening. Light stung her eyes—fluorescents, buzzing and hideous. Tiled walls, a table and two chairs. A man strode in—no uniform, just a dark suit and a maroon tie, sharp-shining shoes and combed-over strings of hair trying to hide a glistening bald patch.

Her hair was full of static, so she was shaking her head and trying to blow the strands free when he laid the by now depressingly familiar manila file folder on the long, polished table. A reek of cigarette smoke and English Leather cologne, a greasy layer of fried food. Smelled like a French dip and fries, with ketchup instead of au jus. Lots of fat, and grease, and an acrid note that said he didn't wash as thoroughly as he could.

Eww. She was hard put to restrain a shudder.

Behind him, a woman. Black turtleneck, black skirt, black blazer, a pair of sensible black pumps with grippy soles. Blond hair scraped back in a tight ponytail, her hazel eyes flat and dead, she moved very economically. No motion wasted. She didn't smell washed-out, though—her scent was blue, like those smelly markers you got in elementary school. The blueberry ones, nothing like real blueberries at all but instantly recognizable.

She smelled, oddly, like Cal.

The real shock came when the man settled himself in the other chair. The woman stood by the door, arms folded. She would have been pretty except for the complete lack of expression, a doll's set stare. The small gold hoops in her ears, the ruthlessly short but buffed nails and the hair all said *businesswoman*—one who would leave a precisely calculated tip just short of insulting. Nothing would be *wrong* with the service, but a slight lift of her eyebrow would tell you that she had judged your effort and found it wanting.

You would have to look a little closer to catch a

glimpse behind that flat gaze, the subtle tension that shouted *hurt*.

She's like Reese. Like me. What did they do to her?

"Ms. Candless." The man with the fried-food aftershave had obviously decided it was time to pontificate. "You've had an exciting week."

Holly's stomach lurched. *I know that voice.*

The last time she'd heard it, she'd been drugged out of her mind.

It probably wasn't the best idea to start talking, but she couldn't help herself. "It was you." *I sound like I've been punched.* "You told them to kill me in my own house."

His pitted face—if he ate French dip enough to reek like he did, no wonder he had bad skin—pursed up like she'd made an embarrassing bodily noise. "The situation was…complex."

"You told them to murder me."

"Well, they died for it. Did Agent Six kill them, or did you?"

She opened her mouth to tell him she'd been too busy trying to stay conscious enough to breathe, but recognized the trap just in time. *Agent Six. That must be Reese.* She pursed her lips instead, just like his prissy little frown, and simply glared at him.

That made him even more sour, if that were possible. Really, he smelled awful. "You also gave our seizure team quite a bit of trouble."

They shot Reese with something. Neither of us smelled them—they were covered in something weird. Was Reese even still alive? Even if he was, Holly was on her own.

Could the other woman smell her, too? Would being infected make her more valuable? Should she tell them?

"Now. You've become very much a liability, Ms. Candless. You are now property of the United States government, and we expect your full cooperation."

Is that the royal we? Holly glanced at the woman by the door. She hadn't moved. She was barely even breathing. Her forehead glimmered a little under the assault of fluorescents. Her skin looked polished, it was so flawless. Not a divot, not an old zit or a rough patch.

Bitch. Holly sagged in the hard wooden chair. She couldn't even pretend this was a bad dream. It was too real, right down to the splatter of dried blood on the back of the man's hairy hand as he picked up the file, tapping it against the table as if to straighten the contents. Was there even anything in there? It looked suspiciously thin.

Holly found her voice again. "Whose blood is that?" *If it's Reese's...no, it can't be. It just can't.*

He frowned a little, muddy-brown eyes narrowing. It was the woman who spoke, instead. Contralto, very flat, somewhat breathy...and terribly familiar, again.

"Sloppy, sir." She didn't move, and the sheen on her forehead had to be sweat.

It was the woman who had called Holly *collateral*.

Everything in the room slowed down to nightmare speed. Even the air thickened, and a spike of pain went through Holly's temples to add to the growling in her stomach and the aches all over her.

Something was about to happen.

The man didn't notice. He merely looked at the back of his hand with that same small frown, like there was a tiny, interesting insect crawling there. Then he sighed and tapped the file one more time. "Three, I think this loose end needs to be tied up."

"It does, sir." The woman's tone was just as flat, and she moved so fast she almost blurred. The spike inside Holly's head gave one last twist, and blood spattered across the tabletop and the manila file.

If he hadn't been burning off the trank, he would have killed the bastards before they even got close.

As it was, he was slack-jawed and slow when the black copter descended. Some of the soldiers even wore a fading ghost of Holly's scent, or maybe he was just high on whatever they'd shot him with. Confusing smells whirling inside his head, walls coming down, everything unsteady and whirling.

He was in the home again, sitting in the green plastic chair in the room he shared with Tommy Flisk and George Octonok. George was a Polack, and his lazy eye wandered; Tommy was a klepto and a talker, too. Kept muttering about setting the night on fire, and Reese was smart enough to know that was a Bad Sign even if it didn't mean anything Antisocial. So Reese just sat staring out the window, institutional fried food a lump in his stomach and his brain a mess of fuzzed yarn, rocking back and forth and humming to keep the chaos outside from spilling in.

A jolt, a snap, and he found he was in restraints, his shoulder almost dislocating with a crack of blue pain as he worked his arm loose. You could yank yourself out of cuffs if you didn't mind losing a little skin; zips were bad but they'd taught him things, oh, yes, they had.

Teach a dog to dig, and he goes and digs.

Where was she? Tranked him up—was she collateral? Or was she taken—insurance to make him behave?

Motion. The world was spinning.

A gush of cold sweat all over him, the drug metabolizing all at once. The little bastards in his bloodstream were just eating it up. Did they like the various things the tolerance tests stuffed them with? They ate everything. Booze didn't dent them, smoke didn't slow them down.

They've killed her.

Dark. It was dark, and there was a metal shelf underneath him. For a second he thought he was in the passage again, leading her along, her gloved fingers tight in his.

You're real to me. Really real.

No, he was in the stockade. High lockdown, cuffed and stuffed. Blinking, unable to clear the grit from his eyes because his hands were tied down. He was working one hand free, the grease of blood filling his nose with red rage.

Someone else was bleeding, too.

The dark was almost complete, but he heard another heartbeat. A harsh acridity—someone else metabolizing the drug. It wasn't Holly.

Reese cleared his throat. He still had to try twice before the word would slip loose. "Cal?"

A heavy slurred mumble in reply. *"No, Trace, don't gooooo..."*

It was Cal. They were in the same boat.

Great. The chains meant to hold wrists to ankles made a soft slithering as he moved a little, testing his body's responses.

Concrete walls, more sensed than seen. The only

light a faint gleam under the heavy barred door. Two metal shelves they would call bunks and charge the poor bastard in the stockade for using. They did things like that to keep you indebted. *Free* was a politician's word, meaning whatever they wanted it to mean and losing all importance when they decided they wanted it to.

The restraints at his ankles took a little more work. Cal had stopped moving, and his breathing had changed. They'd dosed Reese hard, but it was already mostly worn off. He tasted salt, metal, grit and a fading ghost of Holly all over his damp clothes. They'd dragged him through the snow, the bastards.

Cal began moving. Reese worked on his ankles. By the time he got them loose, almost slicing his fingers on sharp metal, Cal had his own hood off.

"Location?" Cal whispered.

South, probably. Arizona? There's installations there. "Dunno."

"They got her?"

"Guess so." *What was your first clue?* Sarcasm was useless, no matter how much it might have made him feel better.

"Then they're dead," Cal said, quietly. "What's our plan?"

Why don't you come up with one? There was a wad of nasty, hairy mucus in his throat; he hawked and spat as quietly as he could and immediately felt better. Probably some leftovers from the drug. He felt at his aching shoulder, hot even through his clothes—healing up. That was good. "Door."

"What?"

Holly probably would have understood immediately. Reese inhaled, deeply, pushing the rage down. *If they've hurt her*... Except he was the one who had dragged her into this. "Getting the door open."

"That first one's a lulu." Cal's short, ironic, half-swallowed laugh wasn't loud enough to be heard outside the room. They were probably being recorded.

Reese found out he didn't care. Where there was a will, there was a way. He'd figure out how to get that door open—or he'd find a way to overpower whoever came through it and keep going until he found Holly.

Or her body. That's what you're afraid of, isn't it?

He told that little voice inside his head to shut up and began to examine the room, holding his stretched shoulder. His hands were bloody and missing some flesh. That might compromise his effectiveness, but—

He froze. So did Cal, who had slithered off his own bunk and begun his own examination of the cell.

There. "You hear that?" Reese whispered.

Cal's wolfish grin was a gleam in the darkness. "Visitors."

The place was huge, full of concrete tunnels either badly lit or glare bright, and it smelled awful. The woman—*Trinity*, she'd said, her mouth pulling into a bitter line, *you might as well call me that*—went ahead, halting and cocking her head whenever she heard someone approaching. Holly did her best to move silently in Trinity's wake, stepping with exaggerated care so her new boots didn't squeak. At least her feet were dry.

Well, dryish.

She was surprised she wasn't aching all over as well as stumbling, but her body seemed to know what to do. She was even further surprised when the woman began to talk to her, in that flat mechanical tone. "Odds are they've been transported already, which will up our chances of escape. Do you have ID?"

What? "I, um, have my driver's license. Reese said not to use it, he told me what to say if… Why?"

"Because I need to know what to do with you," was the crisp, flat answer. Trinity's back was ballet straight under her blazer, and those sensible flats had thick soles that didn't dare squeak. Cold and contained, and her expression hadn't changed when she slammed the man's head down onto the tabletop, breaking his nose and spreading blood everywhere. The man with the fried-food smell might even be dead, that's how hard his skull had hit, and Holly's stomach was queasy just thinking about the sound it had made.

She waited, but Trinity said nothing more. *God, she's just like Reese.* "Are you…you're one of them. An agent."

"Infected. Like you. And yes, they…trained…me."

"For…liquidations?" *I'm getting the hang of the lingo. Great for me.*

"Planning, not execution. They think a woman can't kill." Trinity chose lefts and rights almost at random, but one thing remained constant: they were going down.

Oh, God. "Can you?"

"I believe so." Calmly. "If I have to. How do you think I got here?"

Do I really want to know? "You're…working with Cal?"

"Cal? Oh, Eight. No. They lost him in Boulder, until we got another ping on Six, cross-checking one of his old jobs."

"Six?"

"Your infector."

That's one way of putting it. "He didn't mean to."

"Probably not." She didn't turn around, but Holly felt her attention sharpening. "It doesn't matter. He's high value, they'll see if they can make him play."

Uh-oh. "How?"

"Six was their poster boy. Amped mission fidelity, low emotional noise, everything. If it wasn't for a doctor going insane and trying to kill him, he'd still be working, probably hunting down the agents who went off the rez."

"Off the rez?"

"AWOL. Native. Off the grid."

"Okay." *What is it with these people and the euphemisms?* "He said they might be shutting the program down."

"I do not think it likely. Too useful, even with infection vectors. The infected die out, except for the Geminas."

"Geminas?"

"The complementary ones. Agents lock on, infect the Geminas and have a complete break. They vanish." She sniffed the breeze, a queerly animal movement. Any second now she was going to freeze like a cat, one paw in the air, then go bounding off chasing a ball of yarn.

She even *smelled* like a cat—dry, healthy, with a tang of oil. It wasn't unpleasant, but it wasn't as nice as Reese. As a matter of fact, it reminded her of Cal even more strongly. "Vanish. Okay. Look, why are you even—"

"You're a *civilian*." Disdainful, as if that explained everything. Maybe for her, it did.

Yes, if she was still waiting tables, Holly would definitely peg her as a businesswoman, expecting prompt service and leaving that tiny, precisely calculated tip. No *please* or *thank you*, just that slight judgmental eyebrow lift. She smelled like she worked out, too, an undertone of supple muscles and a faint whiff of habitual exertion.

Another tang, shifting and elusive. It was distracting, to get all this information through the nose. How did Reese handle it?

You smell…good.

The intense color at the bottom of Trinity's scent was odd. Like those scented markers in grade school, the blueberry ones. Holly finally realized what it was. "Why are you sad?"

"I'm not." Trinity kept marching straight ahead. "Not happy, either. I don't feel anything, since the induction. I calculate."

That's so not comforting. Induction? "So what equation am I part of?"

Trinity stopped at a metal door painted with red stripes. Looked like a stairwell entry, and it had the same funny little number pad all the other ones in this hall had. There was no sound as she pressed the keys—3-7-5-2-8—with little taps, but a *chuk* sound broke the hush and she pushed the door open with a quick glance and a sniff to make sure it was safe.

"You're not. I've simply decided to pursue this course, Ms. Candless. I saw how they were willing to have you suffocated in your own bedroom because someone didn't want to sign extra paperwork." A slight pause as they stepped into a dimly lit stairwell that reeked of cigarette smoke. A toilet flushed in the distance, and Holly almost flinched guiltily.

"I started calculating chances," Trinity continued,

"of them liquidating me the same way sooner or later. *That* is why I'm bothering now. Please be quiet, I have to concentrate."

Holly's internal clock had taken a bit of a beating lately, but it felt like almost an hour later when Trinity stopped dead, holding up her left hand just in case Holly didn't get the message. Her right hand reached across her body, quick as a snake, and she drew a very nasty-looking dull black gun. Trinity pointed, and Holly obligingly flattened herself against the wall at the precise spot indicated.

The other woman stood very still, listening so intently Holly held her breath as if to help. The hall was full of echoes—stealthy faraway footsteps, a sudden impalpable charge of urgent electricity.

"Damn," Trinity breathed. Even that word didn't have any inflection; it was just as dry and precise as the rest of her. "Bad news."

You know, I think I'm beginning to dread those two little words, but who doesn't? "Which is?" The concrete wall behind her was repainted so many times the gray-green was slick under her fingertips, an institutional carapace.

"Bronson must have a very thick skull."

Who? "Bronson? Oh, the man you—"

"I should have snapped his neck, but I thought Caldwell…it doesn't matter. Next time I'll calculate better."

There might not be a next time, if what I'm hearing is them discovering we're roaming around. "So now what?" A sudden realization hit her. *Wait a second.*

Six and Eight. "You're Three. All those numbers. Not names."

Trinity turned her head very slowly, and now she had an expression. Dull rage stained her cheeks with a sudden flush, and Holly watched, fascinated, as the color faded and the face became a doll's mask again.

"I *was* Three," she said. "Now I'm Trinity. Please don't call me the former."

God. "I'm sorry." Holly swallowed, dryly. "I won't."

"Good." Trinity set off down the hall again, this time at a quicker pace. "Come on."

They rounded another corner, and Holly stopped so quickly she swayed, her nostrils flaring. *Wait. Is that...* "Reese. I smell him."

Trinity took a deep whiff. "Interesting. Why would they be held here? It doesn't compute. Unless…"

"Unless what?"

"It's more bad news."

"Tell me."

"Generally hostiles are held here, until they're interrogated, or…"

"Or?" *I hate pulling this crap out of people, come on!*

"Restructured through induction, but that liquidates the males. Perhaps they wish to test the Gemini males?" She shook her head, slightly. "Not enough data. The only other reason would be simple liquidation."

"You mean *killing*. We can't let them—"

"Not our problem at this point," Trinity muttered, but another expression crossed her face. This one was odd, as if she was straining to recall the lyrics to a long-ago song. "Odd. There's two agent tracks. I wonder…"

"Reese *and* Cal? It's got to be. They *are* our problem." Her heart leaped at the thought. "We have to rescue them."

"Rescue two fully trained liquidation agents, seventy percent chance of them drugged into insensibility? Oh, that's a marvelous idea. They're probably beyond rescue by now, and the chances of getting away ourselves would go down." A faint tinge of sarcasm. Still, Trinity hesitated, her face changing by another millimeter or two.

A faint, rhythmic stamping began. It grew in volume, and Holly realized it was booted feet. Men. At least six of them. Heading straight for them, from a corridor to the left. "They're coming."

"The best exit is this way. If we find the agents along the way, that will alter the calculations. But—"

It was at that point Holly lost her temper. "Look, I don't *care* about the calculations. It's Reese and Cal. We have to help them. If you won't, I'll do it myself." *Even though I have no idea where I am—but you know what? I can follow my nose, maybe I can move as fast as Reese, and... I'll figure something out.*

My smart girl, her father whispered inside her head.

Trinity shrugged. "They're probably in the A5 cellblock. A dead end. The timescale is—"

"Which way?"

"What?"

"Which way? To this cellblock."

Trinity pointed, and Holly set her chin, squared her shoulders and set off.

Reese's shoulder was a ball of hot red pain, but he stayed still, wedged into the corner of the cell. The socks were too slippery, so he'd shed them, and the soles of his feet gripped the wall as his fingertips used a faint lip in the concrete to keep him aloft. A good core workout, but he could have done without it. Cal, his sweat full of that damn trank burning off, was opposite him, jammed into the other corner, holding himself there with sheer will. The cell door groaned and drew aside, clattering, and the lead for the team outside looked in, a yellow beam from his flashlight playing over the two empty metal bunks. "For God's sake," the leader snarled, "is this the right room?"

"Got to be," someone else said. "Right on the sheet, A-54."

Come on, Reese prayed, his feet slipping by millimeters as he strained, silently, his own acrid sweat stinging as it dripped into his eyes. *Give me something here. Get curious. Where did we go?*

Cloth moving. "Can't have vanished—" The dumb jerk covering the door opening made his first mistake, edging inside the cell as the flashlight beam played around the shadows underneath the bench.

Reese dropped, light as a cat, and then it was a blur, bones snapping and a spray of blood from the one whose nose he broke with a quick hand-heel up, dropping his center of gravity immediately afterward to power through the doorway, Cal landing behind him and the greenstick crack of a neck breaking. Slapping the gun aside, smelling refried beans and pico de gallo on the backstop guy, cheap beer and good steak on another, their uniforms familiar and strange at the same time. A highly trained transport team had a good chance against two tranked, restrained agents—had they expected him and Cal to still be zoned?

The leader managed to squeeze off a shot that whined

and ricocheted down the hall before Cal was on him, the
other agent silent and economical, a strike to the throat
and subtracting the gun as the leader folded down, and
between the two of them, they had just killed four men.
True blue American patriots, no doubt. Just following
orders.

Had one of them shot Holly? Or had that pleasure
been reserved for a higher-up? Was she still alive?

She'd better be.

The only sound was their breathing and soft rustles
as the agents canvassed the bodies for gear. Boots that
fit, still warm, a piece of luck. Ammo, service guns, a
crackling walkie-talkie—someone would get nervous
and start looking for these guys soon.

Cal stiffened, his blond head coming up. His blue
eyes blazed, and the difference between this man and
the one who couldn't shut up back in the cabin was night
and day. Maybe he'd just needed someone to talk to.

Don't we all. Reese heard it too. Six sets of footsteps,
moving in doublequick, almost on them. Something else
nagged at him, but he didn't have time to figure it out.
He was already moving, Cal following to cover. The
gun in his hand was a good start, and a multiplicity of
targets meant that maybe he could neutralize and in-
terrogate one of them. First step was to find out where
he was, and the second…well.

Louder and louder, and he smelled adrenaline, determination, a chemical reek and the peculiar staticky
unsmell of men carrying live weapons. Jingles and little
creaks of gear. A cross corridor ahead, and if he and
Cal could reach it before they did, the ambush would
be simple to—

No.

He dug his heels in, hard. It couldn't be. He couldn't be that lucky.

Faint noise underneath the louder footsteps. Agent-strong, beautiful scents, both female, but one raised his hackles. The other had quite a different effect.

It was Holly. Riding some current of air that almost vanished, and everything in Reese collapsed for a moment before reforming in a different constellation.

"You smell that?" Cal mouthed. He'd stopped, too.

Reese nodded, and the impossible happened.

They surged around the corner at a run, two slim female figures, one all in black, skirt and very practical flats, her hair tied back in a too-tight ponytail and her scent rasping a little unpleasantly across his nose. The other, in an unzipped blue parka and still-damp boots, with a glory of mussed black hair, wild-eyed and fuming with fear and adrenaline, was Holly.

A shout behind them, echoing strangely, and the pop and zing of live fire.

Reese didn't remember the intervening space. He just *moved*, and Holly ran into him, her breath coming high and hard. She was whole, and alive, but both the women reeked of blood and exhaustion.

The other woman, holding a standard issue with the barrel down, moving smoothly and professionally, barely broke stride. "Incoming!" she barked, and Cal bolted straight for her. Weird—the new woman's smell almost vanished into a powerful burst of something from Cal, a blue-tinted wave that might have knocked Reese down if his anchor hadn't been in his arms, coughing as her eyes welled with tears that were probably, if Reese was lucky, at least partly relief.

"Come on!" the stranger said, but Cal grabbed her,

neatest trick of the week, and shoved her against the wall, almost knocking the gun out of her hand.

"Stay there," he snapped, and turned, his gun coming up.

Thank you, God. Thank you. But they weren't out of the woods yet.

Reese pushed Holly behind him and had bare seconds to brace himself before the first of the pursuers appeared.

Chaos. Bullets zinging, Reese yelled, "Get down!" and Holly stumbled aside, fetching up against the wall instead. Her cheeks were slick and hot, the pain in her head had vanished, and deep relief at seeing Reese— mussed and dirty, with blackened fingers and a pair of boots that looked hideously uncomfortable—turned her knees to jelly. Cal was similarly dirty and didn't even bother glancing at her, instead sinking to one knee and steadily aiming at the opening she and Trinity had just run through. Trinity raised her gun as well, sliding along the wall with oiled grace, and Holly realized what was going to happen.

The men chasing them were going to walk right into a shooting gallery.

Uh-oh. She snapped a glance back down the hall, impelled by a gleam at the edge of her peripheral vision.

Everything seemed to slow down. Later, she would wonder if it actually had, or if her newfound senses had played some trick of perception. Maybe she'd just found a cosmic pause button.

Trinity, Reese, Cal. They all wore the same expression—set and thoughtful, though Reese's expression shaded into worry, and Cal's into puzzlement. Trinity's was faintly puzzled, too, but a casual observer would probably just call it blank.

There was a slice of brilliance behind their little group. That gold was electric light, spilling out in a slowly widening scythe, and the shadow behind it filled Holly's throat with cold dread. She was suddenly, completely sure that the shadow belonged to a man with pitted skin and eyes cold and dark as leftover coffee. He would be holding a gun, and when he stepped out he would be able to fire down the hall, right at their unsuspecting backs. They were like fish in a barrel here.

Do something!

But what? What could she do?

I am so tired of being afraid. And another thought, at the same time, familiar and strange.

I want to live.

The shadow was growing closer, because she was running, her boot soles squeaking as a racket started up behind her. Pops and pings, a scream cut off on a gurgle, shouted obscenities.

It was him, the man with the bad skin. Everything on his face was puffing up, dried blood and bruising turning him into a leering grotesque. His mouth had opened, maybe surprised at walking into this chaos. He *did* have a gun, the same kind the others were carrying, and Holly's entire body went cold.

Because its ugly black mouth—and why did it look so big, she didn't have time to figure it out—was pointed directly at Reese's back.

Crunch.

Later she would be amazed that she could remember, very clearly, the sound of ribs snapping as she crashed into Bronson. The gun skittered away, an eye-searing flash as the shot went wide, and Holly realized she was screaming as they hit the ground in a tangle of arms and legs and a hot burst of blood from his wounded face, because her forehead had clipped his broken nose again.

For one blinding instant, she remembered the light shining in her eyes—the rest of the room was black in comparison, and her unresisting body had been strapped to a hard wooden chair. Their voices—Trinity's, Bronson's, someone else's—as they discussed what to do with her. The terse, low conversation as two men carried her up to her apartment, and Reese's face, pale and drawn as he pulled her up from the floor. *Holly? Holly, look at me.*

Reese in a chair, the scalpel bright as he dug something small and silver out of his hip, his face betraying nothing but distance. No pain, not even a wince.

This is probably the man who made him that way.

She thrashed, trying to get free of the tangle, and there was another sickening crack. The man's body sagged, and Holly, blinking, his blood on her face, stared up into Trinity's expressionless gaze.

The blonde woman had shot Bronson.

Next time, I'll calculate better.

Holly's stomach lurched, but Trinity stooped a bit, and her warm hand closed around Holly's. Trinity sank back, and Holly rose in a rush, her head spinning dangerously. They stood almost nose to nose, for a moment, and Holly had time to see a spark of…something… struggle to stay alive in the other woman's pupils.

The flash died. Trinity snapped a glance over her shoulder, her ponytail whipping. Then she was gone, past Holly and running, and she nipped neatly through the door Bronson had used before it closed with a dull, heavy, final thud.

"Holly!" Reese skidded to a stop, sliding a fresh clip of ammo into his gun. "Come on!"

But Trinity—

There was no time. Reese grabbed her right arm and pulled her along. When they passed Cal, the other man grabbed her left arm, and hanging between the two of them Holly didn't have to time to think about that awful cracking sound, the blood and Trinity's blank, horrified gaze.

Getting off a high-security base smack-dab in the middle of the desert was made fractionally easier by the fact that it was the middle of the night and the alarms hadn't started going off. The key fob Cal had plucked from a casualty's pocket matched a nice little sedan full of a ghost of drive-thru meals and the heavy smell of a man who wouldn't ever be eating another one again, Holly went in the backseat, and Cal drove sedately through the base, navigating by feel and instinct, until they found a gate. Flashing Bronson's badge got them through it, and as the klieg lights of the installation faded behind them, Reese could finally let himself sag in the seat, blowing out a long breath.

"She didn't give another name?" Cal asked, again. He couldn't let it go.

"Just Trinity. They called her Three, but she..." Holly's voice broke. Reese reached down to find the lever on the right side of the seat, hitting the seat belt's catch with his other hand. All the way back, and he could squirm into the backseat as Holly scrambled to make room. Cal let out a short, frustrated sound, but twenty seconds later the passenger seat was back up and Reese had Holly in his arms. Trembling, full of sharp fear-smell cutting through the rest of her glorious scent, she was still whole and alive. He buried his face in her hair.

"Christ." Cal snapped the radio on, flipping it to AM and searching through the bands for any news or emergency chatter. "Get a room, you two."

"God," Reese said around a mouthful of Holly's tangled hair. *"God."* True to form, his body wanted to prove she was alive another way, but that could wait.

Everything could wait. She was here, and alive, and everything else was just noise.

She shook like a leaf, but she wasn't crying. She just clung to him, and after a little while Cal cleared his throat. "I, uh, should probably split off from you guys and go find her."

What? Reese's brain started working again. "You think she's—"

"She smells good, Reese." Cal tapped at the steering wheel, once. "We have a freeway. Looks like Utah. Great. So, north or south?"

That was an easy one. "South." *Lost my damn backpack. Need liquid resources and fresh ID. Wonder if that place in Phoenix is still open?* "How good does she smell?"

"Good enough that I'm going to track her down." The other agent sounded very certain. "Ma'am, when we've had some time to calm down a bit, I'll ask you for everything she said that you can remember, all right?"

"She...she's..." Holly shook her head, and the movement against his chest made his entire body ache in the most frustratingly pleasant way imaginable.

"Not now," he said, nice and low and easy. "Not right

now. Just breathe, honey. Everything's okay. I'm here."
Lucky. So goddamn lucky.

"I th-thought you were d-dead." Maybe she was
going into shock. Her teeth were chattering. He hugged
her even harder.

"Not even close." *And even if I was, I'd come back
for you.*

"I hate to interrupt, lovebirds, but we have stuff to
do." Cal peered at the signs flashing by. "They'll be on
us as soon as Bronson's missed."

"Just keep going south. We need to get urban and
vanish."

"Right. Campgrounds around here, too."

"Start of winter. Might be a cabin or two."

"Want to risk it?"

"No. Installation this size has to have a hub near it."

"It's Utah. The hub might be a survivalist compound
full of polygamists."

"Then we'll deal. Does the glove box have a map?"

"I'm busy driving. *Sir.*"

And I'm busy. But he had a job to do. "Holly. Baby.
Be easy, okay? It's over. It's all over."

"N-no, it's not." But she wriggled away from him,
his arms suddenly cold without her breathing weight.
"We still h-have to escape." Her face was a pale smear
in the darkness, her eyes just a suggestion of glitter, but
he could see her chin lift a little and her shoulders go
back. It made his chest feel a little funny. Loose and
weird inside. "I'm all right."

Oh, Christ. Reese lost every battle he'd ever thought
of waging with himself, leaned forward, and kissed her.

She tasted like gunsmoke and citrus and adrenaline,
and everything that was good and beautiful and mad-

dening in the world. Her hands cupped his face, soft and
shaking just a little, and he fell into her for an eternity
before she retreated, breaking free with a low inquir-
ing noise that tightened every string in his body. She
rested her forehead against his, their breath mingled,
and Reese realized she wasn't the only one shaking.

He was, too.

I am never losing you again.

"Good God, you two." Cal rolled his window down,
and the roar of the slipstream married to a burst of sage-
scented, dusty desert chill filled the inside of the car.
"Quit making out on the job."

The next morning found them in a dusty, run-down
back end of Utah, a hotel that might have been flea rid-
den if it wasn't so goddamn cold. For all that, the cash
from the dead soldiers' wallets paid for a room, and the
water was hot. It was enough to keep them from freezing to death, and even though Reese and Cal should
have shared watches, he realized they hadn't when he
woke on one of the double beds, his arms around Holly
so tightly they ached. She was still out like a light, and
what had awakened Reese was Cal's soft movements.

The door shut, almost silently, and Reese took care
not to disturb her as he slid off the bed. They hadn't
even bothered with the bedspread, or taking their
clothes off.

Sleep was the best thing for her right now.

Outside, it was a desert sunrise, the bitter cold turning his breath into a plume, little curls of steam rising
from Cal's forehead as the other man stood staring at
the eastern horizon. The parking lot, cracks in the concrete a map of contract and expand, hosted a sprinkling

of older cars. The dusty Ford sedan fit in perfectly, but it needed new plates. They should have taken care of that last night.

Oh, well. He got tired of waiting for Cal to start talking, for once. "Leaving so soon?"

"Got to find me that girl. Trinity." Stubble rasped as Cal rubbed at his face. "And you've got to stash that one somewhere safe."

Believe me, I will. "And then what?"

"I don't know."

Silence. The sun, just peeking over the horizon, was a smear of crimson, faint scattered clouds taking on a rosy blush. A red dawn.

Finally, Cal spoke again. "You were right not to trust me."

There was a lot that statement could mean. Reese waited, his shoulders tightening fractionally.

"Heming tried to get me, then they nabbed me when they killed Tracy. Bronson sent me out to get you. Figured it took one to catch one, and he convinced himself I wanted to be back in the agency's good graces. Some of the files were doctored, but I managed to grab others, too. I had agency support until the storm hit, then I dug the tracker out of my hip and I thought…well. So they had leads on you up to Boulder. From there all they had to do was run a sweep with travel parameters, and they probably… I don't know. I'm…sorry."

The chill was all through Reese now. The cold of a mission, where an untrustworthy element had now been exposed. There were responses he could give—including tying Cal off. Then he'd have to hide the body and hustle Holly out of here.

For a moment he was back in the heat and the smoke,

the knife clattering on the floor, and the wide dark eyes of two children mixing with Holly's clear, beautiful gaze.

You're really real. To me.

What would a really real man do? He didn't know.

So, then, what would Holly do? Something idiotic, like not killing this man.

Something *good*.

"You had your reasons." Reese's voice surprised him. Thoughtful, and even. "Are you going back into the program?"

"Oh, hell, no." The tension of readiness drained out of the other agent. Had he been expecting Reese to smoke him? "Division's got all the data. They'll make more. Maybe with less emotional noise. We're going to be obsolete."

And you say you're not good at long-range planning. "Loose ends."

"Yeah. You got a plan?"

Not even close. "It seems to me," Reese said, slowly, giving each word particular weight, "that there's a bigger chance of survival if we work together. And it's better for them, too."

"Them?"

"Holly. And… Trinity. You really think she's—"

"She smells good. Damn near knocked me sideways."

"I can relate." Christ, could he ever.

"You're going south?"

Reese nodded. "Come and visit when you've got that girl of yours. We'll see if we can't plan something."

"I suppose if I ask where, you'll just say figure it out.

I'll leave you the car—I'm sure there's something else around here I can bounce with."

"Good luck."

"You, too."

Another pause.

Finally, Reese turned, very deliberately presenting Cal with his back. By the time he stepped back through the door into the dark cave of a small sad motel room with dingy blue-striped wallpaper, Cal was gone.

He closed the door, locked it, and leaned against the inside, listening to Holly's steady, slow breathing. Lifted his hand, staring at the angry red flushes where he'd ripped flesh off escaping the restraints. They were fading, and his hand looked...solid.

Real.

For a moment he shut his eyes. In the darkness, with only her breathing and his own, it was easier to think.

Let me, then. Let me be as real as she thinks I am. Never too late, right?

He hoped so.

When he opened his eyes, he found Holly had awakened. She sat on the bed, her eyes huge, her arms wrapped around her knees.

In two strides he was across the room. Another half step and he was on the bed, and her mouth opened under his. She tasted like night air, spice and softness, her breath tinged with pain and sleep and fear, the sudden spike of musk through her scent reassuring him that even if she wasn't happy to see him, even if she blamed him for getting her involved in this and shot at and almost killed, she wasn't immune to him. He could still get a response.

Was it enough to make her stay with him? Was he going to have to find something else?

He kissed a trail down to her vulnerable throat where her pulse beat, frantic strong. "Don't leave me," he whispered. "Holly, please. I'm sorry. Don't leave me."

"Reese," she whispered back. "Reese."

It wasn't an answer, but it was more than he'd hoped for. He forced himself to stop, to go still. "We've got to get out of here. Are you okay? You're hungry—we'll get something to eat… God, Holly. *God.*"

She blinked up at him. Still wide-eyed, her lips full and a little parted, ripened by the pressure. Just begging to be kissed again. "I'm okay. You…are you all right?"

"As long as you're with me, I'm fine."

Wonder of wonders, she smiled. It was a thin, wan expression, but better than nothing. "I'm with you. But, um, can I use the little girls' before we leave? And for God's sake, can I stop losing all my clothes?"

The tiny car inched forward, a small silver beetle in a line of other beetles, under a sky so brilliantly blue it was hard to remember the color was probably smog-induced. Holly took a deep breath. It felt weird to be wearing shorts, but it was a balmy seventy-five degrees and they were supposed to be a couple on their way to honeymooning over the border. The low-slung blue-silver sports car, bought for cash in Tucson, was no bigger than a postage stamp, but just the sort of thing two crazy newlyweds would take off in.

"Alice Hanson," she murmured. "Of course I didn't give up my maiden name. Alice Hanson. Thirty-six, Norbert, Iowa."

"Good girl." Reese's fingers were warm. The sunglasses hid his eyes, and his half smile was relaxed. His pulse didn't vary, nice and even, and she was learning to keep her own calmed down. It was funny, the degree of control you could exercise over your own body. She'd never thought anything like this was possible. "In a few hours I'll be knocking back beers, and you'll be in a bikini."

"Dream on. I haven't shaved my bikini line."

"I haven't shaved mine either."

Her chin dropped forward, and she smiled into her lap. "I wouldn't mind sitting by a pool. Can we…"

"Can we what?"

"Never mind." She swallowed dryly as the line of cars moved forward again. "What if they don't let us through?"

"We'd have more of a problem going north, babe. In a little bit we'll both have tans and won't stick out so much, though."

"Skin cancer."

"Not with the little bastards in the bloodstream taking care of things."

"Do you really think they would?"

"Christ, will you relax? You're a hypochondriac."

You couldn't even smell the cancer on me. "I am *not*." She squeezed his fingers, and he laughed.

The baked wind, freighted with dust and fried food, slid through the open window and touched Holly's bare knees. She could see the blue veins, a delicate network under the skin. The virus was pretty amazing—she could eat pretty much anything without the nausea now. She could run without getting winded. The headaches and exhaustion had gone away. "You should be nicer to them."

"To who, sweetheart?" He had the two passports—she didn't want to know where he'd gotten them. *Tricks of the trade*, he'd said, *I'll teach you later. For right now, leave it to me.* And the careful, finicky precision when it came to settling the photos in—*don't smile, they don't want you to.*

It was hard not to. "The virus. It helps us out, doesn't it? Saved my life, too."

"Mmh." Noncommittal, but that could be because the car in front of them moved again, and now she could see the guards in their tan uniforms. Their service revolvers glinted, and they looked hot, bored, uncomfortable. The border crossing looked a little more casual than she'd imagined—on the other side, there were street hawkers pressing close to the cars that crept through. Brighter colors than she was used to, fluttering pennants flirting with the warm wind, smoke-steam rising from food carts.

Holly let out a shaky breath. "I should be able to find a job. I can wait tables anywhere. Maybe I'll... I don't know. What are we going to do?"

"One step at a time. Let's just get past this, okay?"

"Okay." She couldn't help herself. Her stress hormones were rising—she could taste them, even though Reese was just the same. Not even his breathing changed. "Reese?"

"What?"

"What would happen if I vanished? Like Trinity?" *Since I'm deadweight you probably would do better without, even though the sex is great. I had no idea you could hold your breath that long, or that I was that flexible.*

"I'd find you."

"What if I didn't want to be found?"

"Are you saying you wouldn't? Now's a weird time to be having this conversation, Holl."

Well, there's never a good time for a conversation like this, ever. "Reese, come on. I'm just asking. If we have a fight or something—"

"I don't ever want to fight with you."

"I know you don't, but things happen. And…you might decide not to…that you don't…" The memories were sharper now—Phillip sitting in the kitchen. *I want a divorce, Holl.* Seeing him holding hands with the other woman at the hearings. Mixed in with that was the throat-clenching panic when she realized she wasn't alone in the small shed at the top of the tunnel's long darkness, and Reese's body slumping as he fell in slow motion—

"Holly. Breathe."

Her heart kept trying to hammer, but Reese's pulse, nice and slow, wouldn't let it. He squeezed her hand again, and when they pulled up to the border guards she was able to offer a smile to the one out her window. The man, stocky and sweat greased, passed a flat judgmental look over her hips and breasts, scanned her face and straightened as Reese engaged the one on his side with a serious expression and the passports, his hand never leaving Holly's.

The panic attack trembled just on the verge of breaking loose. Did she look nervous? Guilty? Something else?

Two stamps, a rill of liquid Spanish and braying male laughter, and Reese took the passports back. He wished them *buenas tardes* and gave a *gracias*, and then they were through. The hawkers clustered the car, but he kept going, creeping forward until they broke free of the press.

Reese let out a long breath. "We're through. Keep breathing."

"I'm fine." Panic retreated. "I'm sorry."

"Don't worry. It's all good. If you aren't at least a little nervous, they think you're hiding something." One hand on the wheel, and he was even driving differently now. The traffic wasn't gonzo, but still, other cars swooped a little too close for comfort as he navigated a tangle of streets that looked just the same as the ones on the other side of the border. It was hard to believe they were in a completely different country. A *limonada* stand on a corner sat in a bubble of ranchero music while Reese waited to join a roundabout's swirl, harsh sunlight glittering off paint and windows as the woman at the stand fanned herself and mouthed along to the song.

Reese was silent for a long time as he drove, until they had cleared the edge of the city and a long ribbon of dusty highway stretched before them. Cacti clustered on either side, and the bilingual signs were in different colors. "We'll make Santa Ana in an hour. I know a place. You can have your first real tequila there, too. That should settle your nerves some."

"I'm sorry." She might have given the whole thing away.

"Don't be. I'm not going anywhere, Holl. Sooner or later you'll get used to me."

"I already am," she said, and that shy, sweet smile of his came back. The knot in her stomach eased, and she settled on the seat and watched a different country roll by.

Two weeks later

From the balcony she could see the cathedral of glowing biscuit-colored stone, floodlit against the night. From here you could believe it wasn't Sinaloa, where people vanished so easily. Every time Reese left the expensive gringo hotel without her, she was on tenterhooks until he came back, and tonight was no different. The weather was beautiful, though he told her in summer it would be too humid to breathe. By then they would be somewhere else. For right now, though, they were in this quiet place with its courtyard full of frangipani and a murmuring fountain. There was a pool in the basement, and the food was incredible. Apparently one of Reese's identities was a gringo businessman who knew his way around, and tonight he was making contacts.

So when the sound came from the balcony, the curtains flowing white in the slow, highly scented wind, she leaped out of the chair, her water glass almost hitting the floor before her hand arrived to catch it. She was still getting used to her reflexes. Under the heavenly aroma from the courtyard came another thread of familiar scent, and Holly actually sagged with relief.

"It's just me," Trinity said, peering between the curtains. The only light was from the courtyard below and behind the slightly opened bathroom door, so she was a shadow among shadows, the vines growing up the building thick and juicy. She'd probably climbed them—there was a reek of sap and crushed green. "Nice place."

"Temporary." Holly straightened. "I'm glad you're okay. How did you—"

"Don't worry, nobody else could. I wouldn't have blown your hide." She was fearfully gaunt, and had dyed her hair to a washed-out chestnut. Her gaze was still flat and dark as ever. Jeans and a gray tank top, muscle moving smoothly on her tanned arms, the other woman took a cautious step inside. "I did have to wait until he left."

"Why?"

Trinity shrugged.

Oh, for God's sake. "So why are you here?"

"I…" A long pause. "I wanted to…check…on you. To see if you were hap—I mean, safe."

"I'm okay." Holly set the glass down on the mosaic-tiled top of the small table next to her chair. "I was just sitting here thinking about a book I left behind." *It was a great one, too. I can buy another copy, though.*

"I also…wanted to apologize."

"For?"

"He almost liquidated you." Trinity made a restless little movement. She really was awfully thin, almost as thin as Holly had been. "And…after that. If I had calculated better—"

She means Bronson. Holly quelled a shudder. "It's fine. Reese says Cal's looking for you."

"To tie me off, no doubt."

You guys and your euphemisms. It helped them, she supposed. If you could say *liquidate* instead of *murder*, *target* instead of *human being*, you were halfway to believing it wasn't such a big deal. "No. Just to talk to you. He said Cal—"

"It doesn't matter." Trinity took another half step into the room. "Tell Six that the program is shelved for now. They still have the data, though, and they will find out how to take emotional noise from the agents. When that happens, the orders for all of us won't be *capture*. They'll be *kill*."

Reese already thought about that. "I know. Look, we're safer if we stick together. You could stay with us. Another agent will help—"

"I am *not* a help." It was the first time her tone was anything but flat, and it was shocking. Trinity's lips skinned back from her teeth, a startling grimace. "They know it's possible to cut the emotional noise out, because they did it to me."

Well. That answers that. Induction, she said. I'd better tell Reese. "Then why are you here checking on me?"

The grimace vanished. Trinity stood, her weight balanced just so, and Holly sensed something. Maybe it was a subtle change in respiration, or something in the other woman's sweat, or maybe it was just the sure instinct that came with years of waiting tables and seeing people in every possible shape, size and mood while they ate, hearing their conversations and predicting the size of the tip. A hesitation, a struggle inside the other woman's contained, impenetrable shell.

"I had to." The words were almost lost under the susurration of the night's breeze. "I had to," Trinity repeated. "Perhaps my calculations are in error, and I am degrading. Be…safe, Ms. Candless. Goodbye."

"Trinity, wait—"

But the other woman was gone, stepping out onto the balcony. By the time Holly got there, she was just a fading smear of agent-strong scent, and it again reminded Holly powerfully of Cal's. Was that why he was looking for her?

Outside, the city growled, and a sharp spatter of gunfire sounded in the distance. The songs in this part of the country sang about the *narcos* and forbidden love, *corridas* and *muerte*. Was the violence any cleaner because it was out in the open?

Footsteps in the hall. She recognized them, and relief poured through her. The key in the lock, and she rushed to unbar the door—because here, you couldn't be too safe—and Reese's smile as he saw her was a balm. He stopped, his nostrils flaring, and she pulled him inside.

"Trinity was here. She just left. Reese, she's—"

"Good." His grin widened. "Cal's in town, too, honey. He's determined, I'll give him that much. Smarter than he thinks he is, too. Were you waiting up for me?"

"Of course. Reese—"

"Let me just be happy to see you, baby. We're moving on tomorrow." He barred the door and took her in his arms. "But that can wait. I, um, found you a ring."

What? "A ring?"

"Crap. I thought I'd get down on one knee, but I blew it. There's a place farther south, I know a priest—they're all Catholic here, I forgot to ask if you—"

Oh, good God. "You're asking me to marry you?"

"Well, we're running for our lives, I suppose I might as well, you kno—"

He might have said more, but by that time, Holly was kissing him, and for that night, at least, the outside world didn't matter.

* * * * *

Read on for a sneak preview of FATAL AFFAIR,
the first book in the FATAL *series by*
New York Times *bestselling author*
Marie Force

ONE

THE SMELL HIT him first.

"Ugh, what the hell is that?" Nick Cappuano dropped his keys into his coat pocket and stepped into the spacious, well-appointed Watergate apartment that his boss, Senator John O'Connor, had inherited from his father.

"Senator!" Nick tried to identify the foul metallic odor.

Making his way through the living room, he noticed parts and pieces of the suit John wore yesterday strewn over sofas and chairs, laying a path to the bedroom. He had called the night before to check in with Nick after a dinner meeting with Virginia's Democratic Party leadership, and said he was on his way home. Nick had reminded his thirty-six-year-old boss to set his alarm.

"Senator?" John hated when Nick called him that when they were alone, but Nick insisted the people in John's life afford him the respect of his title.

The odd stench permeating the apartment caused a tingle of anxiety to register on the back of Nick's neck. "John?"

He stepped into the bedroom and gasped. Drenched in blood, John sat up in bed, his eyes open but vacant. A knife spiked through his neck held him in place against the headboard. His hands rested in a pool of blood in his lap.

Gagging, the last thing Nick noticed before he bolted to the bathroom to vomit was that something was hanging out of John's mouth.

Once the violent retching finally stopped, Nick stood up on shaky legs, wiped his mouth with the back of his hand, and rested against the vanity, waiting to see if there would be more. His cell phone rang. When he didn't take the call, his pager vibrated. Nick couldn't find the wherewithal to answer, to say the words that would change everything. *The senator is dead. John's been murdered.* He wanted to go back to when he was still in his car, fuming and under the assumption that his biggest problem that day would be what to do about the man-child he worked for who had once again slept through his alarm.

Thoughts of John, dating back to their first meeting in a history class at Harvard freshman year, flashed through Nick's mind, hundreds of snippets spanning a nearly twenty-year friendship. As if to convince himself that his eyes had not deceived him, he leaned forward to glance into the bedroom, wincing at the sight of his best friend—the brother of his heart—stabbed through the neck and covered with blood.

Nick's eyes burned with tears, but he refused to give in to them. Not now. Later maybe, but not now. His phone rang again. This time he reached for it and saw it was Christina, his deputy chief of staff, but didn't take the call. Instead, he dialed 911.

Taking a deep breath to calm his racing heart and making a supreme effort to keep the hysteria out of his voice, he said, "I need to report a murder." He gave the address and stumbled into the living room to wait for the police, all the while trying to get his head around the image of his dead friend, a visual he already knew would haunt him forever.

Twenty long minutes later, two officers arrived, took a quick look in the bedroom and radioed for backup. Nick was certain neither of them recognized the victim.

He felt as if he was being sucked into a riptide, pulled further and further from the safety of shore, until drawing a breath became a laborious effort. He told the cops exactly what happened—his boss failed to show up for work, he came looking for him and found him dead.

"Your boss's name?"

"United States Senator John O'Connor." Nick watched the two young officers go pale in the instant before they made a second more urgent call for backup.

"Another scandal at the Watergate," Nick heard one of them mutter.

His cell phone rang yet again. This time he reached for it.

"Yeah," he said softly.

"Nick!" Christina cried. "Where the *hell* are you guys? Trevor's having a heart attack!" She referred to their communications director, who had back-to-back interviews scheduled for the senator that morning.

"He's dead, Chris."

"Who's dead? What're you talking about?"

"John."

Her soft cry broke his heart. *"No."* That she was desperately in love with John was no secret to Nick. That she was also a consummate professional who would never act on those feelings was one of the many reasons Nick respected her.

"I'm sorry to just blurt it out like that."

"How?" she asked in a small voice.

"Stabbed in his bed."

Her ravaged moan echoed through the phone. "But who... I mean, *why*?"

"The cops are here, but I don't know anything yet. I need you to request a postponement on the vote."

"I can't," she said, adding in a whisper, "I can't think about that right now."

"You have to, Chris. That bill is his legacy. We can't let all his hard work be for nothing. Can you do it? For him?"

"Yes...okay."

"You have to pull yourself together for the staff, but don't tell them yet. Not until his parents are notified."

"Oh, God, his poor parents. You should go, Nick. It'd be better coming from you than cops they don't know."

"I don't know if I can. How do I tell people I love that their son's been murdered?"

"He'd want it to come from you."

"I suppose you're right. I'll see if the cops will let me."

"What're we going to do without him, Nick?" She posed a question he'd been grappling with himself. "I just can't imagine this world, this *life*, without him."

"I can't either," Nick said, knowing it would be a much different life without John O'Connor at the center of it.

"He's really dead?" she asked as if to convince herself it wasn't a cruel joke. "Someone killed him?"

"Yes."

OUTSIDE THE CHIEF'S office suite, Detective Sergeant Sam Holland smoothed her hands over the toffee-colored hair she corralled into a clip for work, pinched some color into cheeks that hadn't seen the light of day in weeks, and adjusted her gray suit jacket over a red scoop-neck top.

Taking a deep breath to calm her nerves and settle her chronically upset stomach, she pushed open the door and stepped inside. Chief Farnsworth's receptionist greeted her with a smile. "Go right in, Sergeant Holland. He's waiting for you."

Great, Sam thought as she left the receptionist with a weak smile. Before she could give in to the urge to turn tail and run, she erased the grimace from her face and went in.

"Sergeant." The chief, a man she'd once called Uncle Joe, stood up and came around the big desk to greet her with a firm handshake. His gray eyes skirted over her with concern and sympathy, both of which were new since "the incident." She despised being the reason for either. "You look well."

"I feel well."

"Glad to hear it." He gestured for her to have a seat. "Coffee?"

"No, thanks."

Pouring himself a cup, he glanced over his shoulder. "I've been worried about you, Sam."

"I'm sorry for causing you worry and for disgracing the department." This was the first chance she'd had to speak directly to him since she returned from a month of administrative leave, during which she'd practiced the sentence over and over. She thought she'd delivered it with convincing sincerity.

"Sam," he sighed as he sat across from her, cradling his mug between big hands. "You've done nothing to disgrace yourself or the department. Everyone makes mistakes."

"Not everyone makes mistakes that result in a dead child, Chief."

He studied her for a long, intense moment as if he was making some sort of decision. "Senator John O'Connor was found murdered in his apartment this morning."

"Jesus," she gasped. "How?"

"I don't have all the details, but from what I've been told so far, it appears he was dismembered and stabbed through the neck. Apparently, his chief of staff found him."

"Nick," she said softly.

"Excuse me?"

"Nick Cappuano is O'Connor's chief of staff."

"You know him?"

"Knew him. Years ago," she added, surprised and unsettled to discover the memory of him still had power over her, that just the sound of his name rolling off her lips could make her heart race.

"I'm assigning the case to you."

Surprised at being thrust so forcefully back into the real work she had craved since her return to duty, she couldn't help but ask, "Why me?"

"Because you need this, and so do I. We both need a win."

The press had been relentless in its criticism of him, of her, of the department, but to hear him acknowledge it made her ache. Her father had come up through the ranks with Farnsworth, which was probably the number one reason why she still had a job. "Is this a test?

Find out who killed the senator and my previous sins are forgiven?"

He put down his coffee cup and leaned forward, elbows resting on knees. "The only person who needs to forgive you, Sam, is you."

Infuriated by the surge of emotion brought on by his softly spoken words, Sam cleared her throat and stood up. "Where does O'Connor live?"

"The Watergate. Two uniforms are already there. Crime scene is on its way." He handed her a slip of paper with the address. "I don't have to tell you that this needs to be handled with the utmost discretion."

He also didn't have to tell her that this was the only chance she'd get at redemption.

"Won't the Feds want in on this?"

"They might, but they don't have jurisdiction, and they know it. They'll be breathing down my neck, though, so report directly to me. I want to know everything ten minutes after you do. I'll smooth it with Stahl," he added, referring to the lieutenant she usually answered to.

Heading for the door, she said, "I won't let you down."

"You never have before."

With her hand resting on the door handle, she turned back to him. "Are you saying that as the chief of police or as my Uncle Joe?"

His face lifted into a small but sincere smile. "Both."

TWO

SITTING ON JOHN'S sofa under the watchful eyes of the two policemen, Nick's mind raced with the staggering number of things that needed to be done, details to be seen to, people to call. His cell phone rang relentlessly, but he ignored it after deciding he would talk to no one until he had seen John's parents. Almost twenty years ago they took an instant shine to the hard-luck scholarship student their son brought home from Harvard for a weekend visit and made him part of their family. Nick owed them so much, not the least of which was hearing the news of their son's death from him if possible.

He ran his hand through his hair. "How much longer?"

"Detectives are on their way."

Ten minutes later, Nick heard her before he saw her. A flurry of activity and a burst of energy preceded the detectives' entrance into the apartment. He suppressed a groan. *Wasn't it enough that his friend and boss had been murdered? He had to face* her, *too? Weren't there thousands of District cops? Was she really the only one available?*

Sam came into the apartment, oozing authority and competence. In light of her recent troubles, Nick couldn't believe she had any of either left. "Get some tape across that door," she ordered one of the officers. "Start a log with a timeline of who got here when. No one comes in or goes out without my okay, got it?"

"Yes, ma'am. The Patrol sergeant is on his way along with Deputy Chief Conklin and Detective Captain Malone."

"Let me know when they get here." Without so much as a glance in his direction, Nick watched her stalk through the apartment and disappear into the bedroom. Following her, a handsome young detective with bed head nodded to Nick.

He heard the murmur of voices from the bedroom and saw a camera flash. They emerged fifteen minutes later, both noticeably paler. For some reason, Nick was gratified to know the detectives working the case weren't so jaded as to be unaffected by what they'd just seen.

"Start a canvass of the building," Sam ordered her partner. "Where the hell is Crime Scene?"

"Hung up at another homicide," one of the other officers replied.

She finally turned to Nick, nothing in her pale blue eyes indicating that she recognized or remembered him. But the fact that she didn't introduce herself or ask for his name told him she knew exactly who he was. "We'll need your prints."

"They're on file," he mumbled. "Congressional background check."

She wrote something in the small notebook she tugged from the back pocket of gray, form-fitting pants. There were years on her gorgeous face that hadn't been there the last time he'd had the opportunity to look closely, and he couldn't tell if her hair was as long as it used to be since it was twisted into a clip. The curvy body and endless legs hadn't changed at all.

"No forced entry," she noted. "Who has a key?"

"Who *doesn't* have a key?"

"I'll need a list. You have a key, I assume."

Nick nodded. "That's how I got in."

"Was he seeing anyone?"

"No one serious, but he had no trouble attracting female companionship." Nick didn't add that John's casual approach to women and sex had been a source of tension between the two men, with Nick fearful that John's social life would one day lead to political trouble. He hadn't imagined it might also lead to murder.

"When was the last time you saw him?"

"When he left the office for a dinner meeting with the Virginia Democrats last night. Around six-thirty or so."

"Spoke to him?"

"Around ten when he said he was on his way home."

"Alone?"

"He didn't say, and I didn't ask."

"Take me through what happened this morning."

He told her about Christina trying to reach John, beginning at seven, and of coming to the apartment expecting to find the senator once again sleeping through his alarm.

"So this has happened before?"

"No, he's never been murdered before."

Her expression was anything but amused. "Do you think this is funny, Mr. Cappuano?"

"Hardly. My best friend is dead, Sergeant. A United States senator has been murdered. There's nothing funny about that."

"Which is why you need to answer the questions and save the droll humor for a more appropriate time."

Chastened, Nick said, "He slept through his alarm

and ringing telephones at least once, if not twice, a month."

"Did he drink?"

"Socially, but I rarely saw him drunk."

"Prescription drugs? Sleeping pills?"

Nick shook his head. "He was just a very heavy sleeper."

"And it fell to his chief of staff to wake him up? There wasn't anyone else you could send?"

"The senator valued his privacy. There've been occasions when he wasn't alone, and neither of us felt his love life should be the business of his staff."

"But he didn't care if you knew who he was sleeping with?"

"He knew he could count on my discretion." He looked up, unprepared for the punch to the gut that occurred when his eyes met hers. Her unsettled expression made him wonder if she felt it, too. "His parents need to be notified. I'd like to be the one to tell them."

Sam studied him for a long moment. "I'll arrange it. Where are they?"

"At their farm in Leesburg. It needs to be soon. We're postponing a vote we worked for months to get to. It'll be all over the news that something's up."

"What's the vote for?"

He told her about the landmark immigration bill and John's role as the co-sponsor.

With a curt nod, she walked away.

AN HOUR LATER, Nick was a passenger in an unmarked Metropolitan Police SUV, headed west to Leesburg with Sam at the wheel. She'd left her partner with a staggering list of instructions and insisted on accompanying Nick to tell John's parents.

"Do you need something to eat?"

He shook his head. No way could he even think about eating—not with the horrific task he had ahead of him. Besides, his stomach hadn't recovered from the earlier bout of vomiting.

"You know, we could still call the Loudoun County Police or the Virginia State Police to handle this," she said for the second time.

"No."

After an awkward silence, she said, "I'm sorry this happened to your friend and that you had to see him that way."

"Thank you."

"Are you going to answer that?" she asked of his relentless cell phone.

"No."

"How about you turn it off then? I can't stand listening to a ringing phone."

Reaching for his belt, he grabbed his cell phone, his emotions still raw after watching John be taken from his apartment in a body bag. Before he shut the cell phone off, he called Christina.

"Hey," she said, her voice heavy with relief and emotion. "I've been trying to reach you."

"Sorry." Pulling his tie loose and releasing his top button, he cast a sideways glance at Sam, whose warm, feminine fragrance had overtaken the small space inside the car. "I was dealing with cops."

"Where are you now?"

"On my way to Leesburg."

"God," Christina sighed. "I don't envy you that. Are you okay?"

"Never better."

"I'm sorry. Dumb question."

"It's okay. Who knows what we're supposed to say or do in this situation. Did you postpone the vote?"

"Yes, but Martin and McDougal are having an apoplexy," she said, meaning John's co-sponsor on the bill and the Democratic majority leader. "They're demanding to know what's going on."

"Hold them off. Another hour. Maybe two. Same thing with the staff. I'll give you the green light as soon as I've told his parents."

"I will. Everyone knows something's up because the Capitol Police posted an officer outside John's office and won't let anyone in there."

"It's because the cops are waiting for a search warrant," Nick told her.

"Why do they need a warrant to search the victim's office?"

"Something about chain of custody with evidence and pacifying the Capitol Police."

"Oh, I see. I was thinking we should have Trevor draft a statement so we're ready."

"That's why I called."

"We'll get on it." She sounded relieved to have something to do.

"Are you okay with telling Trevor? Want me to do it?"

"I think I can do it, but thanks for asking."

"How're you holding up?" he asked.

"I'm in total shock…all that promise and potential

just gone…" She began to weep again. "It's going to hurt like hell when the shock wears off."

"Yeah," he said softly. "No doubt."

"I'm here if you need anything."

"Me, too, but I'm going to shut the phone off for a while. It's been ringing nonstop."

"I'll email the statement to you when we have it done."

"Thanks, Christina. I'll call you later." Nick ended the call and took a look at his recent email messages, hardly surprised by the outpouring of dismay and concern over the postponement of the vote. One was from Senator Martin himself—What the fuck is going on, Cappuano?

Sighing, he turned off the cell phone and dropped it into his coat pocket.

"Was that your girlfriend?" Sam asked, startling him.

"No, my deputy."

"Oh."

Wondering what she was getting at, he added, "We work closely together. We're good friends."

"Why are you being so defensive?"

"What's your *problem*?" he asked.

"I don't have a problem. You're the one with problems."

"So all that great press you've been getting lately hasn't been a problem for you?"

"Why, Nick, I didn't realize you cared."

"I don't."

"Yes, you made that very clear."

He spun halfway around in the seat to stare at her.

"*Are you for real?* You're the one who didn't return any of my calls."

She glanced over at him, her face flat with surprise. "What calls?"

After staring at her in disbelief for a long moment, he settled back in his seat and fixed his eyes on the cars sharing the Interstate with them.

A few minutes passed in uneasy silence.

"What calls, Nick?"

"I called you," he said softly. "For days after that night, I tried to reach you."

"I didn't know," she stammered. "No one told me."

"It doesn't matter now. It was a long time ago." But if his reaction to seeing her again after six years of thinking about her was any indication, it *did* matter. It mattered a lot.

Continue reading Sam and Nick's story in
FATAL AFFAIR, available in
print and ebook from Carina Press.

ROMANTIC suspense

Available October 6, 2015

#1867 SECOND CHANCE COLTON

The Coltons of Oklahoma • by Marie Ferrarella

Detective Ryan Colton didn't know that when he set out to prove his sister's innocence, the forensics expert proving her guilt was the woman he'd loved and lost many years ago. This is one fight they'll never forget...

#1868 THE PROFESSIONAL

Dangerous in Dallas • by Addison Fox

When Violet Richardson is kidnapped by the man who has been terrorizing her from the shadows for weeks, it's up to ex-military man Max Baldwin to rescue and protect her from a heist gone horribly wrong.

#1869 HER MASTER DEFENDER

To Protect and Serve • by Karen Anders

It's hate at first sight between agent Amber Dalton and marine Tristan Michaels while investigating a murder, but soon a horrific evil hunts them through the frigid Sierra Nevada mountains, where they must depend on each other to survive.

#1870 LIAM'S WITNESS PROTECTION

Man on a Mission • by Amelia Autin

Bodyguard Liam Jones must shield eyewitness Cate Mateja while she attempts to testify against a human-trafficking organization. It's only a matter of time before danger—and a lethal attraction—takes over his mission.

REQUEST YOUR FREE BOOKS!
2 FREE NOVELS PLUS 2 FREE GIFTS!

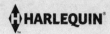

ROMANTIC suspense

Sparked by danger, fueled by passion

YES! Please send me 2 FREE Harlequin® Romantic Suspense novels and my 2 FREE gifts (gifts are worth about $10). After receiving them, if I don't wish to receive any more books, I can return the shipping statement marked "cancel." If I don't cancel, I will receive 4 brand-new novels every month and be billed just $4.74 per book in the U.S. or $5.49 per book in Canada. That's a savings of at least 12% off the cover price! It's quite a bargain! Shipping and handling is just 50¢ per book in the U.S. and 75¢ per book in Canada.* I understand that accepting the 2 free books and gifts places me under no obligation to buy anything. I can always return a shipment and cancel at any time. Even if I never buy another book, the two free books and gifts are mine to keep forever.

240/340 HDN GH3P

Name	(PLEASE PRINT)
Address	Apt. #
City	State/Prov.	Zip/Postal Code

Signature (if under 18, a parent or guardian must sign)

Mail to the **Reader Service**:
IN U.S.A.: P.O. Box 1867, Buffalo, NY 14240-1867
IN CANADA: P.O. Box 609, Fort Erie, Ontario L2A 5X3

Want to try two free books from another line?
Call 1-800-873-8635 or visit www.ReaderService.com.

* Terms and prices subject to change without notice. Prices do not include applicable taxes. Sales tax applicable in N.Y. Canadian residents will be charged applicable taxes. Offer not valid in Quebec. This offer is limited to one order per household. Not valid for current subscribers to Harlequin Romantic Suspense books. All orders subject to credit approval. Credit or debit balances in a customer's account(s) may be offset by any other outstanding balance owed by or to the customer. Please allow 4 to 6 weeks for delivery. Offer available while quantities last.

Your Privacy—The Reader Service is committed to protecting your privacy. Our Privacy Policy is available online at www.ReaderService.com or upon request from the Reader Service.

We make a portion of our mailing list available to reputable third parties that offer products we believe may interest you. If you prefer that we not exchange your name with third parties, or if you wish to clarify or modify your communication preferences, please visit us at www.ReaderService.com/consumerschoice or write to us at Reader Service Preference Service, P.O. Box 9062, Buffalo, NY 14240-9062. Include your complete name and address.

SPECIAL EXCERPT FROM

(H) HARLEQUIN®

ROMANTIC suspense

*Can this Colton cowboy save his wife—and his
beloved ranch—when a killer threatens everything
they hold dear?*

Read on for a sneak preview of
PROTECTING THE COLTON BRIDE
by New York Times *bestselling author*
Elle James,
the fourth book in the 2015
COLTONS OF WYOMING *continuity.*

"Why don't we get married?"

Even though she'd known it was coming, it still hit her square in the chest. The air rushed from her lungs and a tsunami of feelings washed over her. A surge of joy made her heart beat so fast she felt faint. She crested that wave and slid into the undertow of reality. "A marriage of convenience?"

"Exactly." Daniel reached for her hands.

When she hid them behind her back, he dropped his arms. "It wouldn't have to be forever. Just long enough to satisfy the stipulations of your grandmother's will and save your horses, and that would help me get past the Kennedy gauntlet. We could leave tomorrow, spend a night in Vegas, find a chapel and it would be over in less than five minutes."

With her heart smarting, Megan forced a shaky smile. "Way to sweep a girl off her feet."

He waved his hand and Halo tossed her head. "If you want, I can make an official announcement in front of my family."

Megan shook her head. "No."

"No, you won't marry me?"

"No." She pushed past him to pace down the center of the barn. "Your plan is insane."

"Do you have a better one?" he asked. "I'm all ears."

The plan was the same as the one she'd been thinking of before Daniel had woken up. Only when she'd dreamed it up, it didn't sound as cold and impersonal as Daniel's proposal. Somewhere in the back of her mind she'd hoped that marriage to Daniel would be something more than one of convenience.

After yesterday's kiss, she wasn't sure she could be around Daniel for long periods of time without wanting another. And another.

Don't miss
PROTECTING THE COLTON BRIDE
by New York Times *bestselling author Elle James,*
available September 2015

www.Harlequin.com

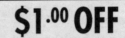
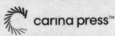